A *Faithful* PROPOSAL

JENNIE GOUTET

SWEETWATER
BOOKS

AN IMPRINT OF CEDAR FORT, INC.
SPRINGVILLE, UTAH

ISBN 13: 978-1-4621-3611-7

Published by Sweetwater Books, an imprint of Cedar Fort, Inc.
2373 W. 700 S., Springville, UT 84663
Distributed by Cedar Fort, Inc., www.cedarfort.com

Library of Congress Control Number: 2019956642

Cover design by Shawnda T. Craig
Cover design © 2020 Cedar Fort, Inc.
Edited by Kimiko Christensen Hammari

Printed in the United States of America

10 9 8 7 6 5 4 3 2 1

Printed on acid-free paper

Dedication

Dedicated to my mother, Cathy Damron, for the frequent library trips and for inspiring me to read everything I could get my hands on.

Chapter One

AUGUST 1812

"We shall arrive within the hour, I daresay. The Pelican assured us we should reach Avebury by two o'clock, which I must say will be a welcome reprieve to this horrid jolting. I swear my teeth are coming loose in their sockets."

Miss Anna Tunstall gave a sidelong glance at her ill-favored companion, not expecting a reply, of course, for she had received little in return for all her efforts these three days past.

Her taciturn companion, however, still had the element of surprise and managed something beyond a monosyllable. "Best be closing that window, miss, as these parts is run by high pads. They'll do over quicker'n ye can stare."

The irritation of a long journey from London with a noiseless young woman, whose grasp at hygiene was tenuous at best, goaded Anna into a retort.

"If there are highwaymen afoot, closing the window won't avert the threat. My, Beatrice, at last you speak. How kind of you to edify me with your conversation, but if you think to frighten me with your Friday face, you are wide of the mark."

Beatrice, a hired companion for the journey and unknown to Anna before they'd set out together, appeared to think she had done her duty in warning the mistress. She lapsed again into silence, pulling the worn cloth traveling bag closer to her chest and looked up to where

1

the frayed yellow squab met the velvet ceiling of their rented coach. Anna's brother, Stratford, Earl of Worthing, had lent them a carriage for their journey, but it had broken an axle at the last stage. Anna had deemed it best to rent another one rather than delay her arrival by awaiting its repair.

Anna raised her eyes heavenward at Beatrice's sullen contribution and allowed herself the luxury of an internal rant. *Emily Leatham, I will murder you for saddling me with such a creature for a traveling companion.* Quickly her humor got the better of her, and Anna turned toward the window as a smile tugged at her cheeks. *If I don't murder Beatrice first.*

Anna had no one with whom to share her private joke. It was the first time she had been away from Phoebe, her twin, for more than an afternoon, and she began to better appreciate her gentle foil. Phoebe had always been a sober, mellowing presence. Anna could indulge in her flights of fancy and humor, and Phoebe checked her when that humor took her too far. Anna sighed. Without Phoebe, she would have to watch her own tongue. How responsible she must now be.

However, it was worth the trip to see Emily Leatham—droll, light-hearted Emily—whose sense of mischief matched Anna's own. They had certainly found ways to amuse themselves in their first London Season before Emily's husband snatched her up. An added benefit to this visit was that Anna would escape a dreary four weeks playing cards with their Aunt Shae, taking slabs of pork in covered baskets to the poor, or accompanying her brother to visit his tenants as befitted the newly appointed Earl of Worthing.

Even the fun of preparing for her brother's wedding held no appeal when she was more likely to be handed the pork slabs than asked to plan the wedding breakfast. Phoebe always had been the industrious one and urged Anna to go visit Emily, saying in her gentle way that Anna would be missed but not needed, a truth that both relieved and stung. Emily hadn't promised higher treats for Anna's visit than what a country village could offer, but at least no one knew Anna there and nothing would be required of her. No, even without Phoebe's comforting and steady presence, Anna had done well to go to Avebury.

A sharp report rent the air and Beatrice gave a shriek. Anna turned with a start, more alarmed by the maid's reaction than the initial noise. Beatrice had forgotten her earlier objection to looking out the window and was now peering out to see the source of the commotion.

"It's jest as I warned yer, miss," Beatrice said. "Them collectors hev come."

Anna hadn't time to assimilate Beatrice's meaning before a shot pierced the carriage from the top of the side panels through the roof. This was much too close for her liking, and Anna's heart began to hammer in her chest. She wasn't prone to anxiety, which was a point of great pride for her, but this ruffled even her sensibility, and darkness threatened to edge onto her vision.

Be calm, Anna told herself. She drew a steady breath and smoothed her skirt while she waited.

The carriage had, by now, come to a halt. There were men shouting outside, but Anna could barely make out what they were saying before the door on Beatrice's side was flung open.

"Out wid 'ee, doxy."

A man's bulky frame blocked the entrance. He was of average height and wore brown clothing and a kerchief over his face and had no distinguishable characteristics other than a pungent odor. With a sharp yank, the man pulled Beatrice out of the carriage, and she stumbled and fell on her hands and knees. Then he turned his attention to Anna, staring at her until she was unnerved by his silent regard.

She kept her voice composed. "Well, sir, must I alight as well?"

The man laughed, an unpleasant sound that would frighten Anna if she allowed it. "Ay. Unless ye want me knife stripping thee along with the squabs."

Anna reached for the door handle at her left, but the man shook his head.

"No, missy—go on. You'll be getting out right here."

It meant moving toward the enemy, and Anna swallowed nervously as she obeyed. Thankfully, the man stepped away from the carriage as she slid across the seat.

"Thee." He waved his pistol at the driver. "Ye stand wid the misses, and if ye be sweet as a lamb I mid let 'ee live."

The driver of the rented vehicle obeyed the summons and stood next to Beatrice, his gaze fixed on his boots. Anna joined the pair, her expression controlled. A second highwayman trained his pistol on their group. The first ransacked the carriage, cutting into the squabs to look for hidden jewelry, which would not be there, of course. This was a rented vehicle. He must not be a very clever robber if he couldn't tell *that*.

Something moved in the trees to Anna's left, and the second highwayman turned to see what had caught her gaze. The distraction was just enough for the driver of the coach to take flight, and she watched in amazement as he cut around the horses and sped into the cover of the trees where the robber could not take aim. *Well, how about that.* Anna had assured her brother she would not need a male escort—not that he would have had time for it with his affairs at Worthing and all his attention focused on his upcoming wedding and honeymoon. Now, without the protection of her family, Anna was realizing just how vulnerable she was, and she began to tremble. The driver had completely vanished into the woods before the thief had finished his search.

"What's this?" The highwayman poked his head out of the carriage. With a glance at his accomplice and then the two women, he laughed. "He left ye, did he? Ha! Liver-hearted." The thief swung down from the steps, his soft leather boots silent when he hit the road. "'Tis nothing to be found. They must be setting snug in yer trunk."

The highwayman came alongside Anna and tilted her chin while the other scanned the edge of the woods, where she thought she'd seen movement. "Unless it's on yer person." He slid one finger along her jaw, and Anna stiffened her spine, refusing to back down from his gaze. For the first time in her insouciant life, she felt cold tendrils of fear creep up her spine.

"It's in the trunk," she said, proud to keep her voice even.

Maybe he would be happy with the jewelry, which would be of no great loss to her. She had done well to leave her most precious items at home, and if this could stave off personal harm, she would accept the loss. All this time, Beatrice had said not a word, but before moving over to the trunks that were strapped on the back of the carriage, the thief crooked his finger at her.

"Thee. Open the trunk."

Beatrice dropped her bundle and followed him to the carriage, where she began to sullenly unwind the straps on the trunk.

"Ye got the look of a dobin rig about ye, girl," the thief said. "What say thee to casting thy lot wid me?"

Beatrice gave a sniff and worked at a stubborn knot until it came free. "Ye ain't got nothing I be needing. I know the likes of ye and what a life wid ye is like. I hev my place in the kitchen and 'tis not one as I'd be leaving."

The thief shrugged. "Have it your way, pullet."

The trunks, now released from their straps, were free for the robber to rummage through. Anna watched her undergarments being flung to all sides, and her fear turned to anger.

"Watch what you do with my possessions," she said. "You need only the valuables. No need to fling my affairs about."

"Ye find the gewgaws then." The robber paused in his rummaging. "What'd ye do? Put them in the bottom of the trunk? Not very accessible-like."

Anna folded her arms. "I'm not going to help someone else to my valuables. You take them but have a care for my things, if you please."

The robber laughed again, this time with real pleasure. "Not often I meet wid a mort such as yerself." He drew her folded gown against his face. "Silk."

After throwing all of the items out of the trunk, he still found none of her valuables. Anna was so astonished, she couldn't refrain from drawing near. The highwayman eyed her and seemed satisfied that her surprise was real. He turned to Beatrice.

"I suppose I know where them sparklers hev gone." He snapped his fingers. "Vixen. Ye'll vamp with me."

Beatrice stamped her foot. "No, I ain't."

The thief grabbed her by the forearm and dragged her to where their horses were tied to a tree, but Beatrice did not go quietly. She shrieked and fought him, greatly hampering his progress, as she continued to scream in short bursts. Anna watched in alarm, wondering if she should attempt to help the girl or flee. *Where was the sack with her jewels and coins anyway? Had Beatrice taken them?* Anna considered what little good she could do in such a situation and was just about to dive into the carriage for a weapon—*her parasol?*—when a hand snaked around from behind, holding her arms in a prison-like grip and clamping her mouth shut. How could she have forgotten there were two of them?

"Ay, poppet," he murmured in her ear. "You'll come quiet now."

Flashes of light pricked at the back of her eyelids as her fear mounted. Anna cast her eyes about at the trees in front of her, searching desperately for help. Surely someone would come. Someone *had* to come. They were near a public road, and Beatrice could summon the dead with her shrieks. Despite the man's threat, Anna screamed—or tried to—but to no avail.

The best she could manage were some muffled cries, which came out amid the whimpers.

Suddenly Anna heard another voice. It did not belong to either of the robbers. "Hoi, Ambrose." She felt the highwayman turn in surprise, pulling her with him. Anna had only time to wonder at the addition to their party before she felt the air stir next to her head.

Everything went black.

Chapter Two

Mr. Henry Aston, known to his chums—but not to his family—as Harry, exited the stables. He led a dray horse that pulled a simple cart. "Easy now, fellow," he soothed as he led the animal between the tight fence posts. "You were just out this morning, but I need you to make an effort for me again." He rubbed the horse's flank before adding, "I know you're thinking the two in there don't know how good they have it, but I assure you they're itching for a good run. They're just not suited to this cart."

Although Harry's speech was humble, his dress spoke of someone of moderate means, and he had the easy, graceful movements of a gentleman. The cart was loaded with items from his kitchen that his French cook, Mrs. Foucher, was pleased to prepare, and he knew she would not despise him for giving away some of her better dishes to the village's poor. Harry did not possess a celebrated chef—none of the ton would pay him a visit and try to steal his cook away. Mrs. Foucher had emigrated with her family during the Treaty of Amiens and had been recommended by the previous rector. Harry counted her as one of the many blessings of his current living situation.

Harry climbed on the seat and clicked his teeth, encouraging the beast to set forward down the lane that wound through Avebury. Today he was not headed toward the Allinthridge Estate or Durstead Manor. He was traveling toward the outlying areas with the modest tenant houses, and then beyond that to the shacks where thieves and poachers dwelled. Harry was determined to break through their leery reception, convinced there was good to be found if only he could coax it out.

The rolling countryside did much to soothe the morning's agitation that had come from receiving his mother's letter recommending yet another eligible female to his attention. Any hope that he could escape his mother's focused attention on his state of matrimony—or lack thereof—simply by leaving London and settling elsewhere had quickly been put to rout. He had been in Avebury eight months, and today marked the eighth letter he had received from her, this time with threats to make the arrangements with Lady Jane's family—who was tolerably pleasing and had at her command twenty-thousand per annum—if he did not make a push for himself. Harry sighed. He would find himself a wife when the right time came. His mother should not think suitable wives dropped down from heaven. *I should have changed religions and joined the priesthood*, he thought in a spurt of rare cynicism.

A greeting from his left had Harry turning in his seat. He squinted into the noonday sun and saw the cheerful face of Mabel Mayne, the squire's wife, walking with her young daughter Amabel.

"Good day, Mr. Aston."

"Hallo, Mrs. Mayne." With a grave nod to the seven-year old girl, he said, "And a good day to you, Miss Mayne. How do you do this afternoon?"

The girl giggled and dropped a blushing curtsy at her mother's bidding. Her mother answered. "Mr. Mayne has promised to bring you a share of the beef he's cured, as well as the berries from our harvest. He hasn't forgotten his tithing."

"Well, give my thanks to your husband and tell him I'll be glad to see him any day. And if he can stay on for a game of chess, all the better."

Apart from the crickets, their voices were the only sounds on the sultry afternoon. Harry thought again how fortunate he was in his living. Good people, beautiful countryside, a noble calling—never mind that his family's opinion differed on this point. He could ask for nothing more than the bounty he had already been given.

"Visiting Haggle End again, are you?" Mrs. Mayne asked. "We brought them some of the lye soap we'd made last week and peeked in on the new schoolroom. The progress they've already made . . . well, it does a body good."

"Indeed. Never mind that only the foundation has been laid. Before you know it, they will be weaving thatch for the roof." Harry gave her a broad smile. "And the soap will be just the thing to encourage the more dilatory toward tidiness. I thank you for your concern for the poor. It does you great credit."

"Well, we can't expect to have you carry the burden on your own, especially when you don't have a wife to assist you. There are some visits better suited to a woman."

"I cannot argue with you, Mrs. Mayne. I appreciate it." Harry tipped his hat. "If you'll forgive my haste, I must carry on so I have time to visit everyone in the row there and beyond. I've brought some of the ragout Mrs. Foucher prepared, and I believe it will be most welcome for those who've had naught to eat."

After bidding farewell to the squire's wife, Harry encouraged his dray to pick up the pace, which the horse did grudgingly. It was summer, and the day would be long, but there were parts of the woods he didn't relish visiting too late in the day. He had already written to his friends in parliament in the short months since he'd arrived about the stretch of road that was frequently attacked by highwaymen. Something needed to be done to protect those passing through. He was well prepared and unafraid today, but why invite trouble if he could avoid it?

Harry's visits to the crumbling thatched houses achieved the goal he'd set of making progress in gaining their trust, and he managed to convey both the goods and his care for them in a carefully balanced timing act that allowed him to visit as many families as possible. As he finished his rounds and drove down the lane toward the shacks and lean-tos that housed Haggle End's poorest, his eyes lit on a familiar and welcome sight.

"Tom, what brings you here?" he called out, addressing the plain figure whom he was more accustomed to seeing near the rectory, though he knew the man had his roots in these quarters. Tom Wardle assisted Harry in caring for his livestock and cultivating his small plot of land.

Tom jerked in surprise at meeting Harry so far outside the village, though he knew Harry's purpose here. Harry had never kept it a secret that he visited Haggle End in hopes of restoring some healthier mode of life to society's less favored. Tom's startled reaction brought to mind his earlier demeanor when Harry had first employed him. For months, Tom's face had worn a mixture of guilt and unworthiness after Harry chose to forgive his theft and employ the man instead. He never wore a look of cunning, however, or Harry would not have trusted him.

"Thought I mid see as how I can help. Like ye be always encouraging me to do." Tom removed his cap and bowed his head as he shifted sideways, so similar to the Tom Wardle of six months ago.

Harry smiled, willing the man to be at ease. Tom knew he was permitted to come to Haggle End whenever he needed as long as his work at the rectory was completed. Harry didn't press the issue, but before moving on, he said, "When you stop by the house, you might find that Mrs. Foucher has kept you some ragout for your supper."

When Harry left the humble dwellings of Haggle End, his mind was still preoccupied by Tom's strange behavior. He trusted him completely, but he wondered if his servant had encountered some worry that he didn't wish to share with him. Tom had shown great improvement since Harry had offered him a chance to exchange his dubious career for an honest one, but apparently he still had progress to make.

Harry moved on toward the row of tents a half-mile farther into the woods, leaving the packed earth road to head down the darker, narrower path that snaked into the trees. When he came to the fork in the road, he spotted a carriage ahead, pulled off to the side and just visible in the clearing of trees. He squinted, surprised at what looked like the effects of the carriage strewn all over the ground.

It is just as I feared. Harry abandoned the idea of any more visits and steered his cart off the road into the clearing ahead. His alarm increased as he spotted what appeared to be a young lady, unconscious in the grass that bordered the path.

Without wasting a minute, Harry leapt down and ran to the inanimate form, falling on his knees beside her as he felt for injuries. He could not tell much without removing her bonnet, but when his fingers brushed the side of her head, she twitched. Pausing only for a moment, he scooped the woman into his arms—her soft, flowery fragrance penetrating his senses— and carried her to the back of his cart, where he lay her down. He climbed up on the cart bed, removed his coat, and flattened it to slide under her head. She moaned, forming inarticulate words. Her eyes were still closed.

As Harry reflected on his next course of action, an unexpected greeting met his ears.

"'Tis a good thing to be seeing thee, pa'son."

Other than briefly scanning the scene upon arrival, Harry hadn't looked to see if he was alone. He now shot his head up and encountered the gaze of a stocky man in a modest vest and brown trousers that were rolled on top of his boots.

Harry quickly dismissed the idea that it might be the thief by the direct way the man was looking at him. He thought he might have seen this man in Haggle End before and squinted up from his kneeling position at the face that blocked the sun. "Eli Smith, is it?" he said at last.

"Ay. I be jest calming the horses, them being nervous creeturs."

"Smith." Harry glanced at the horses tied to a tree further in the clearing and frowned. "I see. If the horses are still excited, the robbery must have occurred not long ago. Did you see who had a hand in it? Where are the people who were with her? She could not have been traveling alone."

Eli Smith lifted his shoulders in a fatalistic gesture. "'Twas on my way home when I found her. She be laying here, log-like."

Harry looked back at the girl, who was obviously gently bred. She wore a soft linen travel dress and a small, neat poke bonnet that showed carefully coiffed blonde strands underneath. Beyond her clothing, the woman was deathly pale. "How came she to faint?" Harry asked, though he had his suspicions. There was no stone near where she'd fallen that would have knocked her out.

Smith screwed up his face as if in deep reflection but only shrugged.

"Well, then," Harry said. "I'd better get this woman to safety. I'll give you a crown to keep an eye on her things until I can get some men to carry them to Durstead, where I'm taking her. Do you accept? You must not let anyone near them, and you mustn't touch them yourself."

"I'm not opposing an honest day's work. Thank 'ee, sir."

"Very well," Harry said, his gaze back on the young woman. "I shall send someone directly."

Chapter Three

*H*arry climbed on the cart and took the reins. Gingerly he turned the vehicle, taking care not to jolt the cart more than necessary. Once on the road, he allowed his horse to pick up the pace. The cart went along more smoothly there, despite the grooves in the earth from past rainstorms.

"If you please, sir."

Harry was startled at the sound of the weak voice and glanced behind him as he pulled on the reins. Leaping from the driver's seat, he ran to see how he might assist the woman and perhaps find out what had happened. He was not prepared for the sight, however, when he peered over the side of the cart. There he met the loveliest pair of celestial blue eyes he'd ever beheld, and his heart stuttered.

"If you please, sir. Where in heaven's name are you taking me? And must it be done in such a ramshackle manner?"

Harry had to lean in to hear what she said, but he caught the flash of droll humor underneath her weak voice. "You've been held up, miss, which I think you must know, and have fainted." He gave a reassuring smile. "I'm taking you to Durstead Manor since it's closest."

"The very place I wished to be," the young woman murmured, closing her eyes for a brief spell. Harry was leaning with his elbows on the sideboard of the cart, and she lay her hand on his arm, adding, "I never faint, sir. You must be mistaken. But my head aches dreadfully. There were highwaymen . . ." Eyes still closed, she drew her brows together and bit her lip.

Noticing her fear, Harry was quick to reassure her of his intentions. "I do believe your losing consciousness was helped along. I will do what I can to discover who was behind this."

The young woman opened her eyes again, placed her hand on the side of the cart, and took hold. At her gesture, Harry ran around and leapt on the back of the cart bed so he could lift her from behind. He now held her arm with one hand and slid the other underneath her back to lift her to a seated position. She smelled of the lilacs growing outside the kitchen of his childhood home, and she turned to look at him, her eyes level with his.

For Harry, all thought fled. When the woman was unconscious, his whole focus had been on getting her the help she needed with all possible haste. With her eyes open, the woman sparked to life, and Harry was mesmerized. Her beauty went beyond the delicate features and wide eyes. It was the intelligence and humor in those eyes that had him spinning. *Here is a soul of unfathomable depth*, he thought.

His arm was still around her, and her face was only inches away. He cleared his throat and attempted a smile. "I'm afraid there is no one to perform the introductions."

The woman appeared neither disconcerted by the familiarity of his arm around her nor affected by his proximity. *It's only my heart that's about to beat out of its chest*, he thought.

She replied, "When we reach Durstead Manor, we may ask Mrs. Leatham to perform the introductions. And then you will learn that I am Miss Anna Tunstall."

"Miss Tunstall," he said, committing the name to memory. *Anna*. "I am delighted to make your acquaintance. My name is Aston, and I propose to set you up more comfortably here in a seated position. We will continue the journey at an easy pace."

"I thank you for your kind offer, Mr. Aston, but I would prefer to sit up properly on the seat beside you. I will not do such an inconsiderate thing as to faint again."

"I should be loath to disoblige you, Miss Tunstall, but I do not think you are ready to sit in front with me. I should be tempted to put my arm around you throughout the journey to ensure you don't fall again. It is better you stay here in the cart bed."

"And be jolted from one side of the gig to the other? Really, Mr. Aston. I will join you in front." She attempted to stand but instantly went white and was obliged to sit again.

Despite his worry that Miss Tunstall may have sustained serious harm, Harry strove to resist the urge to smile at her headstrong, albeit misjudged, determination. The urge proved too strong for him, however, what with the giddiness of his wildly beating heart and his head swimming from an attraction that felt about as pleasant as being hit by lightning. The corners of his mouth crept into a grin. *I might faint dead away myself.*

"How fortunate that my situation affords you some amusement," Miss Tunstall said with a quizzical look.

Harry instantly sobered. "I assure you, I find no humor in your situation. Well," he added, conscientiously, "only a very little, and it is more at myself. My only concern is that you might be made comfortable. And I could see you were a trifle pale to allow for sitting on the bench beside me. However, let me adjust the coat to provide more cushion while you are seated." He did so, adding, "I would remove my neckcloth too, if I thought it could provide enough padding to protect your head to make up for the lack of delicacy. But I'm afraid it won't, so we will ride slowly."

Miss Tunstall allowed herself to be seated with her back to the driver's seat, his coat behind her to provide some support. When she was thus positioned, she adjusted her skirt to cover her ankles.

"If only you were sporting the toggery of a London gentleman, we might have fabricated even a hammock from the cravat. I now see the disadvantages of country life, for you are wearing only a paltry neckcloth."

Harry had as yet to move from her side, and he threw back his head and laughed. When she raised her clear eyes to his and he saw the answering gleam of fun, Harry knew the end to his bachelor days had come. He was done for.

The door flung open when Anna arrived at Durstead Manor, and she could see Emily hurrying as fast as her condition would allow.

"I was waiting for you, alarmed that something might have occurred, and now . . . oh dear! I see I had surmised correctly. Mr. Aston, what has happened, and how came you to be involved?"

Despite a sense of dizziness, Anna took a firm hold of the side of the carriage and pulled herself to a standing position. Mr. Aston did not allow her to make it to the back of the cart before he leapt up and insisted on helping her alight. It was not unpleasant to have this attention, and she liked the sturdy feeling to him. Here was no town fop with buckram padding to ape muscles. He was likely Oxford-educated; he spoke well enough. But he was clearly in trade and not afraid to work. Anna allowed him to assist her to the edge of the cart. Before she could contemplate how to land on the ground, he had already leapt down again—the man was everywhere—and had lifted her by the waist to set her on solid ground.

"Good day, Mrs. Leatham. I was on my way to Haggle End, and I discovered her carriage had been held up. The driver was nowhere to be seen, and apparently her companion was gone as well." He turned an inquisitive gaze to Anna, for she had not told him how she had traveled. She nodded.

"Miss Tunstall had fainted," he continued, "helped along by a blow to the head, I'm afraid." Mr. Aston held her arm as they walked toward the house. Apparently he was determined to see her safely inside, and although she detested feeling like an invalid at any time, she found his strong grasp and the vague scent of soap that followed him pleasant.

"Oh my dear," Emily breathed. "You must have had such a fright. Did the highwayman make away with anything?"

"Well—Beatrice," Anna said. "I'm not sure whether I should pity Beatrice or the highwayman, however. I cannot be sure they were not working together."

Emily gave no other sign than a furrowed brow of having understood as she came to walk at Anna's side. "Your jewels then?"

"He did not have them—"

"Oh, thank heaven," Emily said.

Mr. Aston spoke at the same time. "I did not think to ask. How fortunate."

"No," Anna corrected. "For someone had already made off with them at the last posting house. At least, that is what I must surmise, for I had packed them at the inn, but they were not to be found when the highwayman went through the trunk."

"This must be stopped," Mr. Aston exclaimed. "These *visits* from highwaymen." His arm tensed with indignation as he assisted her up the stone steps and into the house.

Anna shook her head. "There were no truly precious items among the jewels—nothing of great sentimental or monetary value, but I will need to obtain more money. I shall have to write to Stratford."

"I am just thankful you are here and in one piece. Did you not promise me your brother would provide you with an escort besides Beatrice?" Emily asked.

Anna made a wry face. "I refused one."

Emily ushered them into the sitting room, where Mr. Aston eased Anna onto the settee. His face displayed a mix of concern and disapproval. "Your brother should have insisted. It is not fit for a lady to travel alone."

"But I was not alone," Anna said, one eyebrow raised. "I had Beatrice. And the driver."

Mr. Aston pressed his lips together, and Emily smiled and shook her head.

"Mr. Aston, I believe Lord Worthing was no match for his sister. Besides having a fair understanding of how stubborn a sister she can be"—Emily shot an affectionate glance at Anna—"he is fully occupied with bringing his estate into order and preparing for his wedding, which is set for September. I am also at fault because I was aware of the danger on these roads and should have written to Lord Worthing myself to request him to hire an outrider."

"No. You saw fit only to lend me Beatrice." Anna gave her friend a long-suffering glance.

"Oh dear," was all Emily said.

"I must leave you." Mr. Aston addressed both women, but his gaze lingered on Anna. "I would like to see to the retrieval of your trunk and carriage. And . . . perhaps you need a doctor sent as well."

"No," Anna said, while Emily nodded her approval.

"Then I will be off. I will have your trunks sent today, if at all possible." Mr. Aston bowed, and with another dimpled smile, he was gone.

Emily sat at Anna's side. "I've never met Beatrice, but her cousin, Florence, said she might be trusted. You think she was in league with the robbers?"

Anna shrugged. Even that small movement hurt her head.

"I will have to talk to Florence," Emily continued. "She will need to be apprised of the situation."

After musing over the afternoon's events, Emily stood at last and went to the bell. "I will ring for tea, my poor dear. You must have a blazing headache."

After the tea was served, Emily sat on the chair beside the settee and studied Anna in silence. Anna had finally succumbed to the comfort of the cushions. Her head spun.

Emily clasped her hands on her lap. "How do you find our Mr. Aston?" she asked at last.

Anna was certainly not ready to share any thoughts on how she felt about Mr. Aston when even in her private reflections, she could only muster the feeling of being *aware* of the man. She blinked. "No begging for details of the robbery? Only, 'how do you find our Mr. Aston'?"

Emily laughed. "I do wish to know everything, and I am more thankful than you can know that you are *safe*." She grasped Anna's hand. "But I confess your unexpected meeting with Mr. Aston piques my curiosity because before your arrival, I had thought to present you to him. I wondered what you might think of him because *I* thought he might be an interesting acquaintance for you."

"Is he not a farmer? Or in trade?" Anna asked, perplexed. Although she had a sneaking feeling, the matter did not weigh so very much with her as his location did. He was not in London, so there was nothing further to discuss. Nevertheless, her unruly mind continued on its own accord. Perhaps she would not be interested in a farmer, but a man in trade. . . . Her father was in trade, and he was a nobleman. A farmer—well, he might stink of pig by the end of the day, although Mr. Aston did not stink of pig. He did not stink at all. He was . . .

Solid. The word came to her unbidden.

"He is not a farmer, nor is he in trade. He is a gentleman," Emily said with a mischievous smile that did not bode well for Anna. She knew what kind of trouble Emily's smiles could mean.

"How fortunate for him," Anna declared, at a loss for what else to say. Then to fill the silence, and perhaps to cover her confusion, she added, "He did not dress like a gentleman. And he drove the rudest vehicle."

"Oh no." Emily raised her eyes in studied innocence. "He does not like to set himself above the villagers."

"I can see that," Anna said. When Emily offered no further information, she added, "So he is a landowner?"

"He is not," Emily said. She stood suddenly and walked to the escritoire to pick up a magazine, but Anna was not deceived. She recognized the tremor of laughter hidden in her friend's voice.

Anna looked heavenward. "I am sure you will eventually tell me, but since we have many other things to discuss—like being held up at *gunpoint*—what *does* Mr. Aston do, if he is a gentleman but not a landowner?"

Emily took her seat, her eyes brimming with amusement. "Mr. Aston is our rector."

Chapter Four

*T*he rector! Anna would have had more enthusiasm had he been a merchant. Or even a farmer. Her distaste for men of the cloth was high, as they were generally pious, dour sort of men. Or they were hypocrites. She wondered which one Mr. Aston was.

Emily was studying her with an amused expression, most likely because she knew Anna well enough to know exactly what she was thinking. "I did wonder how you might greet the news," Emily said. "But I will say this. John thinks highly of him, and Mr. Aston is unlike any rector I've yet to meet. I believe you will find there is more to him than meets the eye."

"Mr. Aston is of no matter to me."

"Of course not."

Anna was not deceived by Emily's prim voice.

Anna's trunk was returned to her that same evening, by a farmer from the looks of it, and not the town's celebrated rector. Instead she had the dubious pleasure of being poked and prodded by the doctor, who marveled at her excellent constitution and predicted a swift recovery time of two months. He left a variety of medicines for all eventualities and prescribed complete bed rest for two weeks if she did not wish to fall gravely ill. These strictures Anna promptly ignored, although she did take headache powder twice and generally moved at a slower rhythm than she was wont. Her dizzy spells faded after three days.

Alone in her charming bedroom that overlooked the meadow, Anna's thoughts turned to Beatrice, wondering what had become of her. Emily had interrogated Beatrice's cousin, a scullery maid at Durstead Manor who had inadvertently sealed Anna's travel arrangement by mentioning her cousin would be arriving from London on the same day, but she could not shed any light on Beatrice's disappearance. Florence only looked a cross between confusion and guilt, which Anna thought not unusual in the lower orders. Although Beatrice had been a most unpleasant traveling companion, Anna did not wish ill on her, and her last glance of the young woman had not left her with much hope.

In the end, Anna was not prone to worry over matters she could not change and applied her thoughts to the less than pleasant duties before her. She saw that the hired coach was returned to the inn, and she dispatched a letter to her brother, Stratford, to inform him of the broken axle and the loss of her money. Anna set her quill down in deep thought and finally decided not to trouble him with the matter of the robbery, requesting only that he send more money. He could make of that what he would. Why cause him to be overset when, for all intents and purposes, the affair had ended without any considerable harm done?

The week was spent with so much enforced rest that Anna had at last insisted Emily allow her to move about as she wished. Their first outing beyond Durstead Manor was church. Having not had another glimpse of Mr. Aston for five days, Anna would not own to any curiosity when she arose on Sunday morning. But she did dress in a white muslin gown with blue trim, which she knew was becoming to her complexion, and met Emily for breakfast.

"I miss my combs," she said, patting her hair with care over the tender spot on her head. "You said we'd have someone to investigate the theft?"

"Mr. Aston said he'd call on Mr. Mayne to look into it. He is our squire and the village's justice of the peace," Emily said. "He'll see that the matter is pursued until the end."

After filling her plate from the sideboard, Anna joined Emily at the table. "And now we shall see your Mr. Aston in his element," she said with a glance at Emily, who was buttering her second roll. "Is that one for the baby or for you?"

"I told you you'd have to save me from myself, but that will have to start tomorrow. Today I am far too famished." Emily popped a bite into her mouth.

"I can see that, although fortunately for John, the only area that is getting bigger is your middle. You wouldn't want him to come back and find you so utterly changed."

"John will be pleased to come back and find me in any condition so long as I produce an heir." Emily spooned jam on another bite, and it followed the first.

"It might be a girl, you know." Anna raised her eyebrows.

"Wouldn't that be lovely? Just don't tell John I am hoping for one. He has his heart set on securing the estate first."

"You must have a son, of course," Anna said, "but a daughter will bring the leaven." She fiddled with her knife before picking up her bread and buttering it. "So . . . Mr. Aston. Do his sermons last forever as any parson's must who is worth his salt?"

"His sermons are quite good, actually. The only one who falls asleep is Mr. Banbury, and he's eighty-six years old and may be forgiven."

"A lively preacher, then. Does he jog back and forth to relieve his curate of duties in whatever other parish to which he retains the living? Or does he just go once a year to elect board members?"

"Mr. Aston is not a pluralist. He has no other parish. He said he prefers to have one living where he can invest in the village rather than collect tithes on several and leave them without guidance or in the hands of some poor stuttering fool." Emily laughed. "No, he didn't say that last bit. But before the previous rector retired, he had placed a curate here for a full year who could not put two intelligible words together. And his sermons lasted well past noon. Avebury is very glad to have Mr. Aston as a rector, let me assure you."

Anna sniffed and poured cream into the China-blue coffee cup, stirring its fragrant contents with a tiny silver spoon. "Still, Mr. Aston doesn't strike me as someone who would choose the church."

"You admit to some interest in our parson then," her friend exclaimed with lifted brows, a delighted smile hovering on her lips.

"You wrong me," Anna said. "I have no interest in your parson. Can you imagine a drearier living? You must drone on and on every Sunday and be nice to everyone—run after people to beg them for your income. I thank you, no." An image flashed in Anna's mind of Mr. Aston squatting at her side, his humorous, gold-flecked brown eyes fixed on her, his unruly curls making her long to reach out and smooth them into place. "I cannot imagine why anyone chooses this living."

"Because everyone must have a living, of course. But I think Mr. Aston chose it because he cares for the church, and he has good intentions for the village and its outlying dwellers. Hide it though you try, I can see Mr. Aston has piqued your interest, and you are not wrong to put your attention in that direction."

The footman entered, and Emily signaled to him. Anna was not allowed to get the last word. "We will be ready to set out in ten minutes. Have the open phaeton brought 'round. Anna, I must run up and fetch my reticule. I will meet you in the front entrance in ten minutes."

Left to herself, Anna allowed thoughts of Mr. Aston to creep up again. He had seen to everything. He brought her safely to Emily's, then set about retrieving her trunk and possessions from the road. Heavens. He must have seen her stays and shifts strewn all over the road. Anna felt her cheeks heat up, a reaction foreign to her, and stood suddenly. She clenched her jaw and moved to the door. *I will not begin being missish at nineteen*, she thought. *Well. And if he did see a few undergarments? Surely he has sisters or something.*

The carriage was brought to the front, and Anna climbed onto the seat beside Emily. Her friend drove, saying she would do so until she was obliged to carry a baby instead, and the groom rode behind. The lawn still smelled of freshly cut grass from the gardeners' work the day before, and the summer sun warmed Anna's arms and legs through the thin cloth. She breathed in. "It's beautiful here, Emily. Although I could never settle here, I can see why you like it."

"Thank you for coming to stay with me." Emily held the reins in her left hand and squeezed Anna's hand with her right. "I needed you with John away. And although I'll be glad to have my mother stay with me for the birth in September, you're helping to make this summer bearable. I will only have two weeks to contend with on my own. You will meet everyone of consequence today. The squire's family is delightful—Mr. and Mrs. Mayne, who have a seven-year-old daughter, Amabel, and George, who will attend King's College next year. Nothing toad-eating about them. There's the Rigby family, whom I'll introduce to you. They're probably the best family after Lord and Lady Allinthridge and ours. Of the Rigby daughters, the only one I care for is Hester. Her younger sister, Marianne, is considered a beauty and is set on making a brilliant match at her come-out next spring, but she's a flirt. Hester is sweet."

"Was Hester in London this past Season?" Anna asked.

"Yes, these two years past, but she didn't take. I don't know why ever not, apart from the fact she's of a retiring nature. Of course, John did not want me to be in London the whole Season, so Hester and I were not in each other's company much. I believe she is smitten with our parson," Emily said with a mischievous smile.

"Why, if she's retiring, she will make an ideal candidate for a parson's wife," Anna replied in a bright voice. "Mr. Aston is lucky he doesn't have to look far." She opened her parasol to shade her face from the sun.

"Oh no," Emily returned, her voice suspiciously innocent. "I don't believe Mr. Aston returns her regard." No more was said on the subject as they drove the phaeton past the hitching posts and on to the stables.

Having delivered their carriage into the hands of the groom, Emily and Anna joined the crowd gathering outside the closed doors to the church. Anna was surprised by the noise and activity in front of it.

"Will they not make their way in? I've never seen this kind of hue and cry before a Sunday service."

"You have not heard Mr. Aston preach." Emily laughed softly. "I believe through some mischance the doors are still locked. Come, we must pay our respects to Lord and Lady Allinthridge. They hold the living for the parish."

Emily stopped in front of a handsome older couple and waited until they had finished greeting a neighbor. "Good morning, Lord Allinthridge, Lady Allinthridge. Allow me to present my dear friend, Miss Anna Tunstall. She is staying with me this month."

Lady Allinthridge's beauty had followed her into middle-age, and her slender physique revealed a strength that discredited any idea she was pampered. Her husband's square face set on a broad frame gave an intimidating appearance, but he was clearly devoted to his wife and turned toward her whenever she spoke.

"Mrs. Leatham has told us you would be arriving. We've planned a dinner party in two weeks and hope you will make up the number."

"You are kind," Anna replied. "Emily has spoken of it, and I would be delighted to come."

The crowd's rumble grew louder as Mr. Aston swept into the church grounds in a handsome curricle with a matched pair of horses. He handed the reins to a stable hand and leapt down, the movement unrestricted by a clerical robe that had slits sewn into the sides and which revealed tan pantaloons underneath. "Good morning," he called out, unabashed by the bows from the boys and young men. "I know you will forgive my late arrival when I tell you Mr. Barnsworth's sow made an appearance on my doorstep and has taken a liking to my hydrangea bushes."

The crowd laughed, and Mrs. Barnsworth, a faded woman in a neat muslin dress, fluttered forth, saying, "Oh heavens, parson, surely Mr. Barnsworth told you he would be sending it ahead for his tithe."

Mr. Aston took both her hands, his eyes alight with good humor. "I did not receive word but am most grateful for your gift, all the same. I might, perhaps, suggest a different diet for him than hydrangeas, but— where is Mr. Barnsworth today?"

"He is laid up with the gout, Mr. Aston, and regrets not being able to hear the service read this morning," she answered earnestly.

"You tell him he did well to stay home while he's feeling so poorly," Mr. Aston said. "And I will visit without fail tomorrow." He turned to one of the young men. "George, please be so kind as to unlock those doors. Here are the keys."

Mr. Aston reached over to shake the hands of the boys who were lined up to greet him, then turned to Lord Allinthridge and his wife. "A rector who is late does you no credit," Mr. Aston said with a disarming smile.

Lord Allinthridge couldn't keep his stern countenance under such a frank, cheerful gaze. "Well, well, it has never happened before, and it may be overlooked. I must say how glad I am to see you driving a proper vehicle for once."

Mr. Aston laughed outright. "Shall I lay it at your door, then, that the wheel to my cart broke before I'd left the stable? I had no choice but to take the curricle."

Lord Allinthridge was betrayed into a smile. "So it was not just the sow. I had no part in your broken gig, but perhaps providence did. Those horses of yours are badly in need of exercise." The stern landowner actually winked at Mr. Aston and turned to take his wife's arm to lead her into the church.

Mr. Aston turned slightly until he saw Anna, and his eyes widened. That smile that seemed never to leave his eyes was accompanied by two deep dimples on either side of his mouth.

"Miss Tunstall." He bowed and raised his head, his eyes searching hers. "I trust you are . . ." He stopped short, realizing, perhaps, she might not wish her misadventure to be generally known. ". . . well rested after your journey."

He waited for her to answer, but for once in her life, Anna was tongue-tied from the force of his personality. She could only nod. He held her gaze for a few more seconds, his smile widening, before he turned to her friend.

"Good morning, Mrs. Leatham." He spoke suddenly and bowed, as if he had only just remembered he should have greeted her first. Without another glance at Anna, he walked through the church doors.

Anna felt vaguely disappointed, as if he'd taken the sun with him when he entered the doors of the church. She followed in his wake and was glad for the comfort of Emily's arm tucked through hers. Now the service would start, and Mr. Aston would become someone else. He'd be the parson—a strange, religious, droning voice, not at all in conformity with the robust person whose face she greeted after her fainting spell. Lost in contemplation that was not entirely pleasing to her, she followed Emily down the aisle.

Before entering the pew, Anna stopped short. "Emily, never say this is your pew? It is so far back."

Emily nodded. "It is, in a sense. Come sit down. It's that Mr. Aston . . . how can I explain this? Although we have every right to buy our seats in the front like our parents and grandparents have done, he encourages those of us who are able to give up the front seats to the more infirm in the congregation, no matter their social standing. It's easier for them to hear the message, and it's warmer in the winter. It's quite unorthodox, and you'll see not everyone has chosen to follow the rector's lead." She nodded toward the Allinthridges and another family that was just making its way down the aisle.

"That family is the Rigbys. I told you about them. They do care about their standing in the village, except for Hester," Emily whispered. "However, John appreciated Mr. Aston's sentiment and has determined we sit back here."

Anna looked about her, feeling she had much to ponder about this unorthodox rector besides his sunny smile. The church was full, and, indeed, the poorer among the congregation were mixed to some degree with the more wealthy. Turning fully, Anna saw that even the back was filled with the poorest among them. She whispered, "Those in the far back have not been invited forward."

Emily followed her gaze and turned to face front before responding in a low voice. "Before Mr. Aston came, that back area was empty. He does think it's important to protect the congregation from the risk of disease, and those living in extreme poverty do not sit with the rest of the congregation. But he serves them something to eat afterward, knowing they might not have much of anything to eat all week." She stopped short with a brittle smile and blinked a few times. "I tease you about him, but we are all proud of our rector."

Anna looked at her in wonder. She knew there was a depth of feeling to her friend, else they wouldn't have been this close, but she wasn't used to seeing Emily show so much emotion. They had bonded over gossiping over tea and flirting during the London Season. Even at her wedding, Emily was laughing and joking as her betrothed looked on with affectionate amusement. The deeper feelings had been tucked away.

Emily noticed Anna's confusion and said, "Yes, I am a waterworks since I became with child. Just you watch. There is no avoiding it, I believe."

The service opened with singing. Since there was no organ, Mr. Aston stood and raised his hands and began the hymn in a clear voice. Anna rose with the congregation. She sang mechanically, observing those around her as she did so. She knew the words but was never in the midst of such enthusiasm in a church setting. After the hymn, Mr. Aston led the liturgy, and even in this he managed to infuse more meaning into the words she had muttered since childhood. His voice rang out above the others. "As it was in the beginning, is now, and ever shall be: world without end. Amen."

Mr. Aston performed the entire service without the help of a curate. Just when Anna thought he must lose his voice from exhaustion, he gave a short sermon on the account of Elijah at Mount Carmel. "Brethren, if you trust in your own strength, your wealth, your position in society, are you not leaning on idols? And what power do these idols have to assist you?"

With a grave expression on his face, he led them to the verse where Elijah taunted the king's prophets of Baal. "Cry aloud, for Baal is a god," Mr. Aston read in a loud voice, his finger following in the massive leather-bound Bible resting on the pulpit. "Either he is talking, or he is pursuing, or he is in a journey, or peradventure . . ." He looked up from his reading, the grave expression on his face made humorous by laughing eyes. "Perhaps he sleepeth and must be awakened."

Anna was shocked by a sound she had never before heard in a church: laughter. She looked around. Nearly everybody was not only wide awake but also smiling. She turned to the front, her eyes on the man who had stirred this dull crowd to life.

The recessional brought Mr. Aston to the back of the church, and although there was a line to greet him, no one seemed in a hurry to rush out. Small groups of people clustered together in the aisle and shook hands, sharing bits of news.

"Anna, let me present you to Mrs. Rigby and her daughter, Miss Hester Rigby." Emily indicated Anna with a nod. "This is Miss Tunstall."

Anna turned to greet them, examining Hester most carefully to see how she might go on as Mr. Aston's wife. Miss Rigby's face was on the long side, although her expression was pleasant. *She isn't pretty enough for him*, Anna decided. Although Mr. Aston was a man of the cloth, surely he was a man first and must notice these things. A pity for Miss Rigby.

"How do you do?"

Mrs. Rigby did not give her daughter time to respond. "Welcome to Avebury. We are not a large town, but we still have up to twenty young couples for the country dances and more when we combine parties with Beckhampton. We hope you will join us for our rout this Friday." Mrs. Rigby's words were pleasant, but there was a slight condescension to them that didn't please Anna.

"I would be delighted," Anna replied with a tight smile. "Wherever Emily goes, I will follow, of course."

Marianne Rigby had been flirting with George Mayne, the squire's son who had opened the church doors, but she joined them as the line moved toward the front.

"Oh, Emily," she called out in an animated voice. "This is your friend you've spoken of? So pleased to meet you. Emily must have told you that I am Marianne Rigby, and I know you are Anna Tunstall. I will be in London for two months in September visiting friends, so perhaps we will meet there as well."

Marianne seemed unaware they were still in the church—too unaware to modulate her voice—but she had a liveliness to her that Anna could find no fault with. She wondered why Emily had said she preferred Hester.

"With pleasure," she replied to Miss Marianne. Then, in an attempt to draw out Hester Rigby and measure her worth, she turned to the older sister. "Miss Rigby, will you also be in London this fall?"

There was nothing shrinking in Miss Rigby's manner of responding. "Yes, I will be in London as well, although my visits to London are more of a trial to me than to my sister."

Anna had to admit she'd not done the woman justice when Miss Rigby spoke in such an open, natural way. She leaned in toward Anna. "Did you have a pleasant journey to Avebury?"

The question was unexpected, and Anna found herself without a ready reply. She did not want the details of the attack upon her carriage known. The line had moved, however, and she was saved from having to answer, for she was now standing before Mr. Aston and looking directly at him. She had not noticed before that they were the same height, but he didn't appear short. His strong build lent him a power that made him seem taller than he was.

"Miss Tunstall, I hope you enjoyed the service. We have several parish events throughout the week, and you are welcome to join in any of them."

Anna's throat constricted at the thought of a series of parish events as entertainment. Her expression must have resembled that of a trapped animal because Mr. Aston's eyes twinkled with mirth. Had he been provoking her? She could give no answer because he held her captive with an enigmatic smile.

Finally he seemed to take pity on her and said, "There are also several social invitations that go out each week, and I am sure to meet you at one of them. Perhaps the Rigbys' party on Friday."

Anna nodded mutely. Still feeling unsettled and vaguely embarrassed, she made good her escape.

Chapter Five

When Harry greeted the last of his parishioners, he saw Mrs. Leatham drive off with her guest. Miss Tunstall leaned into her friend, their bonnets together, before they broke apart laughing. There had been no time to inform her about the actions taken following her attack on the road, and Sunday morning service was not the place to do it. He would pay a visit to Durstead Manor before the Rigbys' dinner party and needed only to decide which day was best. Perhaps he'd go Tuesday morning so he didn't look too eager.

But he was eager.

"Aston. Ain't you glad to see us?"

Harry spun around, astonished to hear such a familiar voice here, but his ears had not deceived him. It was, indeed, Julian Cranfield. And was that Sir Lewis Faure with him? Ah, now it made sense. Harry remembered that Sir Lewis had a hunting box somewhere in Wiltshire.

"Rusticating, are you, Jules?" Harry raised his brows as he faced them.

Julian Cranfield was a dandy in expectation of inheriting an estate of no small significance from a childless uncle. He liked to dress in a manner befitting one of such consequence, wearing the most elaborate colored waistcoats and displaying every sort of ring, fob, and quizzing glass that could be had, usually all at once. And since, in a manner which Jules considered to be a studied slight, his uncle was proving heartier than expected and tenaciously clung to life, Julian often found himself at point non plus before his modest quarterly pay could be drawn.

Knowing this, Harry added, "I see you've managed to gain the sympathy of Lewis here." He encompassed both of them with a playful nod. "It's a good thing, too. You're likely too run off your legs even to beg coach fare."

"You wrong me, Harry," Julian responded with a wounded look. "Even if the dibs ain't in tune, two months in the country will be just the thing to set me up, and the creditors can't find me here." Julian's next words brought an ironic smile to Harry's face. "I have more sense than you give me credit for."

"And I, less, apparently," Sir Lewis said, with a good-humored shrug. "I always get taken in. But I was right that we would find you here."

"Where else on a Sunday morning?" Harry said.

"Who were those two magnificent creatures who just drove off? I hadn't expected to find anyone here but a bunch of dowds." Julian's gaze followed the carriage disappearing from view. "One looked familiar, but I only saw her profile."

"No one likely to interest you," Harry shot back a little too quickly. "*Mrs.* Leatham is entertaining her friend."

"Whose name is?" Julian asked, still squinting after the carriage in the distance.

Harry frowned. "You're not likely to know her. She is Miss Anna Tunstall."

Julian whistled. "Know her? Don't I ever! She's the new Earl of Worthing's sister—you know, Stratford Tunstall, who inherited from his uncle? Miss Anna Tunstall is the livelier twin who talks in such circles you can't be sure she's not laughing at you," he added a bit naively. "I'm only surprised she has allowed herself to be separated from her sister."

Harry gave a start. "A twin?"

"Identical," Julian confirmed with a nod of significance. "There are *two* of those beauties, but the elder Miss Phoebe Tunstall is the more comfortable of the two. They've had two Seasons, and neither has been snatched up."

"'Too picky' is what the ton says, I believe," Sir Lewis added, studying his fingernails. Harry knew Lewis didn't set much store by what society said.

Miss Marianne had steered her sister away from their parents and come into the orbit of Harry's friends. She dropped her fan. Neither Julian nor Sir Lewis seemed to notice, although Harry thought the ploy was aimed at them. Surrendering, Harry walked forward to retrieve it.

"Miss Marianne," he called out from behind her. "I believe you dropped this."

She turned and put a hand over her heart in a practiced gesture, her eyelids fluttering in the direction of his friends. "Why, Mr. Aston, thank you. I hadn't paid attention." Her older sister shot furtive glances in Harry's direction and had yet to make full eye contact from the first time they met. Miss Rigby seemed less pretentious than her sister, but she barely spoke two words in his presence. She was a most unaccountably shy female.

"Do you have friends visiting, Mr. Aston?" Miss Marianne inquired, rather obviously. "I hope they know they will be welcome at our rout on Friday night. I can have two more invitations brought to you."

Julian assessed Miss Marianne, who was quite comely. "Aston, I do believe you've been remiss in your introductions. Something that should be remedied at once."

Harry obeyed. "Miss Rigby, Miss Marianne Rigby, please allow me to present my friends, Mr. Julian Cranfield and Sir Lewis Faure, who has a hunting box in . . ." He turned a questioning glance to the quieter gentleman, who immediately answered.

"In Beckhampton."

"In Beckhampton," Harry repeated and then turned back in surprise. "I had not known you were so close."

"I haven't been back since Christmas, and you didn't acquire this living until January," Sir Lewis responded. "I was planning to write, but that seemed like a tedious thing to do when you would find out sooner or later."

Harry's face cracked into a grin. "Why then, Lewis, you are my parishioner." He clapped him on the back.

Lewis sent a droll look his way, and Julian added his mite. "Harry's been meaning to talk to you about the tithe."

"No such thing," Harry said. "I've been meaning to talk to you about your soul."

He laughed when he saw Julian's alarmed expression. "Have no fear, Jules. You are safe. I know when a thing is beyond human capacity."

Miss Marianne's lower lip began to protrude as the banter went on without her. "I will talk to my mama. I'm sure she has extra invitations for Friday night."

"Your servants, Miss Marianne." Julian bowed with a flourish, to which Miss Marianne responded with a coy smile. Miss Marianne curtsied, and Julian watched her flit away.

Harry murmured, "Do try to behave yourselves here. I don't need any wolves in my flock."

"Why, Harry," Julian protested.

Miss Rigby had paused before them. "Sir Lewis, I believe we have you to thank for having the Callmans' barn rebuilt after the fire." She spoke with a certainty that made it clear she already knew the answer.

Sir Lewis looked embarrassed by the attention, but he rose to the occasion. "Yes, Miss Rigby, I was made aware of the need, and the solution was simple enough."

"I thank you," Miss Rigby responded. "This family is my particular concern." She dropped an efficient curtsy and left. Harry watched her departure with bemusement. *That's more than she's spoken to me in all the months I've known her.*

Harry waited until eleven o'clock on Tuesday morning, although he was up at the crack of dawn. He didn't know if Miss Tunstall was a late riser, but he suspected she might be and didn't want to catch her unprepared for visitors. He harnessed the chestnut pair to his curricle with a prick of conscience over the fact that the cart, now perfectly repaired, was usually good enough for his parishioners. *I'm trying to impress her.* He frowned. *This is not good. She should accept me for the simple man I am.* Nevertheless, it was in the curricle that he pulled into the Leatham residence.

Only Mrs. Leatham was seated in the morning room. In response to Harry's greeting and inquiring look about the room, she said, "Anna has gone walking since it's such a fine morning. It was a little warm for me to join her in my condition, but I am certain she would be glad to walk with you if you care to search her out. She will not have wandered far from the garden and can probably be found in the open path that leads across the meadow."

Harry stayed a few minutes longer to inquire after Mrs. Leatham's health and whether she had received word from Captain Leatham, before taking up her suggestion. He should have stayed longer; Mrs. Leatham had looked pinched. He wondered whether it was the discomfort of her condition or whether she simply missed her husband and was feeling low at that particular moment. Perhaps it was better that he not intrude upon her privacy. What was done was done, however, and he picked up his pace, eager at the thought of seeing Miss Tunstall.

Apart from one of the gardeners, no one else was in the garden, and no one was visible on the path across the meadow. Surely she wouldn't have wandered in the woods after what had happened to her, although, he supposed, the wooded area so close to the manor held no threat and she must know that. Harry strode toward it, and as he approached, noticed the sheep dog at the base of a tree on the edge of the woods, his gaze fixed on something in the branches.

Oh heavens, not something—someone. Had Miss Tunstall been frightened or hurt? Harry picked up his pace and gave a shrill whistle. The dog, recognizing the call of a master, abandoned his quarry and raced toward Harry, who leaned down to give a stern "No!" before relenting and patting the dog's head to show he was forgiven. When Harry drew near the tree, Miss Tunstall's exasperated expression from her perch brought up a bubble of laughter in him, which he allowed to escape when he saw she was unharmed.

"It seems you are forever to be my knight-errant." Miss Tunstall sat with her arm around the trunk and her ankles crossed below her. Harry kept his eyes trained on her face.

"A role I take on gladly," he replied. "Have you suffered any hurt?"

"Only to my pride. To further my humiliation, I will have to ask you to help me down," Miss Tunstall said. "As it is, I've already ripped my dress."

She was sitting on a low, thick branch and must have climbed up using the knobs on the tree, probably in great fright. Harry reached his hands up. After hesitating, Miss Tunstall stepped on the branch just below and from there allowed herself to fall into his arms. He caught her just above her waist and, without intending to throw away propriety, bore the brunt of her weight as he pulled her against him. He stood there for a moment, stunned, with her body flush against his before he came to his senses and pulled away. He thought he saw her blush, and he was perhaps not the only one who had been affected.

Desperate to return to a more proper mode of address, Harry clasped his hands behind his back and turned toward the house. "Were you heading back?"

"I wasn't, but after the ignominious ending to my walk, I believe I had better." Miss Tunstall shook out her skirt and took her place at his side. "Whose dog was that? Do you know?"

"I believe it to be Mr. Harmon's. He is an overzealous sheep dog and probably thought you were a wayward sheep."

"Mr. Aston, that is an unflattering thing to say." Miss Tunstall's severe tone was belied by her quivering lips. The dog had been examining a lump of dubious substance, and he now came running over to them, his tail wagging. She moved closer to Harry.

"Are you nervous around dogs?" he asked, taking her hand and slipping it into his arm.

"Not at all. We only got off on the wrong foot." Miss Tunstall stopped when the dog drew near and, pulling off her glove, put her hand down to greet him.

Harry waited, prepared to intervene, but he knew the dog meant no harm. When the canine lost interest, he ran off, and they continued down the path in silence. He could ask Miss Tunstall what she had thought of Sunday's service, but that would seem like he was fishing for compliments. Or it might seem as though he were overly interested in the religious tone of her mind, which, admittedly, he was even if it was not precisely his affair. Neither was the right thing to say.

"Are you fully recovered from the incident upon your arrival?" he asked with a sideways glance. Her profile was perfect in his estimation, with a nose that pulled her upper lip into a pucker that begged to be kissed. He whipped his face forward. It would not do to think of that.

"Does anyone in the village know about it?" Miss Tunstall asked, lifting her eyes to his. Her lashes were long and dark for someone with such blonde hair. He was mesmerized by the way those lashes opened and closed over her bewitching eyes. For a moment, over the thudding of his heart, Harry forgot she had asked a question and was flustered when called upon to respond. It was only later that he realized she had avoided his own question. Perhaps she did not like to talk about herself.

"Apart from me," Harry answered, "no one except Eli Smith, a maid who assisted me in collecting your belongings and repacking your trunk, and two other men who took the carriage and hired horses to the nearest posting house. They are discreet, I assure you."

He felt the need to mention the help of one of his maids, wishing to spare her the embarrassment of thinking he had gone through her things. It was true, he had seen a few items that genteel young women kept hidden, and, as he had no sisters, was intrigued by the mystery of them.

"I am relieved. You told Emily there would be an investigation into the matter. Do you think I have any hope of getting my things returned?"

"I've had a response to my inquiry. Squire Mayne, our justice of the peace, has informed me that the Bow Street Runners are investigating a similar matter in a nearby town. I believe they will come here after that. The highwaymen held up an earl last month and have eluded the horse patrol to such a degree they felt the matter would be better served with a proper investigation, which is why the Runners were called in."

Miss Tunstall's arm tensed at his side.

"If you would like, I can be present when they speak with you," Harry said.

Miss Tunstall nodded. "I would be most grateful. I am accustomed to thinking myself quite worldly, but this journey has shown me I live a sheltered life. I am beginning to recognize just how green I am."

"No." Harry remembered the way she fought to sit up after being knocked on the head and the way she teased despite feeling ill. "You have the most incredible courage I've ever seen in a young lady."

"Have you any sisters?" she asked.

He shook his head, and she smiled. "I believe that is why. We are a headstrong sex, Mr. Aston. You must not know many young ladies, particularly if you have been a parson for long."

"Ah." Harry raised an eyebrow. "But you see, I was not always a parson."

Chapter Six

Anna turned to Mr. Aston in surprise. "I detect a mysterious past. How very surprising. Do your parishioners know?"

Mr. Aston laughed and, in a fluid movement, guided her around a stone in the path. Anna was used to the practiced movements of gallantry from members of the ton, but his seemed more like an instinct to protect. Awareness coursed through her, and an unidentifiable longing nudged her heart. The feeling was most unpleasant. She preferred her heart intact.

"My parishioners know very little of my past life, and I prefer it that way," Mr. Aston said.

When she turned to him in astonishment, he added, "No, no, it's not what you think. I have nothing to be ashamed of. I wish only to be judged on my own merit as a rector and a man."

She was not convinced, and it must have shown because he laughed again, the two dimples lending a boyish air to his handsome face. "I trailed a doctor for two years, convinced it was to be medicine for me, to the complete despair of my parents, I might add. I began to have a change of heart at age twenty-three, and that was when I became a deacon and assisted a priest in a London parish before becoming fully ordained a year later."

"And your parents find your life in the church more palatable?" Anna asked, wondering what pushed him to make the change.

"Hardly," he answered. "I believe they would prefer me to be a gentleman farmer."

"Well, that is a worthy calling if one is lucky enough to secure a small estate that produces enough income." Anna turned down the path leading back to the manor, strangely reluctant to bring her conversation with Mr. Aston to a close. He released her arm to allow her to walk ahead of him as the path narrowed.

"I beg your forgiveness for sounding overly pious, Miss Tunstall, but all callings are worthy." Mr. Aston spoke in great earnestness, and it reminded her that despite his easygoing nature and his ability to find humor in most situations, he took his own calling to heart. How unused to such a thing she was.

Mr. Aston continued, "I trailed the doctor and learned a great deal that is useful in my role as a man of the cloth. Sometimes the doctor is unable to attend to his patients because he is away in a neighboring town. I may then step in for the smaller services, especially for the poorer of the flock."

"And does the doctor attend to the poor as willingly as he does to those who may more easily show their gratitude?" Anna thought of how attentive the doctor had been and how cheerfully he had prescribed a great number of medicines—*the better to pad his bill*, she thought.

"Fortunately, for the harmony in our relationship, he does indeed." Mr. Aston turned to her. "And you show what sincerity your heart possesses to have asked such a thing."

Anna opened her eyes wide. "Do not bestow upon me such noble attributes. I assure you, you are wide of the mark."

Mr. Aston raised his hands, acknowledging the hit. "No such thing," he assured her. "I can see you are quite self-absorbed."

Before she could register the quirk of his lips, he took her elbow once again to lead her over a tiny footbridge that crossed the creek and led to the manor.

Anna was obliged to laugh. "Perhaps somewhere in between the two. Neither altruistic nor selfish."

"And perhaps I, too, fall somewhere between altruism and selfishness. I've certainly been accused of both, for I find that, as much as it is fitting to honor one's parents, I have not been able to honor their wishes for my occupation. However, I will say this in defense of my past and present occupation: both a doctor and a parson work toward the same objective—to heal. I just chose to devote my life to the healing that is longer lasting."

Soon they reached the front door. "Hm," Anna said, not quite pleased. This was indeed pious, but she was unable to laugh at him. Mr. Aston was not someone she could allow to make any headway into her heart. Of that she was fully convinced. But when he took her hand in his and bowed over it, the gesture nudged at her awareness again. She found him appealing, despite how adamant her mind was in telling her she did not. It was fortunate she would not be staying for more than a few weeks in Avebury. Mr. Aston made her entirely too uncomfortable for her own good.

"I will bid you good day then." Anna held out her hand.

"Good day," he replied, bowing over her hand and turning to go as if he had been waiting only to be released. He walked toward the stables where a groom was leading out his horses.

This puzzled her. Although Anna had ended the conversation, Mr. Aston's abrupt willingness to follow led her to believe that perhaps she had been mistaken in perceiving an interest from his quarter.

All the better, she thought. But in her mind, she turned over the conversation, giving it more weight than she would have liked to admit.

When Anna entered the house, she felt a change in the atmosphere at once. The house was as quiet as a tomb. Anna had been here exactly one week, and the rooms had always been flooded with light and fresh air, with servants bustling back and forth. Before Anna had left for her walk, she had noticed that Emily hadn't seemed quite herself. Now Anna was determined to seek her out and establish the cause.

She found Emily in the morning room with the curtains drawn.

"My dear," Anna said, walking over to pull the curtains on the rods and let the glorious sun stream into the room. "What has thrown you into such a gloom?" She took a seat across from Emily.

Emily's face was white when she met Anna's gaze. "I have the strangest premonition, Anna." Her voice was barely above a whisper.

Anna was generally unperturbed by the premonitions and fancies people thought they'd had, but Emily's white face and somber tone sent a flash of fear through Anna. Perhaps Anna's fear stemmed from the fact that Emily had always been as carefree as she herself was, and the shift in behavior felt ominous. Perhaps it was simply the danger Anna felt was bearing down on her own heart, where giving in would be inconceivable, but she couldn't shake the foreboding as easily as she would have wished.

"Nonsense," she replied in a bracing tone. "No such thing. What premonition do you believe to have had?"

Emily picked at the fringe of the blanket she had thrown over her legs. "Something has happened to John."

"You cannot know that." Anna lightly shook Emily's arm and forced her to meet her gaze. "You have your daughter to think about and must fix your thoughts on something more positive. Premonitions are only feelings; they are not evidence."

Anna saw a flash of recognition in Emily's eyes, as if her words had hit home. She pressed the point. "Why not ring for tea, then meet with Cook to discuss dinner as you always do? You must be up and *doing* something if you don't wish to fall into a fit of the dismals. Speaking of which . . ."

Anna couldn't believe she was about to suggest such a thing when she knew it would mean entertaining village families who held no interest for her. "Why do we not throw our own party? Or perhaps we might plan an al fresco lunch at one of the nearby places to visit. Is Stonehenge very far?"

As Anna had hoped, Emily seemed to revive at the idea. "I had not thought to throw a party this close to my confinement, but a picnic is a very good idea. I think I can still manage it if it is done soon," Emily said, the dull expression leaving her eyes. Anna watched the improvement with satisfaction.

"It's the very thing," Emily decided after they had discussed menu possibilities for their picnic. She stood with the slightest difficulty over her growing belly. "You are right, Anna. I will shake off such ridiculous feelings, for that is all they are. Let me ring Cook for some bread and fruit, for it is nearing two o'clock and I am famished."

The Bow Street Runners arrived at last on Friday, the day that the Rigbys' evening rout would occur—a party Harry had been very much looking forward to because he would see Miss Tunstall there. He was hoeing the vegetables in the small garden plot alongside Tom Wardle when he saw the two men, meanly dressed, entering his property. Tom must have known at a glance who they were because he gave a nervous jump—an instinctive reaction to men of authority, Harry was sure. He put out his hand to reassure Tom before walking forward to greet them.

"Gentlemen," he called out in a cordial voice. "I believe I know why you are here. Why don't we discuss our business indoors? And as you've had a hot ride, I daresay, I will ring for some refreshments."

The stocky gentleman answered. "A heavy wet'll suit me jest fine. Jimmy here'll 'ave tea."

Harry was not overly put out by their lack of deference; he had his reasons for wishing to remain civil. He entered his house with the two men trailing behind. "We have two visitors, Mrs. Foucher, and will be requiring some of your home-brewed and a pot of tea."

The young cook left to do Harry's bidding, and Harry led the way into the library.

"Would you both be seated?" He faced his guests. "We have been waiting for your arrival. I must ask, how did you know to come here when it was Mr. Mayne who sent the letter?"

The heavier one seemed to be the spokesperson for the pair. "Walt Meade is me name, and this 'ere is Jimmy Howe. Them bully ruffians shot up three other coaches in a week, and we'd had our hands full, as you might say. We was at Mrs. Leatham's 'stablishment, and she said as how we ought to see the parson on account of you discovering Miss Tunstall."

Harry felt a flash of disappointment that he had not been there to assist Miss Tunstall in her interview. He quickly decided to seek her out before tonight to see how she fared.

"What is it you wish to know? How may I help?"

Mr. Meade accepted the glass the servant handed him and took a long draught before wiping his mouth on his sleeve.

"There being a great number of robberies on the King's Road in this wicinity, we 'ave reason to believe the high toby is someone as knows these here parts. We was wondering iffin *you* 'ave an idea." He shot a keen look at Harry and touched his finger to his nose. "Mayhaps prish'ners open the budget wit their parson. Mayhaps you know who is guilty."

"My dear sirs," Harry said with a lift of his eyebrow. "You can hardly expect me to trample on the confidence of my parishioners and disclose sins that were confessed in private."

Meade did not seem abashed by the rebuke. "Well, we *had* hoped as you might say . . ."

Harry shook his head. "I would never do it." After a moment's thought, he added, "However, I might reassure you on that head. No one has ever confessed anything of that nature in my hearing. So if it is indeed someone local—and I would find it hard to believe such a thing, knowing my own parishioners—they have not confided the deed to me."

"Was anyone in the wicinity when you . . . might I say, stumbled on the coach?"

Meade's words triggered surprise in Harry—then a flash of guilt—because Harry knew a temptation to dissemble. He wanted to protect his parishioners, not give them up to law enforcers who looked as if they, themselves, had only just left the darker trade.

Harry answered with reluctance. "Eli Smith was there before me. I don't think he had anything to do with the robbery." He was only half-conscious that he had neglected to mention Tom, whose path he had crossed just before that. But Tom wasn't *technically* at the scene of the robbery.

Mr. Howe scribbled the name in his notebook, and Harry asked, "What did Miss Tunstall have to say when you pressed her for details?" It was an attempt at diversion, but Harry could not resist the call to speak her name, as if saying it would bring her close.

"The squire relayed our questions, and Miss Tunstall gave 'im a description of the gentl'man in our 'earing."

Mr. Meade shared a look with his associate. "She said as how the men's faces was hidden on account of the kerchiefs and said as how there 'us a third gentl'man who'd not been with t'others. He called one of 'em 'Ambrose' before she was snuffed, so to speak. The gentl'man who put his arm 'round her did not smell very good, she said, but what we are to do with *that* information I can*not* say."

Harry could almost picture her saying it, and despite his concern, he had to hold back a smile. "A third gentleman, you say? Does she think this is the one who gave her the blow?"

The men nodded but offered nothing further. Harry was forced to ask, "Then do you have any leads, gentlemen? Any idea what happened to the maid that was carried away? Miss Tunstall's jewels?"

Jimmy Howe, a small, neat man, closed the portfolio he had been using to make notes and spoke his first words. "Can't say as we do. We found the driver as he was about to board a stagecoach back to London. He gave a better description of the highwayman, but he took to heel before he saw the second gentleman accost Miss Tunstall and knew nothing about the third."

Mr. Howe tucked the portfolio in his coat, and Harry wondered that it was not Mr. Howe the spokesman since he was clearly the more educated of the two.

Mr. Howe appeared to read Harry's mind because he gave him a brief smile before leaning forward in his chair. "I prefer for Mr. Meade to speak until I have time to assess people and uncover whatever their mannerisms and thoughtless speech will reveal."

"And as we are staying in Calne," Mr. Meade added with a lowered brow, "we 'ave plenty of haportunity to observe."

Harry sensed distrust through their covert glances and all they did not reveal—if not distrust in him, then at least in the innocence of his parishioners. As to that, he had nothing to add, nor, it seemed, anything new to learn.

He stood. "You know where to find me if you need any further assistance." He paused. "Well, anything that does not conflict with my commitment to the cloth."

Mr. Meade and Mr. Howe stood as well and followed Harry outdoors, where they took their leave. Harry leaned against the open door, watching them untie their horses. So there had been three men total. Two who had initially attacked Miss Tunstall and one who came afterwards and who appeared to be the one to cause her harm. How strange that she hadn't mentioned the number of people when describing the incident and that one of them would arrive late. Then again, Harry had to admit, he had been too out of kelter by the force of attraction to ask for more details.

Harry rubbed his face in his hands. He needed to think clearly about this. Who was Ambrose? Had Harry been wrong in assuming Eli Smith was innocent? Frustrated, he turned to fetch his hat and gloves and set out to visit Durstead Manor.

As he was about to cross the stables, he ran into Tom Wardle and put his hand out to stop him. "Those Runners believe someone local assisted in the highway robbery. There was a third man who was not with the original two. What do you make of that?"

"Well, sir." Tom didn't quite meet Harry's gaze, but that was nothing unusual. Ever since Tom had come into Harry's orbit, he had never seemed able to shake the awareness or guilt of his past. "I believe our village 'tis honest as any."

"I agree with you," Harry said. "And I told the Runners as much. But I don't think it's satisfied them, and I suspect they will be staying in the area. They may even wish to speak to you."

Harry turned to the road, eager to arrive at the manor before it was too late. Surely Emily and Anna would be dressing for the dinner party soon, where he hoped to see them again.

"Me, sir?" At Tom's nervous tone, Harry turned back.

"Well, you in the sense that you are working for me, and I was the one who discovered the incident. In fact, you know the area and the people well, and you were not far from the scene. Perhaps you saw something when you visited Haggle End?" Harry said the latter in the form of a question, but Tom was already shaking his head.

"No, sir. I ain't seen nothing."

Harry paused, willing Tom to confess if there was something to confess. He had preached often enough about forgiveness, the man ought not to be scared. Harry's scrutiny seemed to provoke Tom to answer because he scuffed his boot in the earth and met Harry's gaze.

"I only be fearing them men'll cause trouble in these parts is all. Jest when things be starting to change."

Harry could sympathize. *That* same problem worried him, too, particularly when church attendance had never been so high. They didn't need any highwaymen settling nearby and tempting the weaker members of the flock to a life of crime.

He bid farewell to Tom, pondering just how he might exhort them to resist evil and do good in his next sermon. He continued on foot until he reached Durstead Manor. As he stood before the knocker, he hesitated, wondering if he were intruding on the women's privacy since he could just as easily ask them about the Runners' visit this evening. He consoled himself with the thought that they would surely not wish to discuss something so private in a public setting.

The butler admitted him at once, and as soon as Harry entered the room, his eyes sought out Miss Tunstall. Mrs. Leatham rose to her feet and went to meet him.

"You have heard the news that the Bow Street Runners made their visit here, perhaps? Mr. Mayne brought them and stayed so Miss Tunstall could be spared a direct questioning."

"They told me you sent them to me after your visit. I wish I might have been here to assist you both, although I'm glad the squire was." Harry darted his gaze back to Miss Tunstall. "I had hoped that after a week your jewels, at least, might be found. But apparently, there has been a spate of robberies that have delayed their visit until now."

Mrs. Leatham had taken her seat again, encouraging Harry to take the one closer to Miss Tunstall. It was she who picked up the thread of conversation. "I am not so concerned about my jewels. I took only what I could bear to part with for this trip, as one must be realistic."

"That is wise. I should not like the thought of you distressed over the loss of something of great value."

"No." Miss Tunstall clasped her hands in her lap. "The value was not so very great, although I would like them returned to me, of course. I only wish the thieves may be caught to save others from suffering a disagreeable fate."

"The Runners will continue to make inquiries until they get a promising lead—I have no doubt of that." Harry rubbed his chin. "They think someone local aided them, which I have a hard time believing."

"Impossible," Mrs. Leatham said.

"I told them as much," Harry replied, agreeing with Mrs. Leatham and offering her a smile of approval. She had come to Avebury only three months before him, but her husband had grown up here, and she had quickly made his home and its people her own.

Harry transferred his gaze to Miss Tunstall, and he wondered if she could ever do the same. Could she leave London for a quiet life in Avebury? He wasn't sure. A silence settled over the room, and Harry's thoughts drifted to how he might tempt the enchanting Miss Tunstall to prolong her stay.

"Mr. Aston," Mrs. Leatham said. "Will you be attending tonight's rout?"

He snapped to attention. "Yes, I wouldn't miss it. And you? Will you go?" Harry knew he sounded eager, despite himself.

"We do plan to go, Mr. Aston." Mrs. Leatham smiled at him with an air of mischief. "We might even be on time if we are allowed to dress."

Harry's gaze flew to the ormolu clock on the mantelpiece.

"Good heavens." He leapt to his feet. "I had not realized." He saw Miss Tunstall's eyes twinkling with amusement. "I came only to apprise you of their visit to the rectory, but I will leave at once, for I can see it is much later than I had thought."

The two women stood, too well-bred to say anything to further his discomfort, but Harry suffered all the same. It had been many years since he'd been a bashful schoolboy. When he left Durstead Manor, however, that was exactly how he felt.

Chapter Seven

"Well." Emily spoke the word with such significance, and Anna ignored the weighted meaning in the look that accompanied it, moving instead toward the door.

Not deterred, Emily walked in step alongside Anna. "How kind of Mr. Aston to ensure we were not overly troubled by the Bow Street Runners. He could very well have asked after our well-being at tonight's party."

Anna shrugged. "I am sure Mr. Aston is much too considerate to bring up such a delicate subject in a public setting. He is surely falling upon his training as a pastor to attend to us properly."

Why *did* Mr. Aston come? Was it just to see her, as Emily seemed to think, or was it because he feared to upset her by speaking of it in public? She added, "Not that he was able to provide us with any real help or useful information. He could only say that they would continue their inquiries, which we already knew. Mr. Mayne has the matter well in hand. It is not as if Mr. Aston has connections to any important persons who might see that the matter is properly attended to."

Anna turned the door handle and walked into the corridor. "Then he might be of real service."

"Anna," Emily mildly rebuked as they headed to their rooms to dress. "You set your expectations too high."

Anna refused to make any particular efforts on her appearance for the local pastor, and it did not take long to dress. As the groom brought round the horses, she more closely examined Emily, whose evening gown clung to her and revealed an ever growing middle. "My

44

dear, are you certain of your delivery date? You look as if you could give birth at any moment."

"The doctor has said it is for September, so it must be so. In any case I cannot have John miss the birth of his daughter."

Anna smiled. "No, you certainly cannot. Even if he is convinced it is a son. When does he propose to return? I hope it is to be before you are confined. Shall our visits cross, do you think?"

"It is possible. In the case that my confinement occurs before my mother or John arrive, I shall ask *you* to attend to me in the birthing room. You may hold my hand." Emily followed that with an impish laugh. "You are so easy to read, dearest. Have no fear. I know such a thing would be improper, besides being wholly beside what you could bear. My mother will arrive a week after your departure, should the baby decide to make an early appearance. And John was hopeful he would be here in September, and I believe he will be.

"In any case," Emily continued cheerfully, all signs of her formerly gloomy prediction gone, "I am expecting word from him at any moment that his ship has docked at Portsmouth. He will surely send more precise news of his return then, if he does not show up in person in the meantime."

Anna followed Emily into the carriage and took a seat across from her. "Then we have only to think of amusing ourselves. Let it be a night for frolic and fun. Do you know who will attend?"

"Oh—do you mean, who will attend apart from Mr. Aston?" Emily's lips turned up.

"I do not think of Mr. Aston at all," Anna fenced. "Why should I? You must know I am much too indolent and addicted to society to contemplate such a match."

"And yet I do not think his suit is hopeless." Emily infused a slight singsong to her voice.

Anna sniffed. "I've never known you to be so impervious to reason, but persist in false hopes if you must."

The Rigby house was larger than Anna had expected for a country dwelling that was not a seat. It was an honest square structure, built of perfectly cut grey stones. On either side of the front door were four double windows and a second story duplicate. Upon entering, Anna and Emily were directed to the ballroom on their left, where a receiving line extended into the hallway.

Anna leaned in to whisper to Emily. "I can see why the Rigbys put on airs. This is a very fine house." Emily had only time to give a speaking look before they stood before their hosts.

"Mrs. Leatham, Miss Tunstall." Mrs. Rigby gave a regal nod. "I believe you are acquainted with Sir Lewis Faure and Mr. Cranfield, who are visiting from London." She gestured in the direction of the two gentlemen standing just inside the ballroom, and Anna started at the names, which tripped often enough off the tongues of London Society.

"Why, yes, our paths cross frequently in London. Whatever are they doing here?" Anna had not long to wonder, for as soon as Mr. Cranfield spotted her, he nudged Sir Lewis, who had paused for conversation with Miss Rigby.

Miss Marianne called out to Anna from her place in the receiving line. "Miss Tunstall, if you've any trouble finding partners, you need only address yourself to me." She darted a quick glance at Mr. Cranfield and Sir Lewis. "I will be happy to see that you don't sit out any of the dances, for I know everyone here."

Anna began to think she had more properly taken Miss Marianne's measure by now.

"You are too kind." Her smile for Miss Rigby came more easily, especially when she thought she detected a look of exasperation on her face. Emily and Anna entered the ballroom, where they joined the two London gentlemen.

Mr. Cranfield made a sweeping bow, his floral scent overpowering Anna. "Miss Tunstall, imagine my shock to find you here in Avebury. I would not have thought you'd care to be so far from London—or I imagined you'd have your hands full helping Worthing in the marriage preparations." Mr. Cranfield tapped his cane on the ground and allowed his gaze to dart over the assembly. "Nothing to do but move forward now that the gossip mill has stopped spinning around Miss Daventry."

Anna's lips settled in a thin line. Mr. Cranfield had been referencing her future sister-in-law, whose reputation had been unfairly maligned by all of London Society until Anna had stepped in. She knew better than anyone why the gossip mill had stopped churning out insults regarding Eleanor, and she couldn't resist the satisfaction of asking after the fate of its two principal instigators.

"And have you seen Miss Price? Or Miss Broadmore? They were most adamant in their assertions." Anna smiled sweetly.

Despite Sir Lewis's look of warning, Mr. Cranfield continued blithely. "It's odd now that you mention it. They both retired from Society quite in haste. Miss Price's family decided to leave for an extended visit to their estate in Cardiff with no immediate plans of return. And Miss Broadmore contracted a marriage quite suddenly."

He tugged absently at his shirt points, a puzzled look to his face. "She had always been such a stickler for marriage candidates. I am quite beside myself to know why Miss Broadmore should settle for Mr. Ponsonberry."

"Mr. Ponsonberry? Indeed." *How the mighty have fallen*, Anna thought with satisfaction. This was precisely the sort of news she'd missed since leaving London. Mr. Ponsonberry was a timid, malleable sort of creature, twice Judith Broadmore's age and not likely ever to make a splash in the haut ton. It was equally of no surprise that Harriet Price had felt forced to flee when her own interlude with John Fortescue, one of Society's rakes, came to light. Harriet and Judith's coordinated attempt to destroy Eleanor Daventry's reputation—Eleanor, the one Anna's brother had chosen to marry—could not succeed once Anna had decided to champion Eleanor's cause. It had simply taken a few choice words in the right ears.

It was a most effective counterattack. Just as I knew it would be, she thought. *I was made to lead Society.*

"Who is Mr. Ponsonberry?" Anna was brought back to the present—a society far from London's vicious web—by Mr. Aston's question, cheerfully asked, his frank gaze pinning her in place. Although she had seen him only a couple hours earlier, her pulse kicked up a notch when she turned to find him here.

Still, she tossed her head and replied, "No one of consequence," offering him a brief smile to take away the sting of her words. It was unthinkable for her to give Mr. Aston special consideration when there were London beaux in Avebury.

Turning back to Mr. Cranfield and Sir Lewis, Anna inquired, "What has brought you to this village? However did you find it?"

"I might ask the same of you," Mr. Cranfield answered. "Lewis here has a box in the county, and I've come for some diversion." His gaze settled first on Miss Marianne and then on Anna. He smiled vapidly. "Never did I suspect to be so happily diverted."

Miss Marianne, still in the receiving line, darted jealous glances at their party. Anna sighed inwardly. *Mr. Cranfield will one day inherit a fine estate, but he hasn't two thoughts to rub together. You may have him.*

Mr. Aston stepped forward and filled the small space between Mr. Cranfield and Anna until she was forced to notice him. In a voice harder than she'd yet heard him use, he addressed Mr. Cranfield.

"Are you acquainted with Mrs. Leatham?"

Anna was wondering whether jealousy was behind that firm tone when his question penetrated her senses. *Emily!* With a guilty start, Anna remembered her friend, who had been standing patiently at her side and who was surely in need of someplace to sit and something to drink.

"Oh, yes," Anna interjected, eager to make up for her lapse. "Please allow me to present Mrs. Leatham, with whom I am staying. She is formerly Miss Emily Randall, daughter of the secretary to the prime minister, and now married to John Leatham, a captain of a frigate on the Mediterranean." She bestowed a bright smile on the two gentlemen from London.

"Very pleased to make your acquaintance," Mr. Cranfield said.

Miss Rigby, who had separated herself from the welcoming line that was now receiving the stragglers, touched Sir Lewis lightly on the arm. Her quiet murmur was barely audible. "Captain Leatham was also interested in our project of opening a school in Haggle End. Had you spoken of it with him?"

Sir Lewis shook his head and leaned in to reply to Miss Rigby.

Anna's eyes narrowed at the interchange. *If Miss Rigby is not careful, she might scare off her swain. I don't believe Mr. Aston to be the type to share the affection of his betrothed.*

Even as Anna indulged in this fit of petty thinking, she had to acknowledge privately that not only did she not believe for a minute that Miss Rigby was engaging in a flirtation with Sir Lewis—or that Mr. Aston had eyes for Miss Rigby—there was a pull on Anna's heart, a tug of awareness, that made her wonder whether Mr. Aston had eyes for *her.*

Apparently he was not thinking of Anna at all because Mr. Aston performed the service she should have thought of first.

"Mrs. Leatham, might I escort you to one of the chairs in the far corner? You will feel some of the fresh air there, I believe, and I will bring you a glass of lemonade."

"I would like that above everything." Emily placed her hand on Mr. Aston's arm and smiled at Anna in a gracious way that only increased Anna's guilt. They turned toward the far end of the room, and Anna forced herself to turn back to the two London guests.

"Will you be staying for the entirety of the summer?" Anna asked the men. "When do you head back to London?"

"We will be here until October, I suppose, when there might be some doings in London, eh Lewis?" Mr. Cranfield nudged his friend, who added his murmur of assent.

"I hope we shall have the pleasure of meeting often," Sir Lewis said.

"A summer in Avebury is looking to be more promising than last year," Miss Rigby said. "Already there is no shortage of parties planned, and given the number of invitations that have gone out since your arrival, I believe we have you to thank."

Anna smiled at Miss Rigby's quiet humor, which she thought only Sir Lewis had perceived.

Anna's gaze drifted to Mr. Aston, who stood conversing with Lord Allinthridge. Despite Mr. Aston being nothing more than a country parson, he had managed to outshine the London gentleman in his tailored black coat and a white cravat tied tastefully underneath his handsome square jaw. She forced herself to return to the conversation at hand.

"It will be a pleasure, I am sure."

Miss Marianne had finished flirting with one of the latecomers and lost no time in joining their circle.

"Miss Tunstall, I see you have met our guests," she said. "Mr. Cranfield, the dancing will begin after the sandwiches are served. I hope you will be willing to stand up with all the eligible ladies. And you, too, Sir Lewis."

Mr. Cranfield had discovered the panes of reflective glass that had been built into the door and was examining himself in them. Sir Lewis complimented Miss Marianne on the musicians, asking if they were the group he'd heard about that could be hired from Calne.

Anna's attention wandered again as she scanned the faces in the room, finally settling upon Mr. Aston leaning against a stone arch. His gaze was fixed on her. The unexpectedness of his regard shot a bolt of searing awareness through her, and she quickly looked away.

To his right, Emily was seated, engaged in conversation with Lady Allinthridge. Anna peeped back at Mr. Aston only to see that his focus had not shifted. As their gaze met, he pushed off the wall and stood straight. Anna had the oddest sensation when he stared at her in such a manner. She was determined not to go over.

On their own accord, however, her feet began to make their way across the room. *I will not be deterred by his presence*, Anna convinced herself. *I merely wish to speak to Emily and Lady Allinthridge. I will not make any special attempt to talk to him.*

Anna felt Mr. Aston's eyes on her the entire way across the ballroom until she reached Emily. Without a word, she turned her back on him as she took a seat next to Emily, waiting for her to finish her conversation. The whole while she felt the weight of Mr. Aston's stare.

At last, Emily paused in her conversation and looked at Anna in concern. "You seem to be unnerved, my dear. Is something the matter?"

Mr. Aston had come to stand at Anna's side, so she could not express what was causing her to be more ruffled than usual—not that she would have said anything about Mr. Aston at all, even if there was no one in the room but her and Emily. *How ridiculous I am being.*

"No, no, I am perfectly fine," she answered. "Were you not astonished to see Sir Lewis and Mr. Cranfield here?"

"I did know Sir Lewis had property here because he called upon my husband last fall. I'd not met Mr. Cranfield before tonight, but of course I knew of him. He is Sir Lewis's guest, is he not, Mr. Aston?"

Mr. Aston stepped forward. "He is, indeed. They are friends of mine from Harrow and Oxford, and we renewed our acquaintance in London."

They are friends of Mr. Aston's? Anna thought with shock. She had not realized the gentlemen had met before tonight—or that Mr. Aston's station was such that he could claim such an acquaintance.

Mr. Aston looked at Anna keenly. "How well do *you* know them?" he asked.

Anna ignored the question; the answer wasn't very interesting. She knew them like she knew all society gentlemen—on a purely surface level, although, of course, that could change the minute she decided someone's acquaintance was worth pursuing further. Which could be anyone . . . except Mr. Aston.

Instead she said, "If you knew them from London, I'm surprised *our* paths did not cross there."

"I was not in London at the same time as you, I fear." Mr. Aston smiled in his disarming way. "And when I was, I did not go into society much. I was carrying on my apprenticeship at the time."

Emily and Lady Allinthridge had ceased their conversation, and Anna's neck began to ache from looking up at Mr. Aston. Still, she persevered in a conversation that held some interest for her.

"Do you miss it? Not going about in society? There are many diversions to find there." Her eyes dropped as she looked around. "And this is such an out-of-the-way place."

Mr. Aston waited until Anna's gaze returned, drawing her to him as if they were the only two in the room. Emily had turned away and now leaned over to inquire something of Lady Allinthridge, giving Mr. Aston and Anna some privacy.

"No, I am happy here." Suddenly he said, "Miss Tunstall, will you take a turn about the room with me? I fear this mode of conversation is uncomfortable for you, having always to look up at me. But there are no chairs I might carry over to sit by you."

Anna set her hand in the elbow he crooked down and allowed him to assist her to stand. *His is not practiced gallantry*, she thought when she saw the intention in his gaze. *He does it out of true chivalrous feeling, I believe.*

Mr. Aston pulled her closer as they moved forward through the crowd. The heat of his presence, his brilliant eyes when he turned them on her, caused all rational thought to flee. It was a helpless feeling that made her want to lash out at someone—in particular Mr. Aston.

"I have always known that I was a man of the country," Mr. Aston said. It did not seem as if he was affected by their closeness. "It was never my intention to be a Society gentleman. I do enjoy my friends' society, but as for the endless balls and routs, I cannot stomach such a thing."

"No thought for politics, then? Politics is an interesting calling. You can drive government and Society alike, sometimes over the course of a simple house party."

Anna had found her voice, but as soon as the words were out, she felt she was treading on dangerous ground because it would seem as if she cared—as if what Mr. Aston did with his life would have any impact on her future. The seed of frustration that had sprouted, simply by the fact that Anna was affected by the man, took root when she saw how she'd lost the ability to keep her wits before speaking.

"I may have been misled in my early career," he replied, "but I don't think I was meant to do anything else but ministerial work. I am not one who does it because there is no other living offered to me. I am one who does it because I care to."

Mr. Aston indicated the couples standing on the dance floor, as if sure of her answer before he posed the question. "There is a set forming. Would you care to dance it with me?"

Anna glanced over at Emily, who had been watching them, her clever gaze missing nothing.

"I would be delighted," Anna replied, her mouth set in a prim line. What else could she do? She could not turn him down, as she had no other dances promised. Besides, she admitted to herself with annoyance, he was surely the most interesting person to dance with in the room.

She and Mr. Aston took their places in the line, and when the music began they were no longer able to converse. Every time their hands joined, he caught her gaze, and she was helpless to resist the spark of attraction that resulted.

However, now that she was released from their intimate conversation, Anna had time for reflection. She was able to examine what was in her heart. *Clearly I am not interested in furthering my acquaintance with Mr. Aston. He does not frequent Society. He said so himself. Can you imagine? Life in this little village tending the poor?* She shuddered.

Mr. Aston's steps were graceful as he spun with her on his arm, and his attention extended beyond her to the other couple they danced with. Anna didn't even remember their names.

The music came to an end, and Mr. Aston stopped and faced her with a bow. As he led her off the dance floor, steering her away from Mr. Cranfield and Sir Lewis, he pulled her close to his side again in an intimate way she wanted to object to but could not find her voice to do so.

"Miss Tunstall," he said as they neared where Emily sat, "I will call on you this week."

He did not ask if he could. He simply took her acquiescence for granted, as if she were one of his parishioners and he her ecclesiastical guide.

I will be busy. I will be out. I do not think this is a wise idea. Anna's whole being should have revolted, yet she could only nod in agreement. "With pleasure, Mr. Aston."

What a simpleton.

Disgusted with herself, Anna returned to sit next to Emily, who was now alone. There was no time to reflect on Anna's turmoil of emotions as she was immediately solicited for the next dance and then the five following that. There could not be a huge number of dances as there were not many available gentlemen present, but she was asked for every one.

Miss Rigby, she noticed, had been invited twice by Sir Lewis, and finally by Mr. Aston. Anna furrowed her brows. *Perhaps he does find her to his liking.*

When it came time to leave, she thankfully turned toward the front door. It had been, overall, a rather insipid party.

Chapter Eight

As Anna and Emily waited on the front steps for the coachman to bring the carriage, Anna hooked her arm through Emily's.

"How wonderful to have *two* London gentlemen with us," Anna said. "Mr. Cranfield is most entertaining, do you not think?" It was Anna's best attempt at diversion, and when in a better humor, Emily would have seen through it.

Emily gave a noncommittal *hmm*, and Anna tried again. "Lady Allinthridge told me when we were taking air together that he has turned off no less than five valets this past year because they have been unable to polish boots to his satisfaction."

"A most diverting gentleman," Emily replied, dispassionately.

The absence of the levity that usually accompanied their banter made Anna wonder if, perhaps, Emily had really changed so much. She could not resist asking, "Do you not miss the conversation and gaiety of the ton living here?"

Emily squeezed her arm. "I miss John."

It was Anna's turn to fall silent. Keeping up a brave façade cost Emily, Anna thought. It was not easy to maintain. After a minute's silence, Emily peered at Anna in the dim light of the lanterns, her humor restored, it seemed, at least for the moment.

"You were deep in conversation with our Mr. Aston," Emily said.

Anna gave Emily a look of studied patience. That was the problem of having a best friend who noticed everything, even when she was feeling melancholy.

"I was merely trying to be polite." When the silence stretched, she added, "Nothing more." In the shadows, Anna could feel, rather than see, the smile hovering on Emily's lips, which she ignored.

At last the carriage appeared, and the footman opened the door and helped her enter. Anna then assisted Emily onto her seat.

"I have sat upon something," Emily exclaimed. "There is something here."

Anna reached for the object on the seat and discovered a familiar green velvet pouch. "Here are my jewels!" she exclaimed, untying the silk strands. "And my coins. Nothing is missing. Whoever could have found this, and how did they know to put it here?" Shivers crept up her neck at the idea that a stranger could track her so easily.

The carriage lurched forward, and Emily slid open the window to call out. They came to an immediate halt, and the footman appeared at the door. "Ay, ma'am?"

Emily, who had been examining the pouch for herself, demanded, "Martin, we found this on the seat. Did you see anyone? Were you with the carriage the entire time?"

"Ay, ma'am. That is to say, I believe . . ."

Emily pierced him with her gaze. "Martin, I will not reprimand you, but please tell me how long you left this carriage unattended and if you saw anyone approach it."

The groom's shoulders slumped. "I be always with the carriage but for visiting Peggy in the kitchen. 'Twas p'raps then 'e came, ma'am."

Emily sighed. "Well," she said, "I guess we may now be certain the thief has some knowledge of Avebury if he knew to put the stolen goods in our carriage, and we know *when* the thief had his opportunity. But the question now is, why?"

The next morning, as Anna and Emily ate breakfast in near silence, each lost in thought, the servant brought in letters on a silver tray. Emily took hers and dismissed the servant after he had handed one to Anna. Anna's letter was from her sister, Phoebe, and she opened it with eager hands.

My dearest Anna,

How was your journey to Avebury? You were surprisingly deficient in details in your last letter, and I expect you to be more forthcoming. Surely there is more to be said than Beatrice Slyfeel's sullen nature and the unaired sheets at the posting house. How is Emily?

Do give her my love and tell her we are anxiously awaiting news of the blessed event.

Here at Worthing, as you can imagine, we are in a flurry of activity as we prepare for Stratford and Eleanor's wedding. The most unfortunate thing has happened, though. Do you remember the dress Eleanor had fitted—the one we all agreed to suit her perfectly? Well, wouldn't you know but one of Mr. Purcell's goats broke free and wandered into our yard just as Eleanor's dress for the wedding was hanging to dry. And she ate the dress, if you can imagine! The goat, that is. Stop laughing, as I know you are doing, for it is all quite tragic. Such a shame that this must happen after all the beading had been sewn in. I know you are congratulating yourself for finding other employment so that you could not help with the beading; otherwise all your work would have been in vain. And now only ours is. Eleanor handled the debacle with great presence of mind, but we will now need to have a new dress made up with great haste.

Do not think we are to go to London to do so, however. Aunt Shae has fallen ill, and she has implored me most emphatically to take on full-time care of her if she has any hopes of improving and has added that you must not hurry back on her account as she is appreciating the calm. She is certain you will be delighted to extend your visit with your dear friend for another couple of weeks while she makes her convalescence. Eleanor, as you know, is no great talker, and whether Aunt Shae refers to the burden of your chatter, I leave for you to decide.

Anna could hear the teasing in her sister's words and knew she was trying to soften the blow of Anna's not being wanted. The letter continued.

However, I fear I will be sadly pulled. It is convenient to have Eleanor staying with her aunt at the dower house, so she may be close at hand for the wedding preparations, but I feel it incumbent upon me to provide for her whatever support I can give as our future sister-in-law. Mrs. Bailey has found someone in the village to perform the tasks I can no longer do—you know all my dear projects—and, as for Aunt Shae, my time is quite taken up reading to her, if it's not bringing all matters of wedding detail in such doses that she doesn't feel the need to fly out of bed, to her detriment. Not that she ever felt

the need to fly out of bed for anything, even her own wedding, if our
mother's stories were to be believed . . .

Anna laughed.

"Oh dear." Emily had her letter smoothed out before her, her brows pinched in concern.

"What is it?" Anna asked.

"I've some bad news," Emily said, looking up at last. "My mother has written to inform me that she cannot come as early as she had planned. Perhaps not even for the birth. My sister's children have caught scarlet fever, and Mother fears to bring the infection with her." She sighed. "Not to mention the fact that she will need to stay and help my sister, who is not very useful in these situations. Poor Charlotte."

Anna studied Emily while her mind raced. "Are you saying you will have no help at all once I leave? When did you say Captain Leatham is supposed to return?"

"John said only that it would be as early in the fall as he can possibly get away and promised to give me more information as soon as he had it. I am only surprised I have not received anything yet. I should be getting word from him any day now, as they must have docked in Portsmouth. It will be a relief to have him back on English soil, although his duties will keep him there another two weeks before he can make his way north to me."

Emily frowned and looked down again at her mother's letter. "I fear for my sister's children, of course, but I am brought low by the thought that my mother will not be here to assist me."

Anna had a troubling suspicion that fate was toying with her. What else could explain the arrival on the same day a letter for herself stating that her presence was not needed at Worthing, and another for Emily that indicated a great need for Anna to remain? She stalled for time.

"Does your mother not say when she might be free to come?"

Emily shook her head. "I am not sure even she knows. I believe these cases to last several weeks, especially as they wait to see who else will succumb to the illness. My mother had it as a child, but my sister has not. Of course, my sister's condition must be the priority over mine, but I do not see how I will find the courage to go through my confinement alone." She turned troubled eyes on Anna.

Anna was far from feeling confident about the decision but said impulsively, "I can stay."

Emily studied Anna's face before shaking her head. "No. I know how much you long to return to Worthing and then to London and how difficult it was to persuade you to come to such a far-out-of-the-way place as Avebury." She gave the ghost of a smile. "I cannot ask this of you."

"But I will no longer be going to London because my aunt is unwell and cannot travel there. I will go only to Worthing to assist in the wedding preparation." Anna glanced at the letter containing her sister's neat script. "However, I believe Phoebe has that well in hand."

Remaining here would be a sacrifice but perhaps not as much of one as going to her brother's house, where Phoebe's capable presence was required everywhere and Anna's not at all—not to mention the fact that she would have to whisper and tiptoe so as not to disturb Aunt Shae. At least with Emily she could be of real use, even if it meant staying in a country village much longer than she had originally hoped.

"Nevertheless, you will think it the greatest bore to be here, and I will not ask it of you." Emily gave a decided shake of her head. "I will ask Lady Allinthridge to visit more often. And Hester, too. I will be fine."

Because Anna didn't have it in her to insist on something she was far from confident she wanted to do, she remained silent. She read the rest of Phoebe's letter, but the silence in the room felt heavy.

"I suppose I shall answer this letter, and then perhaps we may take a walk." Anna knew her voice was artificially bright, but she shoved down any feelings of guilt over not having insisted on offering her aid. Emily agreed to a walk, and Anna escaped to her bedroom.

After their exercise, which did much to restore Emily's spirits, they were seated in the morning room when the bell rang announcing visitors. Miss Rigby entered first, followed by Sir Lewis and Mr. Cranfield. Emily pulled herself to her feet to greet them, allowing the gentlemen to bow over her hand, then Anna's.

"Hester," Emily exclaimed, giving her a warm smile. "Did you come together?"

"It was quite by chance," Miss Rigby said. And then with engaging candidness, she added, "To be perfectly frank, I came by to discuss last night's rout." Her eyes twinkled as she shared a look with Emily and Anna. "Now we won't be able to discuss it *freely*."

Mr. Cranfield sat at Emily's invitation, and Sir Lewis followed suit. "You may be sure to speak about anything you wish, Miss Rigby," Mr. Cranfield said, "but I daresay the ladies' dresses, and even the gentlemen's waistcoats, left much to be desired. It is not to be expected that Avebury could hope to equal London in the latest fashion, I suppose."

Sir Lewis exchanged an amused glance with Miss Rigby and said, "I proclaim your party a success, Miss Rigby. I had not thought to find such a diverse assembly of people in a country village. The ballroom, large though it is, was full."

"I am glad you think so. You are accustomed to London Society, and therefore your praise must be valued more highly." Miss Rigby flushed slightly. "Before Sunday I'd never before seen you in Avebury, although I had heard of your connection to the neighborhood. How long have you had the hunting box in Beckhampton? Do you often stay there, or do you prefer London?"

Unlike Mr. Cranfield, who slouched, Sir Lewis sat straight in his chair in a ready pose that seemed to anticipate whatever project was next.

"My father acquired the hunting box, so it has been in the family for decades. I am most often found in London, and it is only since it came into my hands two years ago that I have begun to seek out the calm and solitude of the country." He smiled kindly as he turned to face Miss Rigby. "Although I had not been much in the habit of coming into Avebury, I expect that will change now that Mr. Aston is here."

Anna observed Miss Rigby's answering smile and wondered for an instant if she had set her sights higher than the country parson. Anna had to be fair to her, though, now that she had begun to know her better. Miss Rigby did not strike her as someone who cast out lures for a man simply because he was titled or wealthy. *Case in point!* Anna thought as revelation struck. *Mr. Aston is neither titled nor wealthy, and she has taken a fancy to him.*

Emily put her hand to her back and shifted in her chair. It was an unconscious gesture and one that told Anna the visit was demanding for her.

"This village does grow upon one," Emily said. "If you were to have told me but two years ago that I would live someplace other than London, I'm not sure I would have believed it. It was my affection for Leatham that allowed me not only to move here but to love it. A heart engaged can embrace many changes." Emily leveled a meaningful gaze at Anna, who ignored it.

"And you, Mr. Cranfield?" Anna smiled at him. No matter how foppish he was, she was sure of his support for her own view. "How do you find the village of Avebury? I believe you are as much addicted to London Society as I am."

"Oh, I find that for a short while repairing to the country does not chafe as much as one might think. But I shall be glad to return to London as soon as my repairing lease is over. I have had a tip that Schultz is attempting a new pattern for a driving cape with *eighteen* folds!"

When Anna met Emily's gaze, she was hard put to keep a straight countenance and was thankful for the butler's entrance at that juncture. He came to stand before his mistress, and Anna, who was closest, discerned the barely audible words.

"A rider has come with an urgent missive." The footman handed Emily a sealed letter.

One glance at the handwriting, and Emily's hands began to shake. She stood and managed to keep her voice calm when she spoke. "Gentlemen, Hester, I hope you will excuse me while I attend to this. Anna, would you kindly see to our guests?"

Anna nodded and attempted to brush aside the foreboding that rose in her heart. She knew there was rarely good news in urgent letters. Whether it was from practiced conversation or from pure selfishness, Mr. Cranfield turned the conversation to some young relative he knew of Lady Allinthridge who had set all of London on its ears by his latest escapade. Anna tried to follow, but her thoughts were on her friend. Was Emily's mother writing again with more sinister news? Was this about John's ship?

A silence fell after Mr. Cranfield stopped talking, and Miss Rigby bit her lip. At last, Sir Lewis leaned forward, his hat in hand, and both he and Miss Rigby stood at the same time.

"I had better go," Miss Rigby said. "I came on foot, and I do believe there will be rain."

Mr. Cranfield stood when she did but made no move to leave. Sir Lewis was more helpful.

"Miss Rigby, perhaps I might accompany you in my curricle. Jules, do you mind the wait? You might walk to Aston's house and wait for me there. He is not far."

Thankfully, Mr. Cranfield seemed at last ready to depart. "The very thing. I am sure Harry has nothing else to do and will be glad to see us, eh?"

They took leave of Anna, and she hurried into the library where Emily was seated, weeping over the letter crumpled in her hands.

"What is it?" When her friend didn't answer, Anna knelt beside her. "Emily, tell me what has happened. I must know. How else can I help you unless I know?"

Emily held out the letter, and Anna attempted to smooth it out and make sense of the crossed lines, written in tiny print, and blotched with tear stains. She couldn't understand why it must take so many words to convey whatever message was so devastating to receive.

Anna looked up at last. "Leatham's ship is missing."

Emily nodded.

"Emily, this is far from a lost cause." Anna got up from her knees and draped her arm around Emily's shoulders. "This letter has only shown that the ship did not meet the *Marmion* at their rendezvous port. It does not mean it is lost. I mean. . . . It does not mean *all* is lost. My dear, you must retain your hope."

"There *is* no hope," Emily wailed. "John would not have let me worry. He would have found some means to communicate with me. All is lost."

She began to weep again, and at the sound, a sense of dread crept over Anna. This was not something she could fix with a few well-placed words in the right ear.

After ten minutes of trying to console Emily and feeling utterly helpless at the attempt, Anna crossed the room and opened the door, sparking a flurry of activity from the servants outside. One came quickly to take her request, concern in her face. When the tea set arrived, Anna carried the tray to the table. She poured a cup that included both milk and an extra spoon of sugar and handed it to Emily.

"No matter what happens, dearest, you must be strong for your baby. Drink."

Emily's eyes stared ahead vacantly, and Anna put an arm around her back and held the cup to her lips. "Drink. You will only spoil your dress if you do not open your lips, and I know how carefully you economize."

Her poor attempt at humor elicited no response, although Emily did obey. After Emily had taken some sips, Anna set down the cup and took Emily's hands in her own and rubbed them. "I will help you. You are not alone."

It seemed as if Emily had not heard, but at last her gaze focused on Anna's face, and she nodded.

I will have to find strength somewhere to do this, Anna thought, as a dull throb began behind her eyes. *It may be the hardest thing I have ever done.* Despite her fears, Anna had to hold on to hope and get Emily to do the same. It was the only way she could get through this day and each one that followed. Perhaps the ship had merely run off course and there was a letter on its way to explain the mishap.

This was what Anna would set her mind on.

Chapter Nine

*H*arry paced back and forth in the comfort of his library, the one luxury he allowed himself as he spared no expense on books and the snug chair in which to read them. The library usually afforded him peace, no matter how grueling his clerical duties sometimes were.

But not today. Miss Tunstall had not fallen into his orbit as readily as he would have liked at the Rigbys' soirée. In fact, except for her moving in his direction after their gaze met at the ball—that could be taken as encouragement, couldn't it?—she seemed almost ready to exclude him from the conversation when she had Jules at her side. And she had been a bit stiff in their conversation overall.

He paused in his steps. *Perhaps if she knew who I am.*

No!

Harry had never stooped to using his family connections. He had never even been tempted to. In fact, he abhorred such a thing. So why was he suddenly willing to throw away a lifetime of honorable conduct for . . . for . . . *a soul of unfathomable depth*?

He shook his head and resumed pacing. That was what he had thought anyway the first time he stared into Miss Tunstall's open eyes—that she had a soul of unfathomable depth. Perhaps he had been wrong. Perhaps her eyes were just pretty and blue. But he wasn't usually such a poor judge of character.

The sound of the knocker pierced Harry's fruitless ruminations. It was probably Mr. Banbury who had promised to pay him a visit, refusing Harry's offer to come to him. It was pride that made the older man get on his carriage and make a trip that was probably somewhat uncomfortable for him, but Harry couldn't exactly refuse him.

A familiar voice reached his ears. "I'll just show myself in. Harry won't mind." *Jules.*

Harry strode toward the door and opened it before the footman could announce Julian. Here was just the man to take his mind off a problem that didn't have a ready solution. Cranfield wasn't exactly known for being a weighty conversationalist.

"Alone?" Harry exclaimed when he saw him. "Where's Lewis? I thought you didn't know your way around Avebury."

Julian peered out the front door. "It hasn't started raining, but Miss Rigby seemed to think there was a threat. Lewis is accompanying her home in case it does. I *walked* over from Durstead Manor if you can believe it."

He looked down at his boots and clucked his tongue. "We were paying a morning visit to Miss Tunstall and uh . . . Mrs. Leatham." He followed Harry into the library and took everything in at a glance. "Smaller than you're used to, I daresay. That never seemed to bother you, though. Can't say as I understand."

Harry's heart skipped a beat at the mention of Miss Tunstall's name. A flash of jealousy followed. Harry had nearly visited her today but thought it too soon. He wanted to ask Julian how she was doing this morning but knew he would have to be satisfied with the vision she presented last night.

Still, he could not help but ask, "How well did you know Miss Tunstall in London?"

Julian shrugged. "As well as another, I suppose. She has a reputation for having a sharp tongue, and most gentlemen prefer to enjoy her at a distance."

"And you?" Harry couldn't help but ask, although he knew he was treading on dangerous ground. Julian was *not* a soul of unfathomable depth, but he was not that stupid after all.

As Harry had feared, Julian turned a keen gaze on him. "Stay away, Harry."

"What? Why?" Harry spluttered rather than spoke the words as Julian shook his head.

"She is not for you. She thinks only of the latest modes and, I daresay, herself."

Rich, coming from you, Harry thought.

Oblivious, Julian continued. "Her twin, perhaps—Miss Phoebe Tunstall—would suit you better. Docile sort of girl. Couldn't be more unlike

Miss Anna. Ask her to present you to Miss Phoebe," Julian said, pleased with his idea.

Harry was less so. He was spared from having to summon enthusiasm by the sound of the wheels of Sir Lewis's carriage pulling up to the front door. He glanced out the window and saw Sir Lewis, who wasted no time in handing the reins to the groom standing nearby before he strode up the path.

"Harry!"

Harry met him at the front door, wondering what had lent that urgency to his voice. Could it be that something had happened to Miss Rigby?

"Harry," Sir Lewis said again when they met. "I don't suppose this brainbox has thought to apprise you of the fact that Mrs. Leatham appears to have received an urgent letter." He nodded toward Julian. Although his tone was teasing, his expression was not. "Both Miss Rigby and I fear it is bad news. I promised her I would come and find you, although I assure you I would have done so without her urging."

Why Harry should immediately think of Miss Tunstall, he did not know, but he needed no further encouragement to set out.

"I thank you for bringing me the news. Mrs. Foucher will see to your comfort. Don't wait for my return. I must go." Harry grabbed his hat and cane on his way out the door, harnessed his curricle, and quickly set off to the Leathams'.

When he reached Durstead Manor, the butler hesitated to admit him, which did not surprise Harry. Out of deference for Harry's position in the village, perhaps, Forester seemed compelled to explain. "It is only that my mistress has received an upsetting letter, and I fear she will not be receiving anyone."

Harry nodded. "I am aware of it. I should not wish to intrude upon her privacy, but I would like to offer my services as the rector to someone under my care. If you make Miss Tunstall aware of my presence, she may decide whether Mrs. Leatham is able to receive me."

The butler allowed him to enter and then went to the morning room. Harry's suggestion produced a better outcome than he could have predicted. Soon Miss Tunstall made her way to him in the entryway.

Anna slipped through the door and walked down the echoing hall-way to meet Mr. Aston. He started forward as soon as he saw her, and when she reached him, he took her hands in his warm, firm grasp.

Drawing strength from his touch, Anna said, "Mr. Aston, won't you walk with me outdoors?" Anna felt as if she couldn't bear another moment inside. It hadn't yet begun to rain, but the weather was not promising. "Mrs. Leatham is not well at the moment. We will not go far."

Mr. Aston followed her outside, where the grey clouds seemed to move across the sky as if sped on by a brisk wind. She and Mr. Aston came abreast as they picked their way over the pebbled path along the hedges. After a few minutes' silence, he said, "I hope you will tell me at once what is the matter. Sir Lewis paid me a visit on his way from here and said he feared there had been bad news."

"I am not sure if it is bad or only delayed," Anna said slowly. "Emily received an urgent letter from her cousin saying that Captain Leatham's ship never met for its rendezvous when it was supposed to, and no one has had any news. He was meant to stop at Emily's cousin's place upon arrival before heading north. At the time of her writing the letter, I believe the ship to have been weeks late—more than could be accounted for. Her cousin doesn't think it is just a fancy or that they have decided to go else-where because even the local officers of the navy have expressed surprise. And Emily has not had a letter from Captain Leatham stating a change in his plans. In fact, she's had nothing for months."

Mr. Aston frowned. "How did Mrs. Leatham receive the news?"

"I will not hide from you that she is prostrate with worry." Anna ran her fingers lightly along the box hedges to her right, feeling their feathery touch. "She wept for some time, and I coaxed a few mouthfuls of tea down her throat, which seemed to revive her. I left her sleeping, I believe."

"Do *you* feel there is cause for worry?"

Anna gave a small shrug. "I am not one prone to worry," she answered. "But then, it is not my husband who is away at sea. It is easy to think only positive thoughts when it is not our own comfort at stake."

The only noise was the crunch of their feet on the pebbles as they walked. Anna waited for Mr. Aston to speak, hoping he would not spout some absurdity about how everything would be fine—or worse, that all was assuredly lost.

Mr. Aston looked off to the trees bordering the other side of the garden before taking her arm and slipping it into his, as if they were a great deal more acquainted than they actually were. Mr. Aston had an unfortunate habit of catching her off guard. Anna could not bring herself to pull away, although she felt she should. Indeed, his touch was reassuring.

"I believe we must not despair until there is certain news, and we must do everything in our power to keep up Mrs. Leatham's spirits." Mr. Aston met Anna's gaze directly. "She has told me her mother will arrive soon. Do you know when she is expected?"

Anna shook her head, holding back a sigh. "Now that is what is unfortunate. Emily's mother would strengthen her a great deal better than I. Emily's niece and nephew have come down with scarlet fever. Her mother does not want to leave Emily's sister, and she also fears that she might carry the disease if she comes here, which could prove fatal."

Anna sighed. "I fear she will not have someone with her for some time, perhaps not even for the birth."

Mr. Aston absorbed the news. "I applaud her mother's wisdom. Scarlet fever is quite contagious, and her mother is perfectly right to delay her visit. I shall have to see if Lady Allinthridge can recommend someone in the village to attend to her as she awaits her confinement—someone who can serve as a companion."

He paused, then seemed to pick over his words carefully. "Can you not prolong your stay in Avebury?"

Anna felt the heat from his arm next to hers and knew from something deep inside that his studied indifference hid a very real interest in her answer. She did not dare to look at him but felt that he, too, avoided her gaze.

"I do not see how I can leave. Not now," Anna said at last.

She felt his arm tense next to her and glanced at his face in time to see the smile disappear from his lips. He cleared his throat.

"Avebury will benefit from your presence, I think, as much as Mrs. Leatham," Mr. Aston said. "You will not lack for company while you attend to her."

"That is very kind of you," Anna replied. "I fear playing nurse will tax my good humor. It is one thing to bide one's time on a pleasure visit, taking tea and attending soirées. It is quite another thing to sustain Emily through the fear and potential grief of losing her husband."

"I am fully confident in your abilities," Mr. Aston said, lifting his hand to the sky and studying his glove to see if it was indeed beginning to rain. He directed their steps back toward the house. "In fact, I cannot think of someone more suited to the task. Your humor belies a depth of feeling, and you are not given to hysteria. I think Mrs. Leatham very fortunate."

This compliment was too direct for Anna, and she slipped her hand easily out of his arm. "I believe when the Rigbys and Allinthridges are made aware of the situation, we shall contrive a way to turn Emily's thoughts."

Mr. Aston seemed to accept both her need for space and a turn of conversation. "You will be well supported," he said. "Speaking on an entirely different matter, I received a letter from Mr. Howe, the Bow Street Runner who visited you. He said that yet another theft has occurred on the road coming into Beckhampton, and they are looking into it. They will be taking accommodations nearby, and he promises to let us know as soon as he has more information."

"Oh! That puts me in mind of something." Anna turned to him suddenly so that their faces nearly touched, and her traitorous thoughts were flooded with what it would be like to kiss his chiseled jawline. She whipped her head back. "When we returned from the Rigby party last night, I discovered the pouch with my jewels and coins sitting on the seat of our carriage. They were all there."

"Did you indeed? Have you questioned your driver?" Mr. Aston seemed oblivious to her wayward thoughts, for his tone was natural, a circumstance for which Anna was profoundly grateful.

"Emily did so immediately. The driver said that he had only gone to visit his . . . interest in the kitchen and did not notice anything suspicious upon his return." They were nearing the house now, and although the clouds held still, Anna felt the wind pick up.

"Quite interesting. I cannot puzzle it out." Mr. Aston drew his brows together and fingered the handle to his cane. "I find it hard to fathom the thief's motivation for returning the jewels, unless it was out of a sense of guilt."

"We thought the same," Anna said, stopping to face him. "I do not know if we should call off the Bow Street Runners."

"No." Mr. Aston was decisive on this point. "There is still this latest act of highway robbery to be investigated, not to mention the violence done to you. Even if someone is remorseful, they must show their repentance by their deeds. If other robberies are being committed, it means nothing has been learned nor decided."

"Very well then," Anna said. "We shall wait to see what they find."

Another silence followed, and it seemed as if Mr. Aston was as reluctant as she was to leave. What would she return to? A household heavy with despair. Awareness between them grew as they looked anywhere but at each other, and Anna began to feel stifled by the tension.

"I believe I must—"

"I will not trouble Mrs. Leatham just now," Mr. Aston said at the same time, breaking the spell of what felt dangerously close to attraction, much to Anna's relief. "From what you have told me, Mrs. Leatham is not in a position to receive visitors, even those who might wish to help."

"Not at present. No, I believe you are right." Then, regretting her impatience to see him gone, she added, "However, I hope you will come soon and speak with her yourself. You might find words of condolence and support more easily than I."

"I will come tomorrow without fail." Mr. Aston bowed and left. And because he was facing the other direction and could not observe the turn of her gaze, Anna was able to do what she had not dared do before: feast her eyes on the shoulders that seemed broad enough to carry any burdens that might come his way, including hers.

He clapped his hat on his head and strode down the path to find his groom.

Chapter Ten

Mr. Aston did not return the next day. Emily was growing more and more despondent, and for the first time in Anna's life, there was no ready solution. She was at a loss to know what to do. She sent a letter to her sister to apprise her of her delayed departure, ordered the servants to go about their routine as they normally would, and endeavored to keep Emily's spirits up.

Anna had never known Emily to fall so utterly into despair, but then they had never had to face something like this together. Their entire world consisted of laughter and parties, the way Anna preferred it. It was not that Anna did not know grief. Her mother had died when she was sixteen, and the hole she left behind could not be filled. Mrs. Tunstall had not been considered by the ton to be worthy of their notice because her family had earned their fortune in trade. But Anna's mother was dignified and gentle—a woman of great worth—and her father never lost the opportunity to expound her virtues. Phoebe took after their mother.

Then, shortly before Stratford came home from the war, Anna had lost her father as well. She bit her lip at the memory of those dark days. *That* did not bear thinking of. Anna had always been particularly fond of her father, and everyone said she took after him. He was playful, and his gentle teasing was so subtle that people could never be sure whether they were the target. Stratford used to be like that in his school days, but he had been forced into a role he did not relish and had to bear the burden of the upkeep of a sprawling estate, the loss of his beloved parents, and the well-being of his twin sisters. Anna was glad he had found Eleanor.

Not all Anna's teasing had brought a smile back to his lips. Eleanor had accomplished that.

But Emily's grief was unlike anything Anna had known. How could one handle the loss—or the potential loss; one must not abandon hope—of one's husband with equanimity? Anna's heart grieved right along with her friend. So she opened the curtains, ordered hot water for tea, spoke to the cook about what to prepare for dinner, and read to Emily, who appeared not to hear a single word. The one time she tried to pull conversation out of her friend, Emily just moaned. "John."

Anna, alone in the morning room, was loath to admit it to herself, but she longed for Mr. Aston to come today. *It is so he might assist in the role of a rector.* It was too much to accept that it might be something more, that there might be something reassuring about his presence that she longed for.

But now. Anna stood suddenly. *I am falling into melancholy myself, which will not do.*

The sound of the knocker caused her heart to beat wildly. *Mr. Aston.* She had to refrain from rushing to the door and opening it, which just went to show how desperate she was for company. Because she was a well-bred young woman, Anna waited until Forrester's footsteps reached the door. He opened it and announced, "Miss Rigby."

Anna took care not to let her disappointment show. "How delighted I am that you came," she said, indicating for Miss Rigby to be seated on the sofa next to her. "Emily is resting in her room right now, but I'm sure she'll be glad to hear of your visit."

Hester Rigby removed her gloves and bonnet and set them on the sofa beside her. "I do not know what kind of news Emily received in her letter, but I must own that it has left me unsettled. If it is not breaking a confidence, please tell me what is the matter. Emily has been a friend to me ever since Captain Leatham brought her to Avebury."

Anna did not answer right away. It was not her habit to disclose other people's news, especially to someone she knew so little. Instead she asked, "You are here alone? Your sister did not accompany you? Do you not visit together?"

Miss Rigby gave a small smile. "Saturday, my sister did not come because she was still abed. She tends to keep town hours no matter where we are. Today, however, I am sure she would have come were it not for the fact that Mr. Cranfield called upon my father. Mr. Cranfield did not go into the morning room before I left, but I believe Marianne is waiting there in hopes of meeting him."

"And not you?" Anna said. "Do you not like receiving visitors?"

Miss Rigby shrugged. "I was on my way to the stables when he arrived. My mother sent a servant to call me back, but I asked the stable hand to say that I had already left. It was not hard to do. He knows how much I love to ride and take air whenever I can, and how little I like to sit in the morning room hoping that a gentleman will appear." She finished her sentence with a strong hint of irony that Anna could not help but appreciate.

"I am sure it will not be long before everyone knows," Anna said, having decided at last that Miss Rigby could be trusted, "but I ask you all the same not to spread the word any sooner than necessary. I have a sense that you will keep it to yourself. Emily has not had word of her husband in several months. A mere one or two months would not have caused her a great deal of concern because she knows how unpredictable his chances are of sending word. But a letter came from her cousin carrying news that the ship did not meet its rendezvous point near the Strait of Gibraltar as it was supposed to. Emily is crushed with worry."

Miss Rigby absorbed this news, smoothing her gloves next to her. "Her mother will be here shortly, I believe."

Anna shook her head. "No, I'm afraid not. Her mother is tending Emily's niece and nephews who have caught scarlet fever. Emily has no one coming." After a moment's struggle, she added, "I have promised to stay."

There was another loud rap at the front door, and Anna was not given a chance to find out how Miss Rigby would have responded. They waited in silence until Forrester came to the morning room, this time hesitating before he stepped over the threshold. "Tom Wardle, Mr. Aston's servant, is here and wishes to have a word with you, miss. What shall I tell him?"

Anna was surprised that Mr. Aston had sent someone in his place. Curious, she followed the butler to where Tom stood, his eyes cast downwards. She nodded for him to speak and he did so, holding his hat by its brim and spinning it in slow circles in a nervous gesture. He really was a strange creature.

"Miss—forgiving my presumption—I'm to tell ye Mr. Aston can't come today. One of the p'rishners, Mr. Murris, be not long for this world. The pa'son be sendin' his regrets, though to be sure 'ee will come when he's able." Having disclosed his message, Tom took a step back.

"Please thank Mr. Aston for me," Anna said and waited for Forrester to show him out. She walked back to the drawing room feeling ludicrously disappointed. Of course, a parishioner who is dying must need their parson. But so did she. Or perhaps *she* didn't need him. She didn't need anyone. But Emily needed him, and he would not come today.

Anna schooled her expression into one of calm before entering the morning room. She had no desire to wear her heart on her sleeve.

"It is only that one of Mr. Aston's parishioners is dying, and he is therefore not able to come today. To attend to Emily," Anna added hastily, for fear that Miss Rigby might pick up on the wistfulness Anna was sure her voice revealed.

Miss Rigby's eyes showed concern. "Did Tom say which parishioner is dying?"

"Mr. Morris, I believe," Anna replied, taking her seat and battling to keep up an optimistic front. She would have to bear the weight of the household's despondency alone.

"It comes as no surprise, I suppose. But I am sad for his family." Miss Rigby folded her hands on her lap, and then there was silence.

The air in the room began to take on a leaden aspect despite Miss Rigby's company. It seemed the entire village was cursed. First Captain Leatham went missing, and now villagers were dropping off. Anna took a deep breath.

"That Tom Wardle is a strange fellow. He does not look one in the eye. I know some lower servants might have such tendencies, but they are usually trained out of them. Tom does not appear to have any training whatsoever." She had meant this to be an idle observation, but Miss Rigby latched onto it.

"There is actually a story behind Tom's employment," Miss Rigby said. "I know Mr. Aston would not want this to be widely known, and only a couple families *do* know of it. I know only because I assist families in Haggle End where Tom is well known."

Miss Rigby took a breath and relayed the surprising news. "Tom was once in league with footpads, and he broke into Mr. Aston's home with the intent to steal."

Anna was surprised but did not wish to jump to an immediate judgment. Miss Rigby went on.

"Mr. Aston caught him in the act of stealing his household silver, and rather than turn him in to the authorities, which would have meant certain death or deportment, he urged Tom to seek a more honorable profession. When Tom told him there were none to be had, Mr. Aston promised to employ him and not to breathe a word of what happened. If anyone does know of it, it is only because Tom told people, not Mr. Aston. It's the ones in Haggle End, who know Tom, who were most shocked by his transformation. They had quite given him up for a life of crime."

"For Mr. Aston to offer such redemption *is* unusual, even for a rector. Or dare I say, especially for a rector," Anna said.

Miss Rigby smiled, but her story was not finished. "I was there the day he went to his neighbors' home, the Callmans, because I was carrying medicine for their youngest. Tom marched in and announced he had been employed by no less than the rector of Avebury. Everyone in the house laughed at him, but he assured them it was true."

Miss Rigby smiled softly at the memory. "It has been six months since Mr. Aston employed Tom, and Tom seems to be doing famously. He has not lost some of his natural shyness, or perhaps shame. But it is not for Mr. Aston's lack of trying to reassure him." Miss Rigby gave Anna a look as if to say, *Well, what do you think of that?*

Anna was moved by the story. If there was anything she could not bear, it was someone who was quick to pounce on the faults or weaknesses of another and tear them to pieces. If it had been the vicar in their London parish, she was sure he would not only have denounced Tom to the authorities but would have disparaged him before the townspeople as well.

She supposed Miss Rigby was waiting for her to say something, but Anna did not wish to reveal her innermost thoughts. She merely said, "Your rector appears to be well suited for his position."

"He is a good man." Miss Rigby gathered her bonnet and gloves and stood. "I fear I have trespassed upon your goodness for too long. I must be going back. If I know my mother and sister, they will have had their short talk with Mr. Cranfield and he will be gone by now, leaving me free to do as I wish."

Anna stood as well, almost regretting she had been so little forthcoming with Miss Rigby. She needed a friend while she was here, and she did not want to lean too heavily on Mr. Aston for fear that he might get the wrong impression where her heart was concerned. That was what she chose to believe, in any case. She could not allow herself to think that her own heart was in any danger.

It seemed Miss Rigby was Anna's most likely ally for friendship. There was Lady Allinthridge, of course, but she was much older. Anna did not like to presume to visit her without Lady Allinthridge calling first. Mrs. Mayne was of a retiring nature, and she was also older than Anna.

With more warmth than she had shown since Miss Rigby had arrived, Anna said, "I do thank you for coming. I am not as inviting as Emily, perhaps, but I appreciate your visit. If you don't find it too forward, you may call me Anna."

Miss Rigby offered a sympathetic smile. "With pleasure. And I am Hester. Your situation is not easy, Anna. I will come as often or as little as you like."

Anna surprised herself by saying, "I would appreciate your company when your mother can spare you."

As Hester took her leave, Anna pressed her lips together to keep from saying any more, which might smack of desperation. How she missed Phoebe.

Chapter Eleven

*H*arry had seen to all the details for poor Mr. Morris. It was a mercy for him, perhaps, to leave this world, for he had been suffering for some time. Harry performed the last rites, although he didn't know Mr. Morris well enough to be sure of its effectiveness. Mr. Morris hadn't set foot in his church since Harry had arrived in Avebury. However, Mr. Morris had asked for his last rites, and Harry wasn't one to deny the smallest act of faith of even the most unworthy of his parishioners.

The rites, preparation for burial, and other details had taken Harry two days to complete. As much as his thoughts were with the Morris family and their suffering, there was a constant hum of desire to see Miss Tunstall. However, he spent his first free morning tending to the crops alongside Tom to turn the soil from the excessive amount of rain they had received. Harry knew he was doing what was needed, but his thoughts were fixed on when he might break free to pay a visit to Durstead Manor.

Just as Harry was working the last row, Squire Mayne picked his way across the garden to meet him. Although a visitor would have normally been a welcome sight, Harry experienced a flash of annoyance. He wanted nothing to hinder his departure.

Mr. Mayne nearly slipped in the mud before righting himself. "Mr. Aston, don't tell me you make a habit of muddying your hands this way."

Harry leaned on his hoe and smiled. "Will you think the worse of me for it? No, to tell you the truth, I am only out here on the days I sense it to be an unfair burden on my overworked servants. I am the only one to blame if I refuse to hire enough people to run the property comfortably."

He smiled at Tom, who had only paused in his work to lift his cap to the squire. Tom really did not know how to smile. It was one of Harry's objectives for his rehabilitation.

"Good, good," replied Mr. Mayne. "I like a gentleman who is not afraid to work. I haven't met many." Without preamble, he launched into the purpose of his visit. "I had a letter from Mr. Howe, the Runner. There's been yet another robbery near Calne. This is the fifth since Miss Tunstall's carriage was targeted, but this time there was a murder. The highwaymen appear to grow more reckless."

To Harry's right, Tom took a step forward, as if listening. Harry saw that he had paled at the news.

"This time the Runners found an engraved pistol at the scene, and it does not belong to the man who was killed—a Mr. Thompson, who had apparently been traveling to Swindon when he was waylaid. He was shot through the chest." Mr. Mayne scowled and shook his head. "I hope the men hang who are responsible for this."

Harry said what was appropriate, and the squire continued. "I don't know what kind of carelessness caused the highwayman to take off and leave his pistol behind. The fact is, the man's valuables seemed still to be there, and Mr. Howe thinks the robber was interrupted. In any case, now the Runners have the pistol, and that certainly sheds some light on the case."

"Who does it belong to?" Tom asked. The words seemed to spill out on their own accord. Harry looked at him in surprise. It wasn't like Tom to speak up in front of people he considered above him.

"It was easy to identify because the gun maker is local." The squire addressed the rest of his words to Harry. "The pistol belongs to a Lord Ramsworth. Ah yes," the squire explained. "Our infamous viscount who has done nothing for his estate or his tenants, leaving them in the hands of an absent steward so that the whole of Haggle End has become nothing more than a breeding ground for poverty and vice."

Mr. Mayne glowered at the perfidy of lazy stewards, then looked up as the realization of his words came over him. "Your presence excepted, Tom. You're doing a fine job here."

Tom mumbled something inarticulate. He had reverted back to the shy servant who didn't dare speak.

Harry asked, "So what will the Runners do now? Have they spoken of their next steps?"

"They plan to investigate matters in Haggle End, I believe. I think they will stay in this area to search for leads."

The news gave Harry pause. It seemed only logical that the Runners would focus their efforts here. And yet, Harry had been making headway in helping some of the families turn over a new leaf, particularly the younger set. He did not want the law enforcers to upset the precarious balance of redemption and righteousness he was trying to effect.

"I thank you for coming to tell me this news personally," he told the squire. "It is of real importance, as it affects the whole village."

Mr. Mayne cleared his throat. He was a gruff man unaccustomed to sentiment. It was fortunate his wife was compassionate enough to soften out his edges and practical enough not to mind his forthright speech. "I would not think to keep you unapprised of what affects your parish. I approve of what you're trying to do there." With that, the squire bid him good day and left, raising his hand in a salute.

Harry handed his rake to Tom. "You'll see to putting these away for me? I have somewhere to be, and I am long overdue." He hurried inside, calling for hot water, as he tugged at his neckcloth.

"Mr. Aston is here to see you," the butler announced. Anna thought she might weep with relief. He had come at last.

What had come over her? Was she to be such an easy victory? And here Anna thought her heart would always remain untouched. After all, the more tender feelings were not a necessary component for a brilliant match.

"Show him in," Anna instructed the servant, placing her book on the settee beside her.

She stood when Mr. Aston strode across the room to greet her, taking both her hands in his and asking, "How is Mrs. Leatham?"

Anna did not rebuke his impudence or laugh at his sense of the dramatic as she would have done with any other man—privately, of course. She could only be conscious of the warmth that flooded through her at the sight of him and his firm hands grasping hers.

"I will take you to her," Anna said, her voice not as steady as she would have liked.

She led him to the morning room, where Emily spent a few hours each day because it faced south and was flooded with sunlight.

"Has the doctor been sent for?" Mr. Aston asked as their shoes clipped over the smooth hardwood floor.

Anna stopped and turned to him with wide eyes. "Sending for the doctor did not occur to me. It should have, shouldn't it? It would occur to someone who had the least modicum of common sense."

Mr. Aston offered her a smile instead of a scold. "You are not often ill, are you?" When she shook her head, he added, "Most people don't think to send for the doctor when they manage to weather illness or upset without much fuss."

Anna let a tiny sigh escape her, as she moved forward again and reached for the door to the morning room. "I am not thought to be much use in my family for practical concerns. Either it is a deeply ingrained family prejudice, or I truly lack the skill. But I've always found it easier to let others manage such things if they are so determined."

"I will have Doctor Carson wait upon Emily. He can ascertain whether the upset has affected her unborn child in any way." Before Anna could turn the handle and enter the room, he laid his hand upon her arm. "I've said as much already, but allow me to repeat myself. Mrs. Leatham is fortunate to have you here. I would choose such an arrangement myself— were I a woman," he hastily amended with what looked suspiciously like a blush.

Mr. Aston reached forward and opened the door, then stepped back again, likely realizing the impropriety of proceeding her into a room where a woman was indisposed—and in a house that was not his own.

Anna was tempted to smile as she entered the room, but it was easy to put the urge aside. His words awoke something inside her. She wanted to laugh at him for his tendency to leave off the polite society mask, but she could not. He was too sincere to laugh at.

"Emily, Mr. Aston is here." Anna led the way to the settee where Emily sat, now upright instead of lounging and dressed to receive guests.

Mr. Aston did not wait for an invitation from Anna but went over and pulled a trellis-patterned chair in front of Emily and sat facing her.

"Mrs. Leatham, you have received a shock," he began with a kindness and maturity to his voice that did not match his youthful curls. "I would like to remind you, however, that nothing is yet confirmed regarding your husband's whereabouts. I will do what I can to help strengthen you to face all eventualities. Do you feel ready to try?"

Emily's eyes welled up with tears, but she nodded.

"Good," Mr. Aston said and clasped his hands as if to ready them for action. "Your first priority must be the baby you are carrying. I know your heart too well to doubt that you will do everything in your power to safely bring this child into the world. I believe Dr. Carson will support me in this, but we will not hear of cupping or anything that drains your forces. You will need to partake of all your meals, even if it is only a little, and you will need to walk in the fresh air. We've had a bit of sun lately, which will surely help. Miss Tunstall . . ."

He turned to Anna, who had been observing the effect his dictums had on her friend. Emily was beginning to look more alive, and a spark of determination entered her eyes that had held only dullness before.

"See that the routine in this house is maintained as much as possible, will you? Open the blinds and let the sunlight flood in. See that the meals occur at their usual times. If I am not mistaken, I believe you are doing all this already. And if you can convince Mrs. Leatham to accompany you for walks, please do so."

"If I can," Anna said with a lift of her brow, a smile hovering on her face, for she was beginning to feel that anything was possible.

Mr. Aston's eyes sparkled. "I have no doubt of your being able to do anything you set your mind to."

Without missing a beat, he turned back to Emily. "There is both comfort and tremendous power to be found in the Holy Scriptures, so may I remind you not to neglect them. I am, after all, your rector."

"Yes, Mr. Aston," Emily answered, though her voice was meek. This was another side to her that Anna had not known.

Anna could not be fully reassured as much as she would have liked to be, for it seemed as though, as quickly as it had come, the light of hope had already started to dim in Emily's eyes. *So quickly? What fragile creatures we humans are*, thought Anna.

"And let us hear of a return to your humor and optimism. You are known for it, Mrs. Leatham. Do not borrow trouble. We do not yet know the outcome of Leatham's journey, and each day has enough trouble of its own."

At that, Emily smiled for the first time in five days. To Anna's surprise, her own eyes nearly filled with tears just to see it. She blinked them away. When had she become so weepy?

Mr. Aston sat back. "I might . . ."

He hesitated, and Anna wondered what he could find so difficult to say. Apart from the brief confusion he'd shown before entering the room, he always appeared to know what to say in every circumstance.

"I might be able to get more information on your husband. I have connections in the navy. I will write and see what I may find out," he said.

"I would like that," Emily whispered.

Connections? Who could a country parson possibly know in the Royal Navy?

Mr. Aston did not give Anna time to ponder this further. He stood and bowed before Emily. "I will not overstay my welcome, as I know it can be fatiguing to receive guests. However, I promise to come often to visit. Miss Tunstall, would you have the kindness to see me out?"

She would indeed. After not seeing Mr. Aston at all these past days, the force of her desire to spend time in his company surprised her. They walked toward the corridor, and Anna, anxious to speak of anything other than the potentially looming tragedy of John Leatham, said, "So your last Season in London was the year before I made my debut. We might otherwise have met."

Mr. Aston nodded. "We might have. I was anxious to be gone, however. I had already begun looking for a situation in the country. I filled a vacancy in Bristol the first year for a rector who was getting on in years and wished to tour Scotland while he still had some youth on his side. After that I took another temporary living in Bath. And when that position came to a close, this one was offered to me. I consider myself very fortunate to have acquired it."

"Do you not miss London?" Anna asked in a tone she hoped didn't sound overly intrusive. "It is, after all, where everything happens. It's where the latest ideas are brought out, the latest fashions make their appearance. It is where the most interesting people congregate."

"Now there I will have to disagree with you," Mr. Aston replied as they stepped out into the sunshine. He helped her down the broad steps with the lightest touch on her arm and led her on the path along the gardens that intersected with the public road further down.

"Anything interesting you might wish to learn about human nature you may learn in a small town equally as well as a large one. In such a composite of townspeople you might meet with any fresh ideas or new way of thinking. Only fashions lack, not ideas."

"This is where *you* are wrong, I believe, Mr. Aston," Anna said, gearing up for an amicable battle. "New ideas? What new ideas can possibly spring up from people who meet only with the same people, see only the same faces? It is unthinkable. This is why village life is so stilted." Her provocation was done in a spirit of teasing, but she acknowledged to herself that she was daring him to refute what she believed to be true.

"What of people like Mrs. Mayne, the squire's wife, who merely from reading Hannah More's *Practical Piety*—oh you may roll your eyes, my dear, Miss Tunstall, but have you read the book? It produced in Mrs. Mayne the idea to begin an instructive class for the girls of Haggle End to teach them the duties of a maid so they might have hope of employment. This led to Mr. Mayne's idea for starting a school in the village's poorest quarters where the children's future is poverty at best, thievery at worst. So I had only to lend my assistance, upon my arrival, to a project that was already well under way. I defy you to find one so inspired to new ideas as Mrs. Mayne."

Mr. Aston flashed her a teasing smile. "And Mrs. Mayne told me positively that she never set foot outside of Wiltshire. Oh, you might find the theory in London, but you are not likely to find the heart."

"Yes, I have read Hannah More. Who has not?" Anna replied primly and somewhat ambiguously. Mrs. More's works on charity and goodness had touched something in her, but she did not like to admit it.

She forged on. "Because there is intellect it does not follow that there is no heart. Why, the sister to Lady Raymond did the very same thing. Perhaps not a school, but she took in five climbing boys whose futures were no more promising than the burgeoning thieves in Haggle End. She handed them over to her groom to find them employment as soon as they were of the right age and watched over their progress. The boys are now employed in three other households besides her own. And might I remind you that one does not as easily find the room to house them in London as in the country, and yet Lady Raymond found a way."

Mr. Aston put his hands behind his back as they walked, a smile playing on the corners of his mouth, which annoyed her. She was probably revealing more of her opinions on the subject of charity than she generally liked.

"In addition," Anna continued, stubbornly, "Lady Raymond discerned in one of the boys a particular affinity for numbers, and she did not resign him to the care of the stable lads. She thought that with one so adept, she might make a steward out of him—or at least a schoolmaster where he might serve as an inspiration to others living in workhouses. I defy you to say there is no heart in London."

Something flashed in Mr. Aston's eyes as he faced her. A challenge? No, it looked more like satisfaction, as if she had only confirmed something he already knew about her. The intent look and slow smile he sent her way made Anna's heart thud.

"I dare not oppose you," he said gently. "But I might also counter by saying that here in the country, just because there is heart, it does not follow that there is no intellect. Mrs. Mayne did not produce this idea by aping others who do the same thing. She came to this benevolent idea on her own, simply because she was inspired by the literature she read. And she is a simple, if genteel, country-bred woman."

"I never said country-bred women had no intellect," Anna said, stopping to face him.

"But you thought it."

Anna was silent. She could not deny the truth in his words. Mr. Aston met her gaze before walking forward. Somehow, without her being fully conscious of it, they had already walked some distance and were nearly at the public road.

"Come," he said. "We are not likely to agree perfectly."

Anna needed to have the last word—to regain the ground she felt she had lost in their friendly argument, although she could not have said whether it was the logic that lacked or the defenses around her heart.

"I believe you were not in society long enough to have seen the good in people of the ton and are determined to live your life in seclusion as a result."

She peeked at him sideways as they walked, and Mr. Aston's mouth twisted in acknowledgment—or at least she thought it was in acknowledgment. This conversation overset all her complacency. Anna felt herself urging him to her point of view, but why should she do that? He stopped and turned to face her again, his brown eyes fixed on hers.

"Miss Tunstall, I grant that I am not partial to Society and have, perhaps, a prejudice against those who have a love for it. Nevertheless, I hold out a hope that you will see a different side of country life while you are here that will give you a better taste for it. There is something in you . . ."

Mr. Aston reached for her hand, and she was startled at the touch even though she was wearing gloves. He was bold and she was not accustomed to being led in such a way. But he did not give her a chance to pull away because he merely placed her hand on his arm and continued walking. In doing so, he pulled her close and their steps matched naturally. Both his words and the warmth of his presence at her side tore at her defenses.

"I see something in you that is pure, Miss Tunstall, for all you wish to convince me otherwise. You have not the superficial vanity of the ton."

"Do not attribute to me more lofty traits than I possess," Anna began.

Mr. Aston held up his hand and shook his head. "No. There is a depth to you that I do not often perceive in the women I meet in London. Indeed, in the women I meet anywhere, be it within Society or without. It only inspires in me a strong desire to draw it out."

He stopped and turned to her again, fixed in place. They stood like that until it seemed she was held captive. She could not order him to go further, nor could she turn back to the house. Mr. Aston's eyes were level with hers. Now was the time to back away. To tell him he was presumptuous. To tell him he was pursuing the wrong quarry.

Anna could say nothing, and the silence stretched so long, it became leaden with their nearness. She feared they would kiss, and her heart thudded erratically when he placed his hands on her arms. In the moment he took a step forward, she drew breath as if gasping for air.

He pulled away sharply, and a carriage drew around the bend. Mr. Aston pulled her from the road to let it pass.

They turned back toward the house, in unspoken agreement, and as they walked in silence, a horrible suspicion came upon Anna as she reflected on the dangerous moment that had passed.

She had not only felt fear at the idea of kissing Avebury's rector and committing herself to a path so contrary to all she held dear—the memory of his scent, the vision of his face drawing near, the warmth of his hands grasping her arms all held her captive—to her bewilderment and dismay, the thought of kissing Mr. Aston had also thrilled her.

Chapter Twelve

*H*arry thought of nothing but Anna Tunstall for the two days that followed. Never—*never*—had he been on the point of doing something so beyond the bounds of propriety, something so *indecorous* as kissing a woman in plain view—and one to whom he was not even engaged! It was beyond the pale, and Harry almost could not credit such a thing of himself. *Except*, he thought wryly, *you were standing in these very boots when it happened*. Perhaps he might not be so quick to moralize the next time something of this ilk happened to one of his parishioners.

The pull was too strong, however. There was nothing to it. He simply had to convince Anna Tunstall that the two of them belonged to one another and that they should marry. Harry knew beyond a doubt that she had felt the same tug of destiny, although he didn't like to use such a heretical term.

Then he recalled her words. *I believe you were not in Society long enough to have seen the good in people of the ton and are determined to live your life in seclusion as a result.* Although her statement showed how little she knew of who he was, Miss Tunstall had struck a chord. He didn't readily see the good of people in the ton and did prefer to live his life in seclusion.

Harry stared blankly at the open book he had intended to study on the early writings of Clement of Alexandria and finally closed it. He would not be able to focus as he should today, and he decided to set out for the stream that bordered the Leatham property. He could do with a few moments of quiet reflection.

It was not long before Harry had entered the shaded woods and had found the wooden bridge that connected the two sides of the stream. It

85

was empty. He was somewhat shocked that Lewis and Jules had obeyed his dictum not to out his identity, but he was glad they had. Perhaps they supposed everyone already knew. More likely they thought it a great joke. The advantage of Miss Tunstall not knowing his background was that any display of affection or moments of complicity meant she felt it for him as a person and not for his role in Society.

How his parents had given him such a disgust for the peerage so early on he could not say. All he knew was that he was not like his family. He had never been like them. Perhaps it was the influence of his nurse, who came to care for him after Hugh had left for Harrow. Nurse Maggie had been so different from his mother—gentle and nurturing and everything good. She was the one who had spoken to him of God's great love and His personal interest in young Harry.

He holds the lives of each person, great or small, she would say. Nurse Maggie never sought to be above her station, but her station could not contain her. She had been too worthy for her position, and Harry had felt her loss acutely when she died before he'd left the schoolroom. Perhaps it was a determination to honor her memory, but Harry was forever changed by her mark in his life, and he could only be grateful for it. The more he saw of Society, the less he was interested in joining it.

Despite Miss Tunstall's words aimed at keeping a distance between them—or so it seemed—he was sure she felt something whenever they walked arm in arm. Was it his imagination, or did she draw nearer when they walked down the shared road between their houses, a now familiar path? Harry looked up and drew in a breath. *What it would be like to see her here in one of my favorite places!*

Miss Tunstall was certainly lively in her debates, but she did not lack sense or heart. She might not be willing to go so far as to admit to the wisdom in another point of view, but he saw the intelligence in her eyes and knew she was not closed to his ideas. If only he could see some sign that she was interested in more than just going about in Society, how reassured he would be—how glad. It was perhaps too much to ask to learn where her heart stood with God. If her heart was soft toward the ill-favored and she did not despise the lowly and the meek, there was hope for her yet. The rest would work itself out.

It was time he headed back to the rectory to attend to his affairs, although he was far from feeling at peace about Miss Tunstall. He left the verdant stillness of the woods and joined the public road that led to his gate, his mind still whirling. So far, there had been nothing concrete to prove that his faith in Miss Tunstall was merited. There had been nothing but an inclination of the heart on his side and a strong belief that something on the side of truth and goodness stirred in her—that the purposes of her heart were deep waters. He would hold on to that belief until he was proven otherwise. *And I will continue to seek her out and see if her heart can be won.*

Harry entered the gate and reached the plot of land where faithful Tom was repairing the fence around their vegetable garden. He had already tended to the livestock that morning. Harry never had a moment's regret for having hired Tom. He was sure his property had never looked so well.

Harry turned toward the house. As soon as he entered, Mrs. Foucher came to meet him. "Sir, I 'ave been tinking tings trough."

In general, Mrs. Foucher's accent was barely noticeable, and Harry was often lulled into forgetting her French origin. Only the occasional dropping of the *h* when she was nervous or producing a hard sound on words beginning with a *th* revealed her origins. It seemed that whatever she was about to say made her nervous.

"What is it, Mrs. Foucher?"

"I would like to visit Mrs. Leatham, if you please," she said. "I 'ave made the dinner in advance and will have the meal on the table on time, with your leave."

"Of course." Harry furrowed his brow. "I hope I have never given you the impression that I am such an ogre that you may not take a couple hours off to go visit a neighbor, especially one in distress."

Mrs. Foucher did not give him even a fleeting smile in return, and her accent became less pronounced as she gained confidence. "I believe I may bring some comfort to Mrs. Leatham, for I have been in the same situation. I wish to urge her to keep faith and to keep her spirits up. I also wish to tell her of my willingness to help when it comes time for her confinement should she need it. Dr. Carson is sometimes away visiting other towns, and I should not like her to feel alone."

Harry had alluded to the fact that he considered assisting in childbirth too delicate a task to be undertaken by a man of the cloth, even one trained as he had been. Mrs. Foucher's knowledge was valuable, young though she was, and he was glad she was proposing her aid.

"The very thing," Harry said. "I must say how lucky I am that I had you on recommendation so I didn't have to go and find someone to fill your position. I cannot think of anyone I would rather have as cook in my household. And it goes beyond the delicious meals you create. Your concern for others in Avebury is refreshing to everyone in the village."

His encouragement brought about a rare smile and a blush of pleasure that highlighted a scar along one of her cheeks. She had once told him the scar came from a childhood accident in the kitchen but gave no other details. He wondered if she had always been a kitchen maid since early childhood, but she was so private, he didn't like to ask. And his instinct told him she had been well educated, even if it was difficult to perceive when she spoke English. There was an air of refinement about her.

"You are very good, sir." Mrs. Foucher twisted her hands in front of her. "I would like to ask you something, if I may. Would you accompany me to see Mrs. Leatham?"

"Yes, if you wish. But you do not need me in order to be received. Mrs. Leatham is not at all high in the instep, and she will welcome your company. I am sure of it."

"It is perhaps irregular of me," Mrs. Foucher replied. She paused, then met Harry's gaze before looking away to the entryway where the sun shone through narrow panes of glass on either side of the front door. "I would like if you heard what I have to say. I have never spoken of this to anyone, and recounting the story is painful for me."

Again there was that fleeting glance that didn't fully meet his gaze. "I do not wish to tell the story twice, but I would like for you to hear it as my parson. Perhaps you may take it as a sort of confession, although it is not your practice."

Harry was honored to receive her confession, as he knew virtually nothing about Mrs. Foucher other than her country of origin. He walked to the side table and picked up the gloves he had lain there.

"You need say no more. I understand perfectly. Allow me only to change my coat, and I will come with you."

Mrs. Foucher curtsied and withdrew, leaving Harry with a mix of emotions. He wanted nothing more than to see Miss Tunstall, and his cook had provided him with a perfect excuse. Although he was afraid to annoy Miss Tunstall by being at her house too frequently, it was torture to wait days at a time until he thought it proper to visit her again. With a feeling close to guilt, Harry ran up the stairs and quickly changed his coat.

When they arrived at the Leatham residence, he felt obliged to explain his presence to Miss Tunstall as she came forward to meet them inside the entryway.

"Mrs. Foucher has decided she would like to share her story with Mrs. Leatham if we are not intruding." In the same breath, he added, "She has asked me to accompany her to listen to her story as well, for I know only the barest details."

Miss Tunstall's eyes flashed him a look of relief, which warmed his heart. *She is glad to see me!*

"Your visit is timely, for Emily's spirits are quite low once again. I have not been able to raise them on my own, and I believe your presence will be just what is needed."

Her smile was genuine, and it sent a jolt through Harry. How nice it was to see her smile fully instead of giving the usual ironic lift of her brow. Miss Tunstall had never been so direct in her encouragement, and it gave him cause to hope.

"I am certain Emily will receive you," Miss Tunstall told them. "Let me have a word with her first to be certain."

Harry watched Anna walk toward the sitting room. She seemed to glide rather than walk, but there was a certain energy to her steps. Although she never gave an air other than one of great idleness, Harry felt sure it was deliberately done. He was equally certain that—were there something to be accomplished—she would not delay in doing it. He pulled his gaze away from the closed door to the morning room where Miss Tunstall had disappeared and turned to see Mrs. Foucher watching him. He felt himself redden at her observation. His thoughts were likely only too evident, and he was relieved when Miss Tunstall returned.

"Please follow me. Emily will receive you."

Mrs. Leatham was still pale when they walked in the room. Harry greeted her then asked, "Has the doctor come?"

"He did. All is well," Mrs. Leatham replied in a quiet voice. That seemed to be all she would say about her condition, but it satisfied him.

"You have met Mrs. Foucher, I believe," Harry said, waiting until Miss Tunstall was seated before taking his own seat. "She has asked for an audience with you, for she has something of import to disclose. She has also requested that I remain in the room if you are not opposed to the idea." He looked for confirmation from Mrs. Foucher, who nodded.

Mrs. Leatham appeared to have weakened further since Harry had last seen her, and he wondered if she was eating. Although it seemed to take great effort for her to speak, she said, "It is kind of you to visit, Mrs. Foucher. Might Anna stay with us as well? I fear I oppress her sensibility too often with my own dark thoughts, and I do not wish to deprive her of visitors. But, of course, if you feel that what you have to say is of too private a nature, I am sure she will understand."

Mrs. Foucher assessed Miss Tunstall, who returned her gaze calmly. His cook must have decided there was something trustworthy in her—a feeling he very much concurred—because she nodded.

"She may stay."

Mrs. Foucher spoke as though she were accustomed to giving orders herself, which gave Harry pause. What was her past, and why had he never noticed that about her? He was not accustomed to viewing her in any role but that of a servant. *Then again*, he scolded himself, *a rector must be above such thoughts*. As Mrs. Foucher had fled to England during the brief Treaty of Amiens, it now occurred to him that she might be descended from nobility to have wished to flee the country.

"I thank you for receiving me today, Mrs. Leatham. I came only to tell you that I have some understanding of your situation, and I wanted to urge you to be strong."

Mrs. Foucher sat perfectly upright, her hands clasped on her lap, and only the rigidity of her posture gave Harry an inkling of the agitation of her thoughts. Harry had taken a seat at some distance—close enough to hear what was being said but far enough to give some semblance of privacy to Mrs. Foucher. Anna sat on the sofa beside Mrs. Leatham, and her gaze fixed on Mrs. Foucher was hard to read, although Harry was sure he had detected compassion mixed with curiosity.

"I am from an old French family," Mrs. Foucher began. "My name is Marie-Madeleine Catherine Anne de Vieuxchamps. My father was a viscount in the Burgundy region. When Napoléon began to take back his power in 1802, my father said it was time for us to leave, for it would soon be too difficult to do so and too dangerous to stay. He took my mother, my sister, me and . . . *et bien*, my husband came as well. Antoine was the son of Joseph Foucher, a wealthy merchant in trade, and ours was a love match."

The smile that tugged at her lips made Mrs. Foucher look like a schoolgirl rather than her thirty years. "That my father permitted it shocked everyone but me. My father cared only that my husband would love me, that he would protect my heart, and . . . as you English say, 'set me up in style.'

"Antoine came with us all the way to the border in Calais. He knew enough people on the docks to get us safely on a ship bound for England.

But by way of precaution, he boarded us on a sloop run by smugglers, which would not be detected by the English or French authorities. My husband was going to check on a shipment for his father before coming to join us in time to set sail. I should have known when he did not come at once."

Mrs. Leatham's eyes filled with tears of sympathy, but Miss Tunstall remained almost stoic. Harry could only detect signs of emotion in the frown line between her brows.

Mrs. Foucher's voice broke on the next words. "He told me I must go, that there was a chance he would be held back and not arrive in time before we sailed, and that I must leave with my family, even if he was not there. He would join me afterwards, and I was to wait for him in London.

"As I'm sure you have guessed, Antoine did not come that night. So I obeyed him and remained on the boat with my family, and we set sail. The route was not direct, for we had to land on a hidden spot on the coast of England rather than take the shortest route to Dover. We were together on the boat with the other sailors until the early hours in the morning, and I noticed that some of the sailors had begun to shake with a fever that I would later learn to be smallpox." Her words seemed to stick in her throat, and she pressed her lips together before continuing.

"When we arrived on the coast, we sought shelter, but none was afforded us. My family and I crept into barns to sleep at night as we made our way toward London. In a fortnight, my sister and parents were shaking with the fever as well, and the dreaded spots came shortly afterwards. I do not know why I was spared. The only consolation, I suppose, was that we had, by then, found a barn that was not being used and so were not chased from it as we had been in other places."

Mrs. Foucher's voice was hard, as if to ward off the grief. "Two weeks later, they were all dead. I buried them alone in an abandoned field, digging the graves with a broken sickle left inside the barn."

Mrs. Foucher did not pause in her recital. It was as if, having shown the weakness of tears once, she would not do so again. "We had made no provisions for what to do when we arrived on English soil, and we had no connections. We had been counting on Antoine for that. Those smugglers were not as loyal to Antoine or our cause as he believed, for they had relieved us at knifepoint of the money and jewels we had in our possession before depositing us on the coast. Alone, I wandered from village to village until I found a family kind enough to take me in. I had learned no English growing up, but this family showed me nothing but welcome."

Mrs. Foucher's gaze rested on Harry for a moment. "Fortunately for me, I had spent time in the kitchens at home because the chef was always making *petits-fours* and other sweets to tempt me. I had time to observe his skill, and the good Englishwoman taught me all she knew. I learned to cook from her and even trained as a midwife under her servant. I could not remain with her in Stockwell. I needed to get to London where Antoine might find me."

She looked at her hands on her lap. "I waited in London for six years."

Harry absorbed the details of her story in silence. He wondered if this was helpful for Mrs. Leatham. Was it not just another sad story that would crush any remaining hope? He soon had his answer, for there was more to Mrs. Foucher's story.

"When I left France, I was with child. I never got sick, and I don't know if the smallpox had managed to reach the baby without my falling ill or if it was simply the weight of my grief, but in the fourth month of my pregnancy—a week after I had buried my family—I gave an early birth to a son."

At these words, Mrs. Foucher at last gave vent to her emotions and put her hands in her face and wept. Miss Tunstall went to sit beside Mrs. Foucher and put her arm around her.

When Mrs. Foucher had wiped her eyes on the handkerchief that Harry had leapt up to hand her, she turned a pleading gaze on Mrs. Leatham. "I beg of you, be strong for your baby's sake. I have lost my husband, and I will not have another. I will not *take* another. But how I wished, all these years, that I'd had my son. You do not yet know what has become of your husband. There is still hope. For me, ten years have passed, and I can say there is no hope at all. And so I urge you to be strong for the baby that is growing within you so that he might be a comfort to you no matter what else will come."

Mrs. Leatham wept with Mrs. Foucher, and as the story came to a close, Mrs. Leatham dried her own tears.

"I will take your words to heart," she said, her voice thick with emotion. "Thank you for sharing them with me." This common bond was all that was needed for the two women to understand one another perfectly.

Mrs. Foucher stood, and Harry did as well. "I will escort Mrs. Foucher home," he announced. He thought she might need to speak further about what she had disclosed. It had certainly shed a different light on her situation. Of course, this would mean leaving without having exchanged even one private word with Miss Tunstall, but he needed to be there for Mrs. Foucher.

"I will walk home alone," Mrs. Foucher said, as if she had followed the direction of his thoughts. "You may stay if you wish."

And there it was again—that confidence he had never before seen in her but that he would notice forevermore. He wondered if her elevated station was something he should address and sought the words to do so.

"In that case, if I may," Harry said, addressing the two other women instead, "I will see Mrs. Foucher to the door and return for a short visit."

Miss Tunstall raised her eyes to his and nodded.

As he accompanied his cook of a long line of noble French blood to the main entrance, Harry said with the ghost of a smile, "Perhaps you should not be working for me. Perhaps I should be working for you."

Mrs. Foucher shook her head. "I believe I know who you are better than most," she said, her words leaving him surprised. How much did she know?

When Mrs. Foucher was about to step out, Harry couldn't help but ask the question that had been on his mind ever since her "confession."

"I would like to know why you requested my presence when you told your story to Mrs. Leatham. There was not much of a confession to it in the end. As glad as I am to know your story, I almost felt as though I were intruding on your personal thoughts, for there was no confession of sin necessary."

"Oh, but it was a confession," Mrs. Foucher said with a twitch to her lips, her steady gaze meeting his. "I confess to the sin of pride for wanting you to know that although I work for you and will continue to do so gratefully, in a different lifetime it would not have been so."

With those words, Mrs. Foucher turned and walked down the path toward the rectory.

Chapter Thirteen

*A*nna, relieved to know that Mr. Aston would return and bring a respite to her day, examined Emily's pinched face. "It was quite a story," Anna said, willing Emily to speak what was in her heart.

Emily met her gaze, then turned to face forward without replying. Anna's heart sank. Had Mrs. Foucher's story not affected Emily in the least?

When Mr. Aston rejoined them, he talked of inconsequential matters, but Anna thought he watched Emily more closely than he let on. And every once in a while, Anna felt the weight of his regard on *her*.

At last, he stood. "I do not wish to overstay my welcome should you need rest, Mrs. Leatham."

Anna had been ready to spring up from her chair. "I will see you out."

She and Mr. Aston said nothing as their footsteps echoed through the corridor and they walked into the sunshine, down to the pebbled walkway in front. Anna was tempted not only to walk about the gardens with him as they seemed to have formed the habit of doing but to keep walking and not return to this melancholic household that she had promised to commit to for several weeks, at the very least. It caught her by surprise, this desire to seek out a man's company who was still practically a stranger when she'd never had the remotest desire to do so in the past. But in any case, besides it being impossible, what would she do? Follow him home? She had given her word to Emily.

Anna stopped short as the path met the green lawn and turned to Mr. Aston. At least she could unburden her heart. "It was as if Emily heard nothing of what Mrs. Foucher said."

He turned, and there again was the intent gaze of his gold-flecked eyes on hers.

"You would think Emily would *do* something, that she would pull herself up," Anna continued, knowing she was being unfair. Yet, she felt crushed by the impossible task of having to lift Emily's spirits when there was little hope to be had. Still, Anna could not bear the suspense, the waiting, the inactivity.

"After all, *Emily* had not lost her entire family, and there is still a possibility her husband is alive. Doctor Carson said her baby seems to be perfectly sound. And yet she just sits there." Anna's last words came out in a near sob of frustration.

Mr. Aston took her hand in his, his searching eyes full of understanding. He had not judged her, although she deserved it. The days of trying to be strong for Emily had worn away at Anna's compassion until its strings were at a snapping point.

"Every heart knows its own bitterness." Mr. Aston pressed her hand, and Anna would have found it a presumption if it did not bring her a great deal of comfort. She hung on his next words.

"I believe you have had much to bear of late, Miss Tunstall, and it is not easy to be patient in those cases. No one person will react to worry, grief, or even joy in the same way as another. We cannot ask it of anyone else. We are only the master of our own heart."

He held her hand longer than he should have and looked as though he wished to say more. But in the end, he let go and took a step back. "The Rigbys are hosting another party tomorrow, and I suppose you've had the invitation. As their last party was a success." He gave a wry smile and murmured, "Or they are quite determined . . ."

Anna was left to fill in the blank of what he meant. Was it that they were determined to land one of the London gentlemen for their daughters—and Sir Lewis a baron, no less—or was it to land the local parson?

"Is Avebury so short of people that none but the Rigbys might entertain?" she asked, taking care to keep her voice free from the criticism she was tempted to inject into her question.

"There are not many families. The Maynes could, I suppose, but Mrs. Mayne has no pretension whatsoever and does not often invite for fear people will despise her simple suppers. The Leathams entertained as widely as John's schedule allowed until he left again for sea. The Allinthridges will host a dinner in a week's time. They contribute to society but prefer to leave the burden of hosting to a younger set. So you see, we are fortunate the Rigbys have taken on the role."

Anna saw the sense in what he said and was wondering whether Mrs. Mayne considered *her* to be one who would despise the squire's simple suppers when Mr. Aston went on. "I hope you might go. I would so like to meet you there."

Anna lifted her eyes to his. "I do not know. I cannot leave Emily."

Mr. Aston was considering this when a gleam came into his eyes. "It might be highly irregular, but I can ask Mrs. Foucher if she would be willing to come sit with Mrs. Leatham. Perhaps if both parties are willing, *I* might escort you."

Surely he must know that his escorting her alone would raise too much speculation. It would appear as if they were engaged. Anna froze. *Was he planning to . . .*

Without awaiting her response, Mr. Aston shook his head and smiled. "It would be too irregular," he admitted. "But I will not despair of seeing you there."

Anna was left trying to sift through her feelings about the persistence of his attention. The best she could determine was that she was not entirely sure she objected.

Emily astounded Anna the next day by eating her breakfast downstairs and then announcing her intention of visiting Mrs. Mayne that afternoon.

"Emily," Anna replied, wide-eyed. "I am ready to support you in any endeavor that will help you regain your spirits, but you've had several days of eating very little. Shall we not begin by taking a small walk around the park?"

"I must leave Durstead," Emily said in a tone that sounded so like her old self that Anna did not know whether to rejoice or worry that Emily had slipped into delusion. "We have traipsed the gardens here enough, and it is time to show John what kind of wife he has. After all, if you falter in times of trouble, how small is your strength?"

Anna closed her jaw, which she had allowed to fall open. "Then I am ready to go with you." She hesitated before leaving the table. "The doctor said he is sure you may ride?"

"Doctor Carson said the most important thing is to keep my spirits up through whatever means necessary. He gave his approval for short carriage rides if I'm not the one driving. He had talked of cupping at first, but when I mentioned that Mr. Aston had not thought it necessary, he changed his tune, if you can imagine that. A doctor who listens to a parson."

Anna kept up the light banter, although she felt as though she were living in a dream after a fortnight of carrying on conversations with none but herself. "I must be thankful for it. Cupping, indeed. I cannot imagine it will do you any good to weaken you further. And it might do you ill."

"You must know best, of course," Emily replied with a false meekness. "If only the doctors would listen to you."

"Common sense is gifted, not taught." Anna walked over and gave Emily an affectionate peck on the cheek. As long as her friend seemed to return to her old self, Anna would do nothing to hinder it. "And I see you abound with common sense, so let us set out before it flees."

Emily had not thought to apprise Anna about the purpose of their visit until they had nearly arrived, but the meeting was fixed to continue the work on common projects needed for the school to be established in Avebury's poor community. When they arrived at the Maynes' house, Hester and, to Anna's surprise, Marianne were already in the sitting room with Mrs. Mayne, sewing pinafores for their future maids-in-training. Anna had not seen Marianne since their last party, as she had opted to miss Sunday's service so she might stay with Emily. Before she and Emily were even seated, the reason for Marianne's presence became clear.

"Sir Lewis. Mr. Cranfield," announced the Maynes' efficient servant. Anna was at a loss to understand what might bring them to visit the wife of a local country squire when Hester's eyes lit up and she stood to greet them as if it were her own sitting room, before taking her seat once again in a rather abrupt manner. Comprehension dawned then. Anna glanced at Sir Lewis and thought she saw some return of Hester's regard.

I have missed something, mused Anna.

Mrs. Mayne invited the two gentlemen to sit, saying they were about to have tea but that she would bring something stronger for them if they preferred it. Sir Lewis said that tea would suit him very well, and Mr. Cranfield proffered a small bow as he took a seat beside Marianne.

The door opened again, and this time the servant announced Mr. Aston. Anna lifted her eyes to watch as he greeted the hostess, and then she looked away quickly before he could catch her staring. Her heart beat strangely. Would he take a seat by her? She smoothed the pinafore on her lap, and her fingers trembled slightly as she threaded a needle.

Emily had settled in comfortably and had begun talking with Hester while Sir Lewis took an available seat. When Mrs. Mayne had sat again, Sir Lewis kept up a conversation with his hostess while darting surreptitious glances at Hester. Anna did not wish to be so conspicuous in her own regard for Mr. Aston, so she bent her head and focused on the project even though she was not at all fond of sewing.

Marianne spoke across Mr. Cranford in a low voice filled with affectionate concern that did not fool Anna in the least. "It is a wonder to see Mrs. Leatham here at last," Marianne said. "I understand there has been some trouble with her husband."

"Nothing is certain regarding Captain Leatham, and we must hope for the best." Anna despised platitudes, but she would much prefer to offer them than discuss her friend's intimate life in mixed company.

Marianne made another attempt. "Our dinner party is tonight. We have not received your acceptance, but it is not too late if you wish to come. Everyone in Avebury will attend. Is that not so, Mr. Cranfield?"

After receiving his acquiescence, Marianne turned back to Anna and whispered, "I understand you've not been going out since Emily has been indisposed, but perhaps tonight you will be able to attend."

Anna risked a glance at Mr. Aston and found that he was looking at her. He gave her a private wink, which she thought overly bold of him, although she was tempted to respond with a smile. Mr. Aston was forever taking liberties, and she should put an end to them, except with him it didn't feel like liberties.

"I am still considering it," she told Marianne. "I have yet to see how I might make my way. It is possible I will come with a servant."

She gave no further promises. To her relief, Mrs. Mayne called everyone to attention. "We are all here for a reason, but how much you wish to participate is entirely up to you. The women have sewing projects for the girls' pinafores, which may be finished at home. And the men, if you don't mind playing rustic for a bit, will be tying these bundles of paper together and making stacks out of the supplies that we have procured for each child. I thank you for your help, and as the men's portion should not take overly long, I will wait until we are finished to provide the refreshments."

The conversation drifted into the hum of idle talk as each focused on the projects at hand. Mr. Cranfield captured Marianne's attention, as Anna was sure she wished for him to do. That meant that Mr. Aston was able to switch to a seat not far from Anna and say with a teasing smile, "It is fortunate you are the one given the task of sewing, for I'm sure I would make a muddle of it."

"I am not sure mine will be much better. My stitches have never evoked even the smallest praise." Anna put her attention on the stitch she was attempting to set, but she could feel the weight of his regard.

"You might help me to stack these piles and tie them with bundles of string." She could hear the teasing in Mr. Aston's voice, and she pursed her lips.

"I dare not risk the censure," she replied primly. "As the women are all sewing, I must contribute my mite, poor though it may be."

Marianne had kept up a steady stream of chatter to Anna's left, and Emily was carrying on a quiet conversation with Hester. Anna was glad of it, for Emily needed other company than her. Anna was not always the most patient with her friend's suffering, especially in the frustration of being able to do nothing to alleviate it, but she truly loved Emily. After that initial response to Sir Lewis's arrival, Hester did not speak to him again, but Anna saw him more than once sending discreet glances her way.

"Have you given more thought to attending this evening?" Mr. Aston's voice, more quiet than usual, met her ears. "I am sure it will be too much for Mrs. Leatham, but Mrs. Foucher said she is ready to sit with her so that you might come." His ears turned red. "She thought you might be in need of diversion after sitting with Emily all week."

Anna chose to ignore the implication that Mr. Aston and Mrs. Foucher had discussed her situation. "Emily urged me to go when we drove over this morning. I had not even thought she had read through her invitations." She met his gaze, adding, "I think I will attend and take one of Emily's maids instead."

When Anna saw that the news had pleased him, she bent her head again over her cloth, her heartbeat clipping along at a faster pace. It seemed she could not bear to meet his gaze without sending her heartbeat galloping, and it was proving inconvenient to her peace of mind.

For heaven's sake, I am as giddy as a schoolgirl, she thought, annoyed with herself.

Chapter Fourteen

*T*hat night Anna took extra care with her toilette and was pleased with the way her hair turned out. Normally she stayed clear of the short curls framing her face that were so fashionable in London, preferring a more austere look better suited to one who enjoyed depressing pretension. For the occasion, she allowed Emily's maid to coax her hair into a softer style. The summer air was chilly, and she wore her jonquil spencer to cover her neck and keep her warm.

It was odd to step into the carriage with just a maid, with whom one could not, of course, speculate on the evening's entertainment. Peggy was refined and well trained, unlike Beatrice, yet Anna could not share anything more than the merest commonplaces with a servant. She wondered again what had become of the woman who had accompanied her from London. No one deserved such ill treatment as Beatrice appeared to have met with, and Anna hoped that she had somehow escaped.

Anna missed Phoebe's presence, too, and was learning that not even a friend could replace that. As twins, it was natural they should be inseparable, and Anna had supposed staying with Emily would be very much the same thing. They would gad about, exchanging gossip and laughing at their fellow creatures. How wrong she had been.

Anna stared blankly at the empty seat facing her in the carriage. Despite her feelings, she had to admit that nothing would have stopped her from missing this opportunity to see Mr. Aston again. *Am I indeed falling in love?* She knew the answer, and it frightened her that she did not mind it. Perhaps there was something to be said for slipping into anonymity and becoming part of a small village society where one had only to live a quiet life and look into such frank, smiling eyes such as his every day.

When they arrived, Anna handed her spencer to a waiting servant, and the maid went to join the others downstairs. Peggy was happy, for it meant a night of entertainment for her as well. Anna went straight to the Rigbys to greet them before making her way to the Allinthridges and Maynes, who had also been invited. Mrs. Mayne might not feel up to hosting, but the family was certainly genteel enough to be invited.

George Mayne, whom Anna had seen laughing and sporting with other gentleman his age in the two times they'd met, stood in the corner with his arms crossed, glowering at Mr. Cranfield. The image could not but amuse Anna, though she did not show it. George would get over his calf love quickly enough and would hopefully find a woman more worthy of him. The more Anna saw of Marianne, the more she was convinced the woman was a determined flirt. She must be a trial to have as a sister, Anna thought, glancing at Hester, who, having observed George, took a step in his direction.

"There you are."

Anna turned toward the voice with a smile. Mr. Aston had arrived, dressed with that simple elegance one could only admire. How did a country parson have such excellent tailoring? Not a man in London could equal him for the cut of his coat and the way his clothes molded his physique. His stiff white neckcloth tied with simple elegance only served to set off the rugged jawline, white teeth, and bright eyes.

"Here I am," Anna said, her mouth turning upwards. "I believe Peggy was happy for an excuse to accompany me so she could join the other servants. She let fall that her cousin would be below stairs and would introduce her to the others."

They stood near one of the alcoves in the back. Fresh air poured in from an open window, and their small distance from the crowd lent an air of intimacy to their conversation.

Although there were not a great many people nearby, Mr. Aston stood close at her side and leaned in to ask, "Will you do me the honor of dancing this next one with me? And reserving for me the last one as well?"

Anna knew her heart was at risk. Never had a dance request held so much significance for her. Never had she sought a glimpse of a certain gentleman in a crowded ballroom, only to feel fluttered when he suddenly appeared at her side. Their understanding had grown, and it seemed to hurry them toward some type of commitment, without her even having written to her sister about how she felt. She had made only a mere mention of him in the first letter that went out. Perhaps her second would reveal more.

"You may have the two," Anna said, meeting his smile with her own. How very unlike her all this was.

As they waited for the first set to begin, Mr. Aston asked, "How did you leave Mrs. Leatham?"

"The effort of the morning visit wore her out, as I knew it would," Anna replied, her gaze on the pairs of people moving in front of her. "But I do not believe she is the worse for it in spirit. In fact, I believe I left her a great deal better off than she has been since she received the letter."

Mr. Aston nodded, satisfied. "As promised, I have sent a letter to London to see what I might find out about Leatham's whereabouts."

With such a direct reference to it, Anna had to satisfy her curiosity. "Who do you know so well in the Royal Navy that you can inquire of such a delicate situation? It is not often that someone so far removed from Society has this kind of connection."

"You find me so removed from Society?" Mr. Aston gave a faint look of surprise that made him appear haughtier than she was accustomed. Her heart thudded slowly. She liked this side of him, too. "I was educated at Harrow and Oxford," he said.

Anna sensed she had ruffled his feathers or perhaps that she had struck a blow to his pride. "I did not mean so beneath Society," she amended. "I meant only far in distance. In most cases, to keep a pulse on what is happening, one needs to be in London. Which is why I always wish to be there. I cannot bear for there to be some novelty of which I know nothing."

Mr. Aston did not comment on her last thought, which she had not intended to voice out loud. It would later cause her to wonder if he knew what a struggle it was for her to even consider a connection with him.

He answered only her question. "It is a connection of my father's." With that, Anna had to assume his father was based in London and perhaps knew someone who had contacts in the navy. Lord, but what a private man he was for all his frank and easygoing ways.

They took their places in the set, and dancing with him made her heart sing in ways she had never known. His movements were graceful and easy, but it was how he held her in that strong deliberate way that touched her soul. Mr. Aston knew what he wanted, and although he was compassionate, he was not soft. Anna had never met anyone like him before, and it seemed her heart could not resist the potent combination.

The evening passed quickly, and Anna was deliberate in not showing Mr. Aston too much preference so as to set the tongues wagging, but it was not easy. After she had danced a set with him, she applied herself to smiling just as generously to the others who asked her to dance, even young George Mayne.

At the end of the dance, George, in an excess of nerves, stepped on the hem of her dress, provoking a small tear. As he did not notice and she did not wish to mortify him, Anna curtsied and thanked him for the dance, saying she had promised to have a word with Miss Rigby so he need not take her to the refreshment table. It was the only excuse she could think of. Fortunately Hester was not in ready sight at that moment, so Anna could appear as though she were looking for her.

Anna slipped into a dark, quiet room off the corridor. She went to the windowed alcove where enough light was coming in from the moon and the lanterns that had been lit in the garden. There was a cushioned seat on the windowsill, and she was able to appreciate both the calm and a chance to be off her feet. Using the tiny sewing kit stashed inside her reticule, Anna repaired the hem.

She supposed she could have left the tear with no one the wiser, but she preferred not to be slipshod in any way. And there was always the risk that the tear might become worse and therefore visible. When Anna had finished with her hemming and everything was tidy and to her satisfaction, she put the sewing kit back in the cloth bag and returned to the door. She was about to grasp the handle to exit when she heard the voice of Marianne Rigby on the other side of the door.

"What is Miss Tunstall like in London, then?"

Anna took a swift step back. She had done nothing wrong, but she would not like to be caught alone in a room that was closed to guests. Now she was trapped inside for as long as Marianne—and whomever—decided to remain.

Mr. Cranfield's frivolous voice reached her. "One cannot find fault with her dress. Of course, she's not as lively and charming as you, Miss Marianne."

There was a pause, and Anna could only imagine what flirtation he was employing at that moment. She tapped her slippered foot, willing the couple to move on. She would not be able to leave her sanctuary with the two encamped outside the door.

"Well, I cannot see that she is all that pretty. Hester told me Miss Tunstall is thought to be quite witty by the ton, but I do not see how it can be so. I'm sure I have not heard her utter one clever word in all the time we spent together."

"Oh, I suppose some claim her to be a beauty—you must not pull on my coat sleeve in this way, if you please; my valet has pressed it in just the particular way I like—but Miss Tunstall is not at all to my taste. I much prefer brunettes."

There was again a silence. Anna found herself listening more acutely and hoping their *tête-à-tête* would not lead to their attempting an indiscretion in the room she was hiding in.

"And if she is witty," Mr. Cranfield went on, "it all escapes me, for I do not understand half of what she is saying. I believe Miss Tunstall is one of those who are fashionable for a time but who do not have that quality that will last. Her sister, Phoebe, has already faded out. They've both had two Seasons with not a single offer from what I can see. *You*, now, are likely to make quite a splash when you go to London."

Marianne giggled. "I'm sure I will. And you will be mad with jealousy when you see all the beaux I've acquired."

"I'll be positively green, without a doubt."

The voices faded as the two walked toward the ballroom. Anna was relieved to be able to escape without being noticed. The words had hurt, which surprised her. Normally it did not matter what people thought, but although she expected it from the likes of Marianne Rigby, she thought that Mr. Cranfield, at least, found no fault with her—even if she had plenty to find with him. Still, she'd thought he had held a more favorable impression of her.

Men could not be trusted to tell the truth, she decided. Even as she thought it, a vision of Mr. Aston's trustworthy face floated in her mind. *Here, at least, is one man who does not hide his true nature. I will always know where I stand with him.*

Anna re-entered the ballroom, and Mr. Aston sought her gaze from across the room as if he had been searching for a glimpse of her. He was not so indiscreet as to smile at her, but she saw the warmth in his eyes, as if to confirm her good opinion of him. As promised, he claimed the last dance of the evening, and she could no longer deny that he was the most agreeable of any partner she'd ever had. There were no awkward pauses or dull conversation, and the touch of his hand thrilled her. Mr. Aston had spoiled her for other dance partners.

When their dance ended and it was time to make her way home, Mr. Aston retrieved her cloak, gave orders for the carriage to be brought, and sent for Peggy to come from the servants' hall to join her. All this was done with discretion. He made efforts, she thought, to hide his growing attachment for her from the eyes of others in the room. When he bid her good night, he was focused.

"I will come see you tomorrow," he said, "where I hope I might have a private audience with you." He held out his hand for hers and pressed it most deliberately.

Anna smiled and returned the gesture before climbing into the carriage. "I will be at home."

Peggy was thankfully silent on their carriage ride home, which could not have suited Anna more. There were too many emotions—too many fears she needed to work through, along with a slight sense of shock. But it seemed that happiness carried the order of the day. Tomorrow there would be a marriage proposal. Of that she was sure.

I had better write to Phoebe.

The thought made her instantly sober. To put words to her feelings would make them real. But what would she tell her sister? That she had accepted the hand of a local country parson? Or that she had declined?

Chapter Fifteen

The overall frame of Harry's mind was given to vastly pleasing reflection despite the worrisome news he'd received that morning concerning Captain Leatham. He could not quite call the man a friend, as they'd had only three months' acquaintance before Leatham went back to sea, but the two shared similar interests, particularly in their concern for the poorer among the village. Harry had thought when he'd first arrived that, given time, they could become close.

He dropped the letter on his desk and decided to go for a vigorous walk. It was too early to visit Anna, as much as he wished for it, and he had other calls to make in the village. Walking it must be, despite the distance. He was too wound up from worry and excitement—how unfair it was to feel two such opposing sentiments at once—to envision riding.

Harry chose to call on those parishioners who would not tax him with a depth of conversation he could not, at present, manage. He wanted to conquer the world, or at least, a woman's heart, not sit and make idle chitchat. Not, of course, that his conversations as rector had no substance, he reminded himself severely.

In the end, however, he was too exhilarated to enter into any lengthy discussions during these visits and soon contented himself with the briefest of conversations, delicately refusing all offers of refreshment. The visits made, Harry strode down the path, swinging his walking stick, feeling far more content with himself than he suspected a man of the cloth had any right to be. Yesterday, Anna had all but revealed her partiality for him when she accepted his request for a private meeting. Now he had simply to speak the words.

Anna, will you . . .

"Good afternoon, parson." A black carriage, whose stately progress from behind had escaped his notice, stopped beside Harry. Lady Allinthridge leaned toward the window to address him. "Would you like to be taken up, Mr. Aston? You've no carriage, and it looks like rain."

As comfortable as Lady Allinthridge's company generally was, Harry could not bear being tied to a carriage and conversation that would both occur at a sedate pace.

"I thank you, Lady Allinthridge, but I am enjoying this fine weather too much to settle for a carriage ride." He smiled up at her.

She looked dubiously at the sky and then returned her gaze to him. "I cannot say I understand, as I find the air to be too sultry, and a downpour is imminent. However, you are a grown man, and I won't insist. It is quite futile to argue with men, I've discovered."

Harry laughed. "It is most unfair, isn't it? When women have so much sense and we refuse to take it into account?"

"You will hold at least one woman's opinions dear when there is a Mrs. Aston. But I shan't tease you on that subject. Good day, Mr. Aston."

A smile tugged at Harry's lips, as he bowed and continued on his way. He was glad Lady Allinthridge wouldn't tease him, but he had a pretty good inkling nothing had escaped her notice regarding his feelings toward Anna.

The skies could no longer hold the rain, and as he continued down the path, there was a crack of thunder. As if it had received its cue, the rain began to batter the earth. Harry trudged on, his spirits not dampened by the pounding rain. He was only slightly bothered by the thunder when it precipitated a sizzling flash that came too close for comfort. He was near the edge of the woods then, so he ran for its cover, knowing it would be safer than in a meadow where he was the tallest target for the next bolt of lightning.

Harry was more sheltered in the wooded area, but the rain was so heavy that not even the branches provided him with much cover. His cravat began to wilt, and the moisture seeped through his hat. His cream pantaloons were splattered with drops of mud, and even his coat was drenched through. He took off his hat, thumped it against his arm to shake off the raindrops, and put it back on his head. As Harry exited the stretch of woods on the other side and his house came into view, he began to whistle. Oh yes, he looked a sorry state, but there was no one to witness his discomfiture, and Mrs. Foucher would insist he take hot tea before the fire.

Perhaps today Harry would allow her to coddle him. He could use a period of quiet reflection to sort through the best way to convince Miss Tunstall to marry him. She was not an easy victory, she who loved glittering balls and London Society and had a sharp wit. But Harry read characters well, if he could admit this without giving himself over to the sin of pride, and he knew there was something genuine underneath Miss Tunstall's needle-witted speech. He now knew she was not wholly indifferent to him. Despite the downpour and his disheveled state, Harry grinned.

There was no one to greet him when he entered his residence, which was not unusual. The footmen carried on multiple duties as he directed them, so Harry leaned his cane against the wall. To his surprise, he heard a voice coming from the library. Not a member of his small staff would have allowed someone to enter when their master was not at home, so the noises of company were most peculiar. Harry strode forward briskly and opened the door to the library. There, in Harry's own chair, seated before a roaring fire and sipping a warming drink, was his brother, Hugh. A delayed gust of wind blew behind Harry, and he shivered. If he hadn't been feeling the cold before from having been thoroughly wet through, he now was.

"Hello, Henry." Hugh swirled his drink lazily. "Do come in and close the door, would you? I've only just warmed up from my journey and don't wish to catch cold from an errant wind."

Harry closed the door mechanically, trying to recover his speechlessness. "I had no word you were coming."

"I didn't send word. Mother and Father were applying pressure— well-intentioned, no doubt—to accompany them to Bath, where they'd hoped to introduce me to the daughter of Sir Jillard. I believe they've abandoned hope that I will make the push myself." Hugh crossed his leg and folded one hand over the other. "I had better plans for my time than to encourage the fruitless hopes of a debutante and instead decided to visit my younger brother."

"How kind of you," Harry managed, attempting in vain to keep the bitterness from his tone. His mind reeled at the sight of Hugh sitting in his favorite chair. A familiar feeling of helpless rage rose up in him, the one he had spent years trying to stamp out by devoting himself to the study of lofty spiritual matters.

"Would you care for a drink, Henry?" Hugh gestured to the bowl of punch, which was still steaming. The warmth would be nice, but Harry wasn't sure he could choke it down or that he could survive the conversation with his brother in the length of time it took him to drink it.

"I will join you after I've had a hot bath. Jasper!" Harry opened the door to the library and called out to his footman in a harsher voice than he'd intended. "Have a bath made ready for me." Jasper nodded and left swiftly to make the preparations. Harry would have to apologize later for his tone.

"Yes, you need a bath, dear brother." Hugh offered him a cynical smile. "You look like that drowned puppy of yours we fished out of Aldgate's pond. I don't see how you came to be so improvident as to be caught out in such a storm. I arrived just as it broke, but I would have been well shielded in my carriage, of course."

Harry tossed his hat to a chair, strode toward the bowl, and poured himself a small glass. Chilled through, he now realized he couldn't survive even the fragment of a conversation with his brother without it. He sipped, his back to Hugh as he stared through the window, which still had rivulets of water streaming down. His brother's arrival meant putting off his visit to Miss Tunstall today, and he would have to send her a note to apprise her of his change of plans. Harry would not state the reason. She would find out about his brother soon enough. Was her affection secured to such a degree that she could resist his brother's rank? His heart, so light before, was now as heavy as lead.

Harry learned that Hugh, having grilled Mrs. Foucher in her own tongue for information on the people currently residing in Avebury, had a particular interest in accompanying Harry on his visits the next day—most notably to see Miss Tunstall, whose name he recognized from London. It would be impossible to refuse his brother's accompaniment. Harry would need to attempt to divert Hugh's focus from Miss Tunstall, as well as find a way to have private conversation with Mrs. Leatham regarding the news he had learned.

He had small hopes of being able to have a private conversation with Miss Tunstall. Harry exited the house and headed to the stable, seeking solitude in whatever brief snatches it was offered.

He never did compete well next to Hugh. It was not just the title Hugh held, although that alone would have done much to prejudice people to his side. It was also his handsome, debonair manner and practiced charm that made him pleasing to women. If it were just the shallow women who were drawn to him, Harry could bear it. But it was not. The very first woman Harry loved, Rose Sutherlin, had fallen under Hugh's spell. By the time she realized Hugh was not interested in anything more than a flirtation, it was too late for Harry to take her back. Rose had made her choice, and it was not Harry. This was not something he could overlook.

Rose was their neighbor, and although she had grown to be a beauty, it was the elegance of her mind and her love for the poor that attracted Harry to her. At that point, the idea of entering orders had not yet occurred to him, but he did think that he would like a life where he and his wife would live to serve God and mankind together. For all Rose's lofty ideals, they had not helped her choose Harry over a marquess.

Rose had been tempted by the world, and if she could be led astray, anyone could—particularly a woman of Miss Tunstall's stamp who actually courted the world. Harry froze at that thought. *He* could not deny that Anna loved the ton, loved London life, for she had told him so herself. Surely she would favor the eldest son of a duke, the Marquess of Brookdale, over a second son who had all but formally renounced his claims upon the peerage.

These thoughts plagued Harry as he looked about for the groom and then finally harnessed the horses to the curricle himself while his brother stood by idly, imperially, studying the polish on his boots as he waited on the dry path far from the stables. Harry needed to find out how Mrs. Leatham was doing and then decide the best way to relay his news. This was the first order of business, but he was eager to set eyes on Anna again. He was resigned to there being no private meeting with her today, but perhaps he could learn whether she felt any more at peace in her role as consoler and supporter in a small village far from London. He found himself earnestly hoping that village life would grow on her.

As they were leaving the rectory, Tom Wardle lifted his hand to gain Harry's attention. "Pa'son, the sow be having her young today. I mid call on the help of Mr. Moore. Mayhaps 'e will be needed if the delivery be a difficult one."

"Ask him if he is free, but if he is not, it is of no matter," Harry replied. "I believe I will be able to do all that is necessary." With a nod, he snapped his reins and rode off, conscious that he had not been as gracious as he usually was with Tom.

"My, what an exciting life you lead." Hugh folded his arms and leaned back on the seat pleased with himself, apparently, for having put his insignificant younger brother in his place. Harry began to regret that he had chosen to take the curricle and not the old cart, which would have served Hugh right.

Harry managed to make his voice mild when he replied. "It is of no matter. I have no one to impress."

"A stroke of good fortune, for you impress no one." Hugh's voice was every bit as mild, but it held a hint of malice, a subtle undertone to his words. Harry always wondered how everyone was so taken in by his brother, title notwithstanding.

"I never did understand why you despised me so much." The words flew next out of Harry's mouth, as if they had a life of their own. He clenched his teeth, and despite the flood of irritation and hurt that coursed through his veins, he was careful to keep his posture relaxed and the reins slack. It was not for the noble reason that Harry was a man of the cloth that he kept his anger in check; it was only because he knew his brother would pick up on it and despise him for it.

"We have no brotherly relationship," Harry continued, "but we might at least be civil. You will inherit, and I am very glad of it. I have no interest in the title."

"You mistake me. It is not jealousy. It is merely that you do not attract my notice." There was that goading, taunting voice that had shadowed Harry since he could remember.

"And yet you are here," Harry replied dryly. He, too, had been raised by a duke.

Hugh looked idly over the expanse of meadow that encircled Durstead Manor. "I came, dear brother, because I promised our mother that I would assist you in your attempts to find a wife."

Harry's mouth dropped open, and he turned to Hugh. "I am perfectly capable of finding my own wife, I thank you. What of your own, Hugh? Should not you be concerned with having a child?"

"Who's to say I don't have several?" Hugh said, quizzically. He shrugged. "One day I shall settle down and produce an heir, but since our mother needs to see at least one of her children wed, and without delay, we shall start with you."

"You're barking up the wrong tree." Harry could not trust himself to say more as his frustration crept out in increasing measure at every word. He knew his cheeks were flushed in anger no matter how hard he tried to master his feelings. It was therefore not in the very best form that he pulled his curricle up in front of Durstead Manor.

Chapter Sixteen

The butler showed Harry and his brother directly into the morning room, where Mrs. Leatham and Miss Tunstall were seated. Miss Tunstall's first look was of pleasure when she saw Harry, and he watched with unease as her expression changed to curiosity when her gaze turned to his brother. He had been planning on telling her. He hadn't thought too carefully whether that conversation was to take place before or after the proposal, but he would have told her. In any case, it would come out now and not in the way he'd have chosen.

"Mr. Aston, it is good of you to come." Mrs. Leatham sounded more like her normal self, but her eyes skittered from him to his brother as if the sight of another guest fatigued her. "Please forgive me if I do not stand. I am quite tired in my state."

Harry went and bowed over her hand, then did the same for Miss Tunstall. His heart thudded at the sight of her, but when he thought of what he was about to reveal, his neckcloth began to choke. "My brother . . ."

Two words and he was about to fall off the cliff. Only Lord and Lady Allinthridge knew of his true identity and had respected his desire to be a simple *Mr. Harry Aston, rector of Avebury*, even if they could not understand it. Now, before long, the entire village would be undeceived, so he gave it up.

"Please allow me to introduce the Most Honorable, the Marquess of Brookdale, son of His Grace, the Duke of Kirby. This is Mrs. Leatham and Miss Tunstall."

For a long moment, Miss Tunstall stared at Harry, eyebrows raised, before her gaze flitted to his brother. Was she furious with him for having held this back from her? Perhaps it was a point in his favor that he was to be found among the peerage and she would look upon his suit more favorably. *No.* Harry frowned. *If that is the only reason she wants me, then it is better I am undeceived before taking an irrevocable step.* Still, Harry knew he paled next to his brother's height, exquisite manners, and finery.

At last Miss Tunstall drew a breath, and it seemed her good breeding set in, for she turned to Hugh and curtsied. "I've heard much about you, my lord. How odd to meet you outside London."

Harry was not reassured by her words. Of course, she had heard of his brother. Would she think less of Harry because of the association? Or worse yet, would she view him at a disadvantage next to his brother?

Mrs. Leatham gestured to the chairs near her. "Won't you please be seated?"

Harry then noticed the strain around her eyes and forgot his own worries. "How do you go on?" he asked Mrs. Leatham, taking a seat and eyeing his brother, who chose the seat closest to Miss Tunstall.

"It seems I have some days of courage and some days where . . ." Mrs. Leatham stopped short. She turned to face the window in silence, examining its view. In a heroic effort at courtesy, Harry thought, Mrs. Leatham turned to Hugh and said, "I apologize for discussing such uninteresting matters as my personal affairs, but your brother is of great comfort to me."

"Indeed, I hope to be," Harry was quick to assure her. He glanced at Miss Tunstall when he felt the weight of her regard, but he had never seen her expression so closed since he had first made her acquaintance.

"In any case, Mr. Aston," Mrs. Leatham continued, "it seems as if these are the days of lesser courage." She spoke quietly, as if seeking a private audience with Harry.

Hugh, in the freedom granted to one with his position in society, and fully in the manner of his usual flippancy, said, "You need not fear I will disturb you for long. I am accompanying my brother on his visits, but I will not trespass upon your hospitality."

He stood and bowed before Miss Tunstall. "Would you care to take a turn with me out of doors, Miss Tunstall? We might let your friend and my brother talk in confidence in this way."

A surge of possessiveness rose up in Harry at the thought of his brother taking Miss Tunstall on a walk where they would hold private conversation and Hugh would likely offer her the support of his arm. But what could

Harry do? His place was indoors with Mrs. Leatham, providing his support as her rector, while his brother—*confound him*—was attempting to gain ground with the most eligible female in the village. Never mind that he likely knew where Harry's interests lay and had made Miss Tunstall his target for no other reason than that.

Miss Tunstall stood. "A very short walk, then, my lord. I do not like to leave Emily for long, even in the capable hands of your brother."

She wore a mask. Or perhaps it was her voice that revealed none of the warmth she had shown in Harry's presence before. He wished nothing more than to take Miss Tunstall aside and explain his previous reticence in claiming his family name, a name he had been forced to reveal, thanks to his brother's unwelcome visit.

The door clicked shut behind him, and Harry was still ruminating on these things when Mrs. Leatham said, "You need not fear that I will change my regard toward you because of your family, Mr. Aston. May I still call you that? I believe I understand perfectly why you sought to keep it a secret. There might be some who will toad-eat, but I have confidence in Avebury's residents." Her smile was feeble, but Harry was touched that, despite her own concerns, she sought to support him.

"Thank you for your reassurance. It is true that the implication of my brother's arrival has preoccupied me, but I did wish to speak with you today." Harry pushed the thought of his brother with Miss Tunstall further from his mind and focused on the news he needed to convey.

"Now that my secret is out, you will not be surprised to learn how I was able to gain information on your husband's frigate." He had almost said 'fate' and caught himself in time. "My father's friend is the First Lord of the Admiralty and therefore in the best position to have the very latest news. Yesterday I received a letter from him with their initial findings about the HMS *Cornwallis.*"

Mrs. Leatham had moved forward to the edge of her seat, and her words came out breathless. "I am most obliged to you. Please go on."

Harry had too much compassion on her to delay words that would likely inflict more harm than good. "Your husband's ship was supposed to rendezvous at Gibraltar. The Admiralty has not yet received news about what was found. However, I learned that your husband's ship missed an earlier rendezvous point in Morocco, where they would have been informed of a squadron of enemy ships on their direct route with instructions to change course."

Mrs. Leatham gave a sharp intake of breath.

Harry continued, hoping his next words might not remove all her hope. "That they missed the first rendezvous is not worrisome, I am told, as unfavorable winds could have been behind their failure to dock. It's a notoriously difficult coast to navigate. So I would not necessarily take this news as a sure sign of some calamity having befallen him."

"But if they missed it, there was a likelihood they encountered enemy ships on their path, which might be the cause behind the ship's disappearance." Mrs. Leatham understood the crux of the problem at a glance, and Harry nodded somberly.

"That is true," he replied, "but it is only one piece of information. It does not do to despair while they are still investigating the affair. We must hold on to hope until we have something definitive."

"The wait for news is interminable," Mrs. Leatham said. She swallowed and clutched the shawl draped over her lap until her knuckles turned white. "I know I must be strong for my baby, for John's heir. This is what pushes me to get up and find something to occupy me, even to receive visitors. Not everyone, of course, but some."

Her gaze rested again on the bucolic scene through the window, and he was sure the green must soothe, whether or not she was aware of it. "So I will get up, and I will do what is right, but I believe I have very little hope now."

The wretchedness of her situation sat on Harry like a weight. He could not find the words to comfort her.

Anna led the way outside with Mr. Aston's handsome and distinguished brother—*a marquess!* Chin lifted, she decided perhaps it would be wise to give him all her attention and put aside thoughts of Mr. Aston. After all, *he* had not shown himself to be as frank and honest as he first appeared. Why else would he hide his identity and leave her looking like a fool when it was revealed to her?

Her foot wobbled when she left the stone steps and began walking on the pebbles, and she righted herself with an impatient jerk. She paused to restore her emotional equilibrium as much as her balance.

With an urbane grace he wore like a cloak, Lord Brookdale extended his arm. "Allow me."

Anna placed her hand in the crook of his arm, comparing the marquess to his brother. Lord Brookdale was taller and, though well built, not nearly as sturdy as Mr. Aston. Similar in coloring to his brother, Lord Brookdale was, from an objective point of view, the more handsome of the two. His features were more evenly placed with green eyes rather than brown, and his smile held a hint of seduction. Although her attraction to Lord Brookdale was of a shallow nature, it would be foolish not to give him her attention.

"My lord, I confess to my astonishment that Mr. Aston is the son of a duke. Nor could I ever have imagined that you were his brother. From all I've heard tell of you, you lead a large life, and there is not a social gathering in London to which you are not invited. Whether you will grace the event with your presence depends on the society, I assume. I cannot in any way connect your family to a simple country parson." She was careful to keep her voice placid and not reveal that she had more than the most cursory interest in Mr. Aston.

Lord Brookdale lifted his eyes to study the trees, it seemed, and replied in a voice that hinted at disapproval. "Henry is the despair of our parents. He wants nothing to do with the family holdings, and my father is forced to look to hired help to run the property that was destined to be his. Our esteemed parents have sent me here to try to talk sense to him, to urge him to marry well and claim the living that was meant for him."

They walked slowly, unlike the brisk pace she walked with Mr. Aston, and she felt an urge to drop his arm and walk at her own rhythm. She wondered if he would follow. In the end, however, she walked at the pace he had set.

"Do you think your parents will succeed? I am under the impression that Mr. Aston has a mind of his own and won't marry to please someone other than himself."

Anna could think of several examples in which Mr. Aston had a mind of his own, particularly when it came to carrying young women who were perfectly capable of descending from a cart on their own. Anna pressed her lips together. She would not think of such things. Clearly she meant very little to him since he did not see fit to take her into his confidence about something so basic as his true identity.

"Henry is stubborn, but he will give in," Lord Brookdale said. "He knows what he owes his family. I believe he has entered his current profession out of spite and that it is nothing more than a ploy to gain attention for himself. He was always like that—always looking for ways to set himself apart from the rest of the family."

Before Anna could register the dismissal of Mr. Aston's wishes and passion, the marquess tapped his cane on the pebbled ground, turning as if to admire the scenery or choose another direction for their walk. He appeared as if he had no other ambition than to spend the afternoon walking with her, but she knew better than to think it. She knew of his reputation.

As if to confirm her fears, he rounded on Anna with the full force of his piercing gaze. "But let us talk of more interesting subjects. What brings you to this out-of-the-way place? You, my dear, are clearly a diamond of the first water and do not fit in such a backwards village as Avebury." These words were accompanied by an attractive smile that was more mesmerizing than Anna would like to admit.

She steeled herself. "If I were a diamond of the first water, my lord, you surely would have found a way to make my acquaintance in London where even the cream of Society must be considered lesser mortals. But to answer your question, I am visiting Emily Leatham, who is a friend of long date. It was meant to be a short social visit to span the time until her mother arrived, but I find I cannot leave her while she is in such a difficult situation."

"You take too much upon yourself, Miss Tunstall. You must know that Mrs. Leatham can very well look after herself. She is a grown woman, after all. I imagine you will not stay here long?" He had moved forward again, and Anna followed blindly.

She felt at once the justice of his words and the irritation of them. It was true that even as good a friend as Emily was, the sacrifice Anna was making for her was generally something one performed only for family. Lord Brookdale's tone was pleasant and measured, but it stood in stark contrast to Mr. Aston's passionate goodness. Never could Anna have imagined that she would prefer the conversation of a local country parson to his more distinguished brother. The thought gave her chills, and she began to fear for her sanity.

To think! I had almost been waiting for a proposal yesterday. Thank goodness he did not come. This new development can only be fate intervening to save me from a ruinous step.

Anna changed the course of their conversation. "You say it is worry for Mr. Aston that has brought you here—concern for your brother's situation. But I do not believe that, alone, would have brought you. You strike me as a man who will do exactly what he wishes, without much regard for filial duty or the finer feelings of another, even a much beloved brother." Anna said the last words with an ironic lift to her brow, for she *thought* she had quite taken his measure. She also had the distinct feeling she was playing with fire.

If he caught the irony, he did not admit it. "You have seen through me. It is true, I would not have come if the journey did not align with my own purposes to escape a matchmaking scheme my parents thought to set up. But while I am here, I might as well amuse myself. I've learned that Cranfield and Faure are in the neighborhood, and now I find that you are here as well. Perhaps my stay will not be as onerous as I had initially imagined."

Lord Brookdale's gaze had been fixed ahead, but at this he turned and gave her a speaking glance. It stirred in her the desire to meet the challenge, although she would do well to proceed with caution. There was something attractive about the marquess despite his clearly selfish nature. Perhaps he could be tamed. Perhaps she might also amuse *herself* while she was in Avebury rather than moon about waiting for a brown-eyed country rector to pay his addresses to her. It could not hurt to try, in any case.

"Well, you are in time for the Allinthridge party, which will occur on Friday night. This will be similar to the company you keep in London, excepting, perhaps, the absence of all the Corinthians and rakes you usually associate with." She bestowed upon him a serene smile, and he laughed in such a natural way as to sound almost human.

"My reputation precedes me," Lord Brookdale said. "But do not think you may poke me at will without finding in return that my bite is just as ferocious." He said it pleasantly, laughingly even, but she did not doubt its veracity for an instant.

Perhaps Anna could not play with this man as easily as she thought. She managed to raise a quizzical brow once again and offer a mild reply that hid the slight quake inside. "I have no thoughts of play at all, my lord. I am only here to accompany my friend. Shall we not turn back? I believe Emily will be glad for my return, and I'm quite sure, given your brother's prodigious talent as Avebury's rector, he has already managed to impart whatever words of strength and comfort she needs."

"Undoubtedly." Lord Brookdale smiled at her as he took her arm once again, and she felt the full force of his seduction. Small wonder he left a trail of broken hearts behind him. To her relief, he followed Anna's lead and turned to walk back to the house with her.

She kept up a light flow of conversation about Avebury's residents that allowed her to master her disordered thoughts. Through the inconsequential chatter, her mind was spinning about the enigma that was the Duke of Kirby's two sons. They reached the house just as Mr. Aston was exiting.

"I was right," she said in a low voice. "Your brother is quite effective."

Lord Brookdale leaned down to murmur, "I have no doubt you are correct about a great many things." It was not what he said, which was of no consequence. It was the possessive manner in which he said it that pulled at her in a way she could not like and could not resist.

Mr. Aston did not have his usual smile and friendly demeanor, but then, neither did Anna.

"Well, Hugh," he said, "do you continue with me to visit the squire, or do you go back on foot?"

"I believe I have already been graced with the best company Avebury has to offer, and I will not try to top it. I will return, therefore. However, might I suggest, dear brother, that you visit Lord Allinthridge with me in attendance. They will wish for me to pay my respects, particularly as you owe your living to them."

Anna saw a muscle tighten in Mr. Aston's jaw. Although she was not in charity with him at the moment, she didn't blame him. There was something goading about his brother's manner of speaking that was entirely absent when Lord Brookdale addressed her. It lacked respect and set himself up as infinitely superior to his younger brother. Anna did not know how Mr. Aston bore it. For all that, however, she had to admit that there was some charm to Lord Brookdale. If nothing else, life in Avebury would be more amusing with him here.

Chapter Seventeen

As Harry returned from making his morning rounds, he deliberated over whether he ought to confront Hugh and make his position clear regarding Miss Tunstall. She was not available for his brother to take. However, that his brother already knew the direction of Harry's heart seemed likely between Hugh's apparent conversation with Mrs. Foucher and Harry's own overly expressive face. Hugh was likely to play the gallant with Miss Tunstall simply because he wanted to win.

Harry had only just entered his library, where Hugh sat comfortably once again in Harry's chair, when his footman announced a visit from the Bow Street Runners. The squire had warned Harry that morning that the Runners were coming from a neighboring town for a visit, although the squire told Harry they had more pressing concerns in Calne.

"Hugh, can you please give us a minute?" Harry knew his brother preferred to be addressed as Brookdale when they were in the presence of others, but Harry was not interested in catering to Hugh's wishes. He couldn't resist feeling pleased with the look of annoyance Hugh shot his way before moving slowly to the door. His brother would do well to remember this was not his house nor his library. Perhaps then he would take himself off the more quickly.

"Please sit down," Harry told his guests when they were alone. "I assume you have news, or you wouldn't be here."

"You might say as we 'ave news," Mr. Meade said. "Or you might say as we 'ave questions."

Harry could not fathom what they were after, as he thought their first interview had been thorough. He leaned back in the comfortable chair his brother had recently vacated. "Well, is it questions or is it news?" he asked. "The two are not the same thing."

Mr. Howe, the more clever of the two, spoke. "In searching the area a second time where Miss Tunstall was held up, we found a red handkerchief that was attached to a bush." He held the torn and dirtied object up for Harry's observation. "Do you know who this might belong to?"

Harry studied it. It resembled the one Tom Wardle wore, although, come to think of it, he hadn't seen it on Tom as of late. But then, it was so ordinary an article of clothing that it could be anyone's. "I have seen many like it," he said. "It is quite a common thing, you know."

"Not meaning no disrespect, Mr. Aston, but can you think of a partic'lar person who owns this piece of clothing?" Mr. Meade leaned forward.

"What makes you think the article belongs to a villager and not the robbers?" Harry countered, a spirit of defense for his congregation's poorest springing up in his breast.

"We can't say as for sure," Mr. Howe said, "that the two are not one and the same."

The question had yet to be answered, and Harry was tempted to lie. It seemed ridiculous to throw Tom to the wolves simply because he had a past, particularly when Harry was sure of his innocence. However, all forms of falsehood were abhorrent to him, and he needed to trust in Tom's innocence enough to take a chance.

"My own hired hand has one like it," he replied. "As does perhaps every male tenant in the vicinity. If you ask me, there is no point in pursuing this as credible evidence."

"No disrespect intended, but you 'ad best let us do our job the way as we know how." Mr. Meade tucked the piece of evidence back in his coat pocket.

Mr. Howe had been closely observing Harry and must have seen the annoyance Harry had been unable to hide. "Now, Walt," he said. "It will not do to insult the son of a duke."

Harry looked up in surprise. Mr. Howe said, "Yes, my lord. We've received answers from the London office to our inquiries about all the villagers, including Avebury's rector. Your honesty regarding Tom Wardle is appreciated, as is your trust in his innocence. But, as my associate has said, we must continue the investigation in the way we see fit."

Harry was not pleased at the reference to his family coming from an unexpected quarter, but it would not be the last. Soon the entire village would be talking of his connection to the peerage, and people would look at him with a false reverence he had not earned. In this case, however, if it could help his friend Tom, then Harry would lean on his social standing.

"I do trust entirely in Tom's innocence. Our acquaintance is not of long date, but he has never been anything but an excellent servant. Do you have any other news on potential suspects?"

"None. We know only that there is likely to be continued robberies until we catch the culprits. There have already been several more since Miss Tunstall's carriage was attacked on the road, and two, I'm afraid to say, were of a more violent nature than hers. We are still looking for Beatrice Slyfeel, the maid who traveled with Miss Tunstall and who seems to have disappeared entirely."

Mr. Howe closed his notebook, where he jotted down whatever observations he was able to glean, signaling to Harry that they had what they had come for. He hoped they were satisfied where Tom was concerned.

Harry stood. "Well, if that is all, I will see you out."

As Harry watched the Runners exit the small wooden gate that enclosed the front of his property, he thought about broaching the subject of the robbery with Tom. It was difficult, though, and he couldn't think of a way to do it that wouldn't give Tom the impression that he did not trust him. He *did* trust him. It might make Harry naïve—his brother would certainly think so—but if he were to stay true to his own principles, everybody deserved a second chance.

After some reflection, he decided not to trouble Tom by bringing up their visit. In the end, it was not necessary. Tom came around the rectory and stood beside Harry at the door. "'Twas them Runners again." He stared at the departing guests rather than at Harry, and his posture was hunched as if afraid of a blow. "They be finding something?"

Harry shook his head. "They discovered a red kerchief snagged in the branches of a bush in the vicinity, but it could belong to anybody. You, yourself, have the very one," he added.

Tom's gaze dropped to his feet, making him look guilt-prone. "I hope they find 'em. But I hope jest as much that whoever they be, they hev a chance at a new life like me."

With those quiet words, Tom bowed and headed in the direction of the stables. Harry was reassured once again of his innocence and thought that perhaps his continual urgings for Tom to receive grace had reached his servant's heart after all.

By the next day, all of Avebury knew of Harry's title. To their credit, many of the families did not change their behavior toward him as Mrs. Leatham had predicted. But for some, including the Rigby family, the attention was more pronounced. Harry felt it as soon as he entered Lord and Lady Allinthridge's party Friday night, and Mrs. Rigby left the conversation she was having to greet him as he walked in the door.

"Mr. Aston, you sly creature," Mrs. Rigby said. "And here we thought you were merely a gentleman. But no—a nobleman. Avebury is very fortunate to have you as our rector."

It took all of Harry's control not to respond in the way he wished— one that would not be very Christian-like.

"I've always wished to be known for who I am," he answered in a pleasant tone, "and not by who my family is. I hope this will not change among my parishioners."

Mrs. Rigby did not appear to have heard. "And will your brother be joining us? Ah! There! I believe I have just spotted him. I trust you will perform the introductions so he may feel free to mingle with our best families." She stood on her toes, the feather in her hat brushing Harry's face, as she peered over the crowd and tracked his brother's progress.

"Certainly. Perhaps I may start with you and your daughters," Harry said in a spirit of mischief. He knew that was what Mrs. Rigby most wished for, and he thought he might serve his brother a turn as well. Miss Marianne was a most determined flirt.

"Oh, why yes," Miss Marianne said, stepping forward at his words. "I'm sure we are all thankful to make his acquaintance."

No better time than the present, Harry thought. He signaled to his brother, who made his unhurried way over, and performed the introductions. True to form, Hugh, having seen that Marianne Rigby was comely and ripe for a flirtation, wasted no time in beginning one. *Good!* thought Harry. Perhaps now he will leave Miss Tunstall alone.

Speaking of which, where was she? He was long overdue for a talk with her. He had to know what she thought of his apparent change in status. He did not know if Mrs. Leatham would accompany her this evening, and he had not dared to seek Miss Tunstall out to see if she would come on her own. Well, he would have, but he had not had the chance before his brother swept in and occupied all her attention.

It was therefore with much gratification that he spotted both Miss Tunstall and Mrs. Leatham entering the party ten minutes later. He wasted no time going up to them. Bowing before both, he addressed Mrs. Leatham first.

"You have come. I admire your fortitude and hope it will be a strengthening evening, and that the crowds will not cause more distress. How do you do, Miss Tunstall?"

Miss Tunstall did not reply and indeed did not look best pleased with him. It was Mrs. Leatham who answered.

"Lady Allinthridge has promised me a quiet room where we will be only a small number. Miss Tunstall urged me to come, and I cannot but think she is right. Until there is more news, I must be concerned with keeping my spirits up so that I might be strong for the child."

"Your husband will be proud of you." Harry spoke reflexively, his gaze on Mrs. Leatham but his thoughts on Miss Tunstall's cold reception. A look of hope followed by despair flashed over Mrs. Leatham's face, and Harry realized that he was the author of such misleading hope. How could her husband be proud of her if he was dead? That's what Harry got for following the selfish inclinations of his own heart. He was furious with himself but after a beat decided not to try to rectify his error.

"Oh, there is Mrs. Mayne," Mrs. Leatham said when an awkward pause settled over their group. "The very one I wished to see. I beg you will excuse me." With a smile that seemed forced, she left, and Harry was alone with Miss Tunstall.

He took a step closer and caught her gaze but was not encouraged by what he saw. "I had not dared hope to see you here, but it seems Mrs. Leatham has improved."

"Was this one of those pranks you spoke of, my lord?" Miss Tunstall's face was set in a pleasant expression, but her tone of voice was chilled. She had come straight to the point. He would give her that.

"Please," Harry said. "Do not address me as 'my lord.' I took on this profession, even chose to leave London's society precisely to avoid such pretension."

"But it is not pretension." Miss Tunstall's voice was harder than he'd heard it. Even when he was just a stranger, she'd reserved more warmth for him in her gaze, more teasing in her voice. "It is part of who you are. I am surprised you kept it from everyone in the village and that even Sir Lewis and Mr. Cranfield refrained from mentioning it. Emily told me she had not known."

"Not everyone. Lord Allinthridge knew, of course, since he gave me the living, and although he did not think the secret would keep long, he was willing to keep it at my request. I believe Lewis and Cranfield would have blurted out the news, but I asked them not to. To my astonishment they listened. They likely just viewed it as another one of my pranks."

"So it *is* a prank." Miss Tunstall lifted an eyebrow.

Harry shook his head, letting out a sigh of frustration. She should be glad he wasn't concerned with position. Anyone who cared the least bit about authenticity would be.

"Those days are over. I have always been under pressure from my parents to play a role in society that was of little interest to me. I am as different from my family as can be, and were it not for the physical likeness, would doubt that I even belonged to them."

He couldn't resist adding what was occupying his thoughts. "You ought to be glad at the discovery. Better a person choosing to hide his peerage under a cloak of obscurity than an imposter pretending to be somebody."

"I do not like being made the fool, Mr. Aston. If you had considered me worthy of your regard as an acquaintance, you would have told me."

Acquaintance? Was that all? Their brief interlude was interrupted by Lord Allinthridge, who had finished greeting the last of his guests. "Well, Mr. Aston, your secret is out, as I told you it would be. I am only surprised it lasted until now."

"Yes, you did warn me." Harry kept his gaze on Miss Tunstall a moment longer, but she had turned her face away. He fought to keep the discouragement at bay. He had most certainly not won this round.

Hugh was making signs of disengaging himself from Miss Marianne, and Harry did not need to overhear the conversation to know it was being done in such a way that she would not feel slighted. He also knew it meant his brother was likely headed over to claim Miss Tunstall's attention instead.

It was therefore with a distracted air that Harry added, "However, I could not have expected my brother to demean himself by coming to Avebury just to visit me." He looked up and saw the faint air of surprise on Lord Allinthridge's face at Harry's having publicly aired his hostilities with his brother.

He hastily corrected himself. "Of course, it is always a pleasure to receive a visit from one's family." *Oh, goodness. This is getting worse and worse. I will soon have to forfeit my position once the true state of my heart is revealed.* And here he thought he had escaped the oppression that came with his family connections by running away to Avebury.

Miss Tunstall had remained as he stood in conversation with Allinthridge, and when Hugh joined them, she lifted her face to smile at him. Harry's spirits were further depressed.

"Miss Tunstall, you are ravishing." His brother leaned in to take her hand in his and bow over it, as if they were the only two in the room. *Blast him!* "You are, by far, the most entrancing woman at this soirée."

Harry was afforded some gratification when Miss Tunstall responded in dampening tones. There were too many people ready to cater to his brother's will.

"How flattering you are, my lord, and how gratifying it is to hear the words trip off your tongue—words, I am sure, that have only ever been addressed to me."

Without missing a beat, his brother replied, "I may engage in a bit of practiced flirtation, but I can see with you that will never do. I must only offer words that are sincere."

Watching them, Harry said in a dry voice, "I applaud you, brother. If you are sincere, it will be for the first time."

Now it was Miss Tunstall's turn to look at Harry in surprise. He felt a flush creep up his neck. His brother did not bring out the best in him. He was behaving like a sulking child for her to see. What a hopeless thing this evening turned out to be.

When he followed the crowd in for dinner and was seated across from Miss Tunstall and Hugh, where he watched their heads bent together in conversation, he thought it the crowning touch to a disastrous evening.

Chapter Eighteen

*T*hree days later, Hugh sat at the cloth-laid table having a leisurely breakfast. Harry was setting out for his morning visits. Afterward he would spend time on Sunday's messages and work with Tom in the garden and in the stables. He had come to love his simple daily routines that were a healthy mix of spiritual and worldly labor. The pleasure was somewhat tempered when confronted by his brother's idleness.

Harry retrieved the freshly baked bread Mrs. Foucher had left for him on the sideboard and faced his brother. "How long do you plan to stay?"

His brother's presence cut up his peace. He did not like the idea of Hugh, the marquess who had a reputation for leaving a trail of broken hearts in his wake, meddling with Avebury's inhabitants. That had always annoyed Harry, but now there was an even greater consequence to Hugh's focused flirtations. Not only would Harry be left to pick up the broken pieces of any young lady who had been hurt by his brother, but his brother's behavior might also reflect negatively on Harry. How had he lulled himself into thinking he could escape his family's sins?

"I have not decided, dear brother." Hugh leaned back with a self-satisfied smile, and he lifted the coffee pot to serve himself a second cup. Harry was amazed he found the energy to do even that. "Are you asking because you enjoy my company and wish for me to stay for some time? I can, you know."

Harry's lips went into a straight line. "You know very well there is no great love between us, and the sooner you take yourself off, the better it will be for both of us."

"Tsk tsk. Such harsh words coming from you, a man of the cloth. Do your parishioners know that you harbor this bitter root?" Hugh's tone of amused cynicism grated Harry in a way few things could.

"There has never been cause to reveal it to my parishioners *if* a bitter root does indeed exist." He knew it existed. "Only you are able to bring out these darker attributes in those whose lives you touch."

Harry had asked a question, however, and he forced himself to stand his ground. He would not leave until he had a response.

"Well, that is a signal honor." Hugh took a sip of coffee, looking for all the world as if there were no place he would rather be. Harry knew he had to get a hold of his temper. There was only one person on this earth who could make him come close to losing it, and that was his brother. There had been too many taunts, too many brutal words in their shared history. With a quiet prayer, he pushed the frustration down and waited.

"I may stay a while. Avebury is a quaint little village, and today I intend to grace its commerces with my visit. As for its inhabitants—or its visitors, I should say—they are equally as lovely. As there is nothing happening in London at present, why not amuse myself here?" Hugh lifted his eyes to meet Harry's gaze, and Harry saw mischief that bordered on malice.

"I wish you would not dally with anyone here under my protection." Harry knew better than to single out Miss Tunstall. "But you have never been one to follow my wishes. So please, stay as long as you want."

He turned to leave, and Hugh's words followed him. "How nicely irony fits you. You almost seem human, like one of the family."

Harry did not deign to reply but left to seek out Tom, who he knew would be in the garden. "Tom, will you be going to Haggle End today?"

Tom leaned on his pitchfork, rubbing his chin before answering in his own time, the way he always did. "I mid vamp if ye'd like."

Harry nodded. "I was supposed to go and relay the squire's specifications on how the rooms were to be laid out in the school since he has gone to Calne. However, my brother's stay has complicated things. I do not wish him to know everything I'm involved in, for it will reach my parents' ears and cause me nothing but headache." He hesitated before adding, "I also feel I must pay more attention to the villagers while he is here."

Tom squinted in the direction of the house. "'Tis thought yer brother ain't like ye. Be more a wolf among sheep, he be." Harry only shook his head wearily. How close to the truth Tom was.

Harry had almost reached the stables when he heard footsteps on the packed earth. He turned to see that Sir Lewis had arrived. For once Sir Lewis was without Jules, much to Harry's relief. His renewed acquaintance with Julian Cranfield only served to reinforce his feeling that the folly and frippery one accepted in a school chum could not stand the friendship of grown men who should be more sober in years. He didn't know how Lewis could tolerate his presence for more than a day.

Sir Lewis shook Harry's hand. "Hallo, Harry. I'm glad I caught you before you've left. I've come to find out more about the school you've started building. I would like to take a part in supporting the endeavor."

Harry raised his eyebrows. "The school *I've* been building? The Maynes, rather, and to some extent, Leatham. It was their idea to begin with, and they have been more involved than I ever was."

"With your help, though, if I'm not mistaken, and I don't know them well enough to approach them myself. It would be too big a project for the Maynes, and Leatham left too soon after it was started." Lewis's voice was mild, but it was clear he wouldn't accept being fobbed off.

"I had hoped to hide the particulars of my involvement from the congregation. How did you know I had any hand in this? Especially when you haven't managed to set foot in Avebury before a few weeks ago?" Harry gave him a droll look.

"I've come to Avebury, just not since you've had your living. Miss Rigby told me of how the school came about, and I suppose she had it from Mrs. Mayne, for they are quite thick." Lewis shrugged. "Word gets around, you know. All it takes is for you to visit the school once and people's tongues start wagging."

Harry supposed village gossip was not worse than the ton. At least it was not generally ill-natured. He just didn't like that people knew he was contributing his finances. His right hand should not know what his left hand was doing.

Lewis continued. "Miss Rigby wishes to visit the school for herself, but a lady must not go into the area unaccompanied. As I said, I have increasing interest in this project, too, since I plan to spend more time in Wiltshire."

Harry suspected there might be some tender feelings toward Miss Rigby, but he did not ask. Lewis would share his inclinations in that direction when he was ready.

"I asked Tom to go in my stead today to carry out Mayne's instructions on the size of the rooms," he said. "Do you wish to accompany him so you can have a look? Perhaps you could give your opinion on the rooms they are building and see whether the men we chose are being diligent in their work."

Lewis looked up as Tom carried the rest of the tools past them to the gardening shed. "Why not? I hadn't wanted to go without some sort of introduction, so your proposal is timely. I don't think the tenants of Haggle End will look upon me with a friendly eye if I show up unannounced. I can also assess how easily I might bring Miss Rigby there without compromising her safety in any way. She visits tenants on the outskirts, but her parents have forbidden her to go as far as the school."

Sir Lewis frowned and added, "A sentiment I very much concur. But it will be a good thing if she might go accompanied. After all, there are not just men who need tending to in Haggle End but also women and children."

"Very true. Knowing Mrs. Mayne, I'm sure she has already thought about how to bring that about. Let us talk with Mayne this week and even Lord Allinthridge. Perhaps they will know of others in the village willing to volunteer their services in Haggle End to advance the project more rapidly. I want nothing more than for everyone in Avebury to be gainfully employed and living under better conditions. It was what Leatham expressed, too, before he left."

Lewis looked at him with speculation. "Will you be going there today? To Durstead Manor, I mean?"

"It was my intention." Harry wondered what that had to do with the project. "I had promised Miss Tunstall I would look in on Mrs. Leatham as often as I can. She does seem to be improving in strength at times, but it must come as no surprise that her spirits are often depressed. Some circumstances are more overpowering than our strongest will."

"If I didn't know you and your life better," Sir Lewis said, "I would believe you were speaking from experience."

"You know all too well I have led a pampered existence," Harry retorted with a wry look. "But that does not mean the condition of the heart and the lives of others do not touch me."

"You are well suited for your profession," Lewis said.

Their attention was diverted when Hugh exited the front door and walked to the stables, swinging his cane. *My, but he is ambitious today,* Harry thought.

Lewis watched his retreating form. "So your secret is out. How did Miss Tunstall take the news?"

Harry pulled his gaze off his brother to look at Lewis. "Why do you speak of Miss Tunstall?"

"I have eyes in my head," Sir Lewis retorted, a grin lurking on his features. "I have known you since you were ten, and I have never known you like this. I wish you happy."

Perhaps Harry should have teased Lewis about Miss Rigby after all, since apparently all discretion was thrown to the wind. However, he answered sincerely. "I would like to say you are right, but victory is far from sure. Perhaps you may just wish me luck."

"Luck then."

Sir Lewis turned as Tom led the dray horse out of the stables. Harry gave him instructions to accompany Sir Lewis to Haggle End, then went to get his hat and cane. It was indeed time to pay a visit to Mrs. Leatham and ascertain the state of Miss Tunstall's heart.

When Harry called at Durstead Manor, he learned that Mrs. Leatham had gone into the village center and that Miss Tunstall had accompanied her. He left and went in that direction.

Knowing it was where Hugh had intended to go, Harry was certain his brother must have coaxed Miss Tunstall and Mrs. Leatham to the village commerces as well, and the idea bothered him to no end. He, himself, had not had enough time to properly court Miss Tunstall. There had been such complicity between them before his brother arrived on the scene, and before—Harry had to own—the village was *au courant* about his bloodline.

Harry had no regrets about having chosen to hide his pedigree from the villagers because the anonymity was essential to his livelihood. They needed to see him as approachable. It was imperative they not set him on a pedestal, as he knew they would be likely to do once they found out. However, he questioned whether he was not wrong in having kept Miss Tunstall from his confidence. If she was somebody he intended to marry, he ought to have let her know who he truly was. Her cold reception showed him just what she thought of his lapse in judgment.

But how could he fight against it now? She had closed off to him, and the two times they'd met, Harry had not been able to regain his footing. He was engaged in these not-so-pleasing reflections when he saw the squire exiting the office of his man of business.

"Squire, I was coming in search of you." A country wagon ambled by, and Harry crossed the street after it. "You probably know the Runners came by once again with a flimsy piece of evidence. I'm sure they showed it to you first."

"They did, and I told them Tom Wardle had the very one." He saw Harry's mutinous look and quickly changed the topic.

"However, I have more pressing news for you. I received word that another robbery was committed on Bath Road, closer to Avebury than to Calne, and it was a theft of no small sum. The victims were traveling in a simple black coach that should not draw suspicion, but their purpose in traveling was to transport a small trunk of the king's gold. The highway patrol believe the high pads knew when this carriage would travel because it came at an unusual hour, but the robbers were ready for it. These men will hang for it when they're caught, and they *will* be caught."

Harry thought about what Miss Tunstall had endured at the robbers' hands and felt an uncharacteristic desire to pummel someone. "When the Runners came a few days ago, they mentioned their suspicion about there being someone local mixed up in this business. I cannot credit it. You?"

The squire rubbed his chin, and after a moment's reflection said, "I believe there is some possibility of it."

He shot a calculating glance Harry's way. "Don't take it amiss, if you please. I know you have your heart set on the redemption of this parcel of land just next to Haggle End. But I know hardened criminals. I've been the justice of peace here for eighteen years and counting. I have yet to see a criminal really turn over a new leaf, your Tom excepted. But even with Tom, I regret to say, I have my doubts. You can dress a sow, but it's still a pig. Not that Tom's a bad creature," he hastily amended.

The thought of having to defend his decision and convictions regarding the redemption of people with a criminal past fatigued Harry, but with unwearying patience he replied, "I understand your thoughts. They are similar to many in the village. As for me, my hope is that I can prove you all wrong. Tom will never be more than a laborer. He wasn't raised with the knowledge, and he's too old to start book learning now. But he's an honest man, and that's good enough for me. However, these children in Haggle End and just outside it . . ."

Harry paused and met Mr. Mayne's gaze. "Despite your reluctance, I must thank you for your gift and contribution toward the building of this schoolhouse. You may not have great faith in the possibility of their redemption, but you have a mustard seed at least, because you're doing something about it. That is good enough for me, and it is good enough for the Lord. These children . . . if we can just get them young enough, there's no limit to what they might do."

"I will not disagree with you there, Mr. Aston. My wife has been urging the same thing, and it's only for her that I've lent my support."

The sound of a carriage rumbling down the road had them both turning their heads. Harry saw that the coach was marked with his brother's crest. To his dismay, but no great surprise, he saw that Hugh rode with both Anna and Mrs. Leatham. His suspicion had been right.

The squire frowned when he spotted the carriage. "I should have said 'my lord,' I suppose. I've just taken to calling you Aston and must learn the new way."

"I beg you will not," Harry said. "Can you imagine if the congregation takes to calling me 'my lord'? They will always feel there is a great distance between us when there is no distance at all. And there is only one Lord. We are all fellow creatures under the same authority. So kindly continue to call me Aston as you were."

The squire nodded and turned his gaze back toward the vehicle that had pulled up in front of them.

"Well, Henry, I see you are doing your duty to your parishioners." With a glinting smile, Hugh added, "I've taken two of the lovely ones off your hands, so you need not worry about them."

Harry ignored him and went over to the carriage. "Miss Tunstall, may I help you alight?" He lifted his hand, and she gave him an indifferent look before setting her hand in his and allowing him to assist her. It was not a very promising start.

He then turned to Mrs. Leatham. "Please allow me to assist you as well. It was wise of you to make your journey in my brother's well-sprung carriage. You would not have been overly jolted in it."

"Thank you, Mr. Aston. It is true. I barely felt the bumps on the road. And I must say the fresh air is doing me a world of good. Your brother persuaded us to join him in his shopping excursion, which was very obliging of him." Mrs. Leatham smiled at Hugh.

"James, see to the carriage, as we have some purchases to make. Ladies, I have only one errand to run before I am yours. Henry will see that you are attended to until I return." Hugh was playing the gallant again, and unless someone knew him very well, it would be hard to distinguish the lack of sincerity in his speech.

"What condescension," Harry said under his breath when Hugh left. His brother was never one to perform services without expecting something in return, and Harry wondered what that return was. He suspected it had something to do with Miss Tunstall.

"Have you also purchases to make then?" Harry asked her. He was wilting under the heat, and Miss Tunstall looked as if the heat of the day hadn't touched her in the slightest. A waft of lilacs drifted in his direction.

"Only a few. I had not planned to stay this long in Avebury, and I do not want to be short of resources. But I am mostly here to assist Emily in choosing whatever she needs." Miss Tunstall still spoke with a stiff voice. Although she had answered him, he could not scale the wall she put up.

"A very good plan." Refusing to be daunted, Harry offered his arm to both ladies, wishing he could walk with Miss Tunstall alone. Only if they spent time together could he reach the vein of warmth he knew was hidden. But, of course, he could not leave Mrs. Leatham.

They had not gone farther than across the street when his brother came walking in that measured step that showed the world they might wait on him.

"You have too many on your hands. Allow me to take Miss Tunstall, and you may help Mrs. Leatham."

Harry observed the maneuver without surprise, but it did not annoy him any less for it. He called on all his reserves to offer Mrs. Leatham the grace she deserved.

"I am glad for this moment to find out how you are doing. I see that you are not in want of courage, for you have agreed to come out."

His brother had begun murmuring to Miss Tunstall closer than propriety should allow, and Harry pressed his lips firmly shut. He could not hear what Hugh was saying. When he glanced back at Mrs. Leatham, he noticed tears had sprung to her eyes.

"I stay strong for him—for my husband," Mrs. Leatham said. "I also do it for my baby. I do not want my child to be born to tears but rather hope. And that is what I fix my eyes on. I pray this hope is not an illusion or something weak and fragile but something one can latch on to."

Now she had Harry's full attention, and he turned to look at her in wonder. "Mrs. Leatham, you serve as an example for how to bear up under trial. Although I would not wish this affliction upon you or anyone else, I hope you might be comforted by the fact that you are an inspiration."

Mrs. Leatham squeezed his arm but did not reply. The four of them had reached the haberdasher's shop, where Miss Tunstall gave Harry a cool nod before entering the shop.

The door shut behind her, and Hugh turned back to assist Mrs. Leatham. "Henry, I am sure you have some pressing visit that cannot be put off. You need not trouble yourself from here."

"Good day, then, Mrs. Leatham," Harry said.

Of course, he could stay and force his notice on Miss Tunstall, but he was not foolish enough to think this was a battle he could win. He preferred to withdraw and try his tactics another day.

Chapter Nineteen

Anna had grown used to being solitary in Avebury. From her earliest recollection, she rarely spent time alone, and even when she was visiting friends in London, Phoebe was never far. For the first time she knew what it meant to be alone—to have no one with whom to share life's little amusements or lay some worry to rest simply by finding something to laugh at.

Mr. Aston was becoming something akin to a worry, but she found nothing to laugh at. Why had he hidden his true identity, and why had he stayed away from her since? Perhaps now that he was reminded of his peerage, he considered her beneath him. But what, then, could explain Lord Brookdale's continual attention?

She had to credit Lord Brookdale with an exceptional delicacy in coaxing Emily to join them. He spoke with just the right degree of persuasion in addressing the need for her to accompany Anna for propriety's sake, and the perfect weather that would make the trip not too taxing. He let it fall that it would give him pleasure to learn more about Captain Leatham's projects in the village and his rise in rank in the navy. His address was so perfect, Anna could almost believe he was truly interested. And, of course, the surest way to touch Emily's heart was to ask her to expound upon her husband's virtues.

The weather was once again fine today, and Anna, dressed to go riding, was nearly at the front door when Emily called to her. She turned and entered the morning room where Emily was seated with her hands clasped on her lap, her face resolute.

"Anna, I wanted to tell you something." She paused. "I can see you are dressed for riding. Can you spare me some of your time?"

"Of course." Anna took off her gloves and sat beside Emily. "I hadn't realized you were here. You often rest now in the afternoons. I assure you, you have my full attention."

"You are such a good friend to me." Emily squeezed Anna's hand as her eyes filled with tears. A few minutes passed before she could continue. "I wished to tell you that I am quite sure John will not return—"

Anna could now allow her to finish. "Emily, you cannot know that. It is too soon to give up hope."

Emily shook her head and squeezed Anna's hand again, silencing her. "It does not help me to hope in this case. I know that might seem strange to you, but *hoping* keeps me prisoner to a state of anguish. At any moment I might get word that my husband is lost to a watery grave and that my hopes are dashed for good. I need to push through this state of uncertainty lest fear and grief take control of my future. I must do this for my baby and for myself."

Anna opened her mouth to speak but then closed it. There was nothing she could say. Emily was right. The greatest likelihood was that John was dead. The realization nearly stole her breath. How could Emily bear it? How could she bear knowing her husband would never return? Anna's own eyes filled with tears, and a lump formed in her throat.

"How may I be of help to you?" she asked quietly.

"Do not leave me until my mother arrives." Emily turned a pleading gaze on Anna. "That is all I ask. I will focus on not falling into a deep melancholy." She broke off with a laugh that turned into a sob, and Anna had a hard time fighting against the sadness that threatened to engulf her at witnessing her friend's pain. She took both Emily's hands in hers.

"I will not leave you," Anna promised.

Bright white clouds filled the sky, and Anna felt a steady breeze when she finally left Durstead Manor and headed for the stables. She needed this ride even more after her talk with Emily to restore the equilibrium of her mind. If Emily was brave enough to refuse to fall into a state of decline, Anna must be no less courageous.

She set off at a brisk pace over the meadow and toward the road that had brought her to Avebury. She was accompanied by Emily's groom, a quiet man. Despite his advanced age, he was so shy he could barely string two words together in her presence. Anna was so distracted by her talk with

Emily that she rode toward the scene of her attack without being aware of it and without being checked by the groom. Perhaps he was too shy to call her attention to it, but surely the location was less than desirable.

The sight of the clearing took her by surprise, and she knew at once where she was. The bushes had been trampled upon, and Anna saw the grouping of silver birch trees into which the hired groom had disappeared. An unmistakable ball of fear settled in her stomach. What if the robbers preyed upon this location regularly? She had been attacked, but much worse could have happened. Anna reined in while the groom pulled his horse up at a respectful distance, and she tried to force deeper breaths to enter her lungs.

"Miss Tunstall, it appears to be my lucky day."

Anna turned her head at the sound of Lord Brookdale's voice and went limp with relief. She would not be left prey to any highwayman who chanced upon her, with only a groom too old to defend her should the need arise. The relief was swiftly followed by the realization that if Lord Brookdale chose to force his attentions, the groom would not be of much help. But surely Lord Brookdale was a gentleman.

Anna forced a smile, deciding as she did so that she would say nothing of what had happened here. The attack was too personal to talk about with someone she did not know well. Besides, Mr. Aston was already fully aware of the details, and that was enough.

"What brings you to these parts, Lord Brookdale?"

"I had stopped first at Durstead Manor, but as you were not there, I set out for a ride, thinking that I might still chance upon you. Imagine my surprise at finding you *here*. On the road that leads back to London."

Their horses had fallen into step alongside one another, and he added in a teasing voice, "Are you tempted by it?"

It took a minute for his question to register. *Oh! The road to London.* Anna wondered if he had been right. Was that why she had chosen this road? Because it led to London? She was certainly missing London's conversation. Perhaps her longing to leave did not run as deep as she might have supposed, however, for her next thought was that she missed Mr. Aston's conversation.

"I might ask the same of you," she replied lightly. "In fact, I am astonished you are still here after a week."

Lord Brookdale looked ahead, and she admired his profile. He truly was an attractive man, and his self-assurance was pleasing. Every eligible female in London had been setting her cap at him ever since he had made his appearance in Society, she had been told. What a triumph if he were to set his sights on her. *Good heavens. What was she thinking after imagining herself to miss Mr. Aston's conversation? Was there ever a more undecided female on earth?*

She supposed so. *Females are notoriously undecided*, Anna thought uncharitably, rather piqued with herself for falling into that category.

"Let us just say"—Lord Brookdale turned briefly in her direction to meet her gaze—"I have found reason to stay for a time."

His look was significant enough to convey he had meant it for her, and she felt the flush of victory. Or was he just trifling with her? In any case, Anna knew little of her own heart in this matter, and it was best she stayed silent.

When she gave no response, he cast her a sidelong glance and said in dulcet tones, "I wish to congratulate you on successfully scotching the rumors regarding Miss Daventry."

Anna turned in her saddle to look at him. "How do you know I had any connection whatsoever with the rumors regarding Miss Daventry?"

Lord Brookdale shrugged, looking pleased with himself. "When a huge scandal erupts, one of my friends hastens to regale me with all the *on-dits*, particularly when it pertains to a rival."

"A female friend, then," Anna mused with a lift of her eyebrow. "By rival, I can only imagine you mean Miss Broadmore. Harriet Price has not even had a complete Season."

He nodded. "You have judged correctly, Miss Tunstall."

The movement of the horses was soothing on the quiet path, and Anna allowed it to lull her until a question sprang up in her mind. "And how did your friend attribute the success in scotching the rumor to me?"

"She had merely to follow the progression of your visits that morning from all the tales that flowed her way and see where the conversation led from there." Lord Brookdale was now looking at her with interest to see how she took this bit of news.

"I am surprised she was able," Anna said with asperity, "for the type of female friend you speak of is not generally welcomed in the *haut ton*." As soon as the words left her mouth, she regretted them.

"*Touché*, my dear." Lord Brookdale did not seem put out by her insinuation and merely laughed. "I do have other female friends."

"*Married* ones, most likely." Anna knew she was treading on dangerous ground with the direction of her conversation, for it showed an unflattering knowledge of Society's underbelly. And she was probably wrong. Lord Brookdale would be no one's cicisbeo. He just laughed again, sounding more human—and more attractive. It was time for Anna to change the subject.

"It was kind of you to invite us to go into the village with you. It did a world of good for Emily."

They had left the cover of the woods and were now on the open road, with the silent groom trailing behind. Anna could not help but turn her head to the left where the road led to the rectory. She would have liked a glimpse of Mr. Aston coming from that direction but wasn't sure it was to her advantage to be seen riding with the marquess. Mr. Aston would think it was by design that they had met.

"I was glad to be of service," Lord Brookdale replied. "You may send a note around to the rectory at any time you need something, even something as simple as coaxing Mrs. Leatham out. Henry is busy with his duties and cannot always perform such little services. Life with him is rather wearisome."

It was true. Lord Brookdale had come twice to Durstead, and Mr. Aston had not even come once since he had first introduced his brother. Surely Emily merited his time as one of his parishioners in deep need. Anna drew her brows together. *Would* life with him be wearisome?

"I appreciate your offer and will not hesitate if the need arises," she said.

The next day, the butler announced Lord Brookdale once again as Anna and Emily sat in the morning room. Anna couldn't understand why the marquess was so assiduous in his attention and Mr. Aston seemed to have retired from the lists. Only pride kept her from asking. Perhaps she had only imagined Mr. Aston's interest.

Then she remembered what it felt to be near him, to be held by him, even if he was only assisting her to alight. Her memory flooded with the vision of them facing each other on the public road, with her standing nearer to him than she had ever been with a man, the air buzzing with the force of their pull.

"Miss Tunstall?"

Lord Brookdale's gaze was on her, and she flushed with the knowledge of where her thoughts had led. Anna smiled feebly and looked to Emily, who, after the initial greeting, had seemed to withdraw from them.

"I brought you something that might interest you." Lord Brookdale handed her the pages of *The London Gazette*, looking amused when she gasped and seized them eagerly.

Anna scanned the columns of news items. "How I've longed for a recent copy. How did you get one? *Hmm!* What do you know? Lord Liverpool has issued another bill to parliament that is sure to bring things into order, winning him many *friends*, to be sure. . . . Oh, I see the Duke of Clarins is to be wed. But who *is* she? Who could have heard of a Kathryn Martin? Such a common name. And here—"

The sound of the knocker interrupted her perusing, but she didn't look up until the butler announced, "Mr. Aston."

It seemed Harry had never had a busier spell. Fortunately, there were no more deaths, but there had been christenings and marriages to be performed from among the humblest of his flock. He could not find it in his heart to refuse them or to exact the fee they owed for his performing these services. He did not begrudge them for the fee, but he did for the time it took him to perform the rites and sacraments. He confessed his divided heart to God, but the knowledge that Miss Tunstall spent all her time with Hugh while Harry was kept busy doing the Lord's work was a bitter pill to swallow.

The sight of her sitting at Hugh's side when he entered the morning room at Durstead Manor did not help, although he thought he detected the slightest tremble in her hands when she stood. Had she missed him? His eyes flicked from his brother's face to hers, and he took her hand in his and raised it to his lips.

"Henry, you are at last awake and about." Lord Brookdale had remained seated and was twirling a quizzing glass between his white fingers.

"You know very well I rise before you and have been out since dawn. How do you do, Miss Tunstall? You are looking very well." His eyes searched hers, but she met his gaze with only the fleetest of regard before sitting.

Harry bowed before Mrs. Leatham, who returned his greeting in a subdued tone. As he sat, he noticed the newspaper that Miss Tunstall had let fall on the sofa. She picked up the paper again but did not open it. "The Society pages?" he asked.

He knew there was censure in his tone, and Miss Tunstall lifted her chin with a challenging gaze. "As you see."

"I must suppose it was the object of your visit then, Hugh, since your paper came with the morning post." Harry strove for a neutral tone, but his brother looked at him keenly, his eyes missing nothing.

"It was not the only purpose of my visit," Hugh replied. He took the newspaper from Miss Tunstall's hands and opened it. Leaning in and pointing to an article in the paper, he murmured, "And here it is."

Harry shifted in his seat at the intimate picture they presented and was not pleased when Miss Tunstall's expression lit up at what Hugh had showed her.

"And so there it is. Miss Judith Broadmore married to Mr. Samuel Ponsonby." She shook her head.

Harry took a breath and turned to Mrs. Leatham with determination. "Has Dr. Carson been by to see you again?"

"Just yesterday," she replied. "He said everything continues to be as well as expected." Mrs. Leatham looked as though she would say more but glanced at his brother and closed her lips.

Miss Tunstall looked up suddenly and turned to Hugh with narrowed eyes. "What could possibly make Judith Broadmore someone's rival, and why did she rush into this precipitous marriage? Surely it was not over any mischief of mine, for I only meant to make her take back what she said about Eleanor."

"No, not even a person of your influence could have brought Judith Broadmore to meet someone of Ponsonby's ilk at the altar. I will answer you. Judith was seen one too many times in the company of Sir Delacroix, the Frenchman, who was forced to flee to France. Do you know him?"

Harry thought Miss Tunstall's color rose at hearing the name, and he felt a vague sense of alarm. What connection could she have had with a man who was forced to flee the country?

Hugh went on. "I believe my lady friend shared the gentleman's attention but refused to fly with him. Delacroix left Judith without notice, in great haste, and in a delicate situation."

Miss Tunstall gasped.

Harry could stand it no longer, nor could he help but include Miss Tunstall in his look of reproach when he said, "Hugh, have you nothing better to do than to bandy about people's names?"

Hugh turned to him with a sneer. "They are only receiving what they deserve. *Le remords est la seule vertu qui reste au coupable.*"

Mrs. Leatham met Miss Tunstall's inquiring eye and came out of her quiet contemplation to explain, "'Remorse is the only virtue left to the culprit.' It was Voltaire who said it."

"This is what comes of being addicted to Society." By force, Harry controlled his voice, but he clenched his fists on his lap. "Bit by bit we give up pieces of our soul, and for what? A few choice morsels that taste well as they go down until it is our turn to be chewed up by Society."

Miss Tunstall's eyes snapped dangerously. "What is it to you, Mr. Aston, if I wish to read the *Gazette*? Have I not the right to know what proposal Parliament has set forth as well as someone who is still in London? And if I wish to celebrate the news of friends who have married or rejoice in the downfall of one who has done ill by my brother and his fiancée, that is entirely within my rights."

"It is the 'rejoice in the downfall of someone' I take exception to. This is what comes of courting Society. It leads to moral ruin," Harry said bitterly.

Hugh had been watching the interplay with some amusement, having surely noticed the tension around Harry's mouth and the bright spots of color on Miss Tunstall's cheeks. He leaned back. "I enter fully into your feelings, Miss Tunstall. You may be sure I enjoy the downfall of those who deserve it and who are too simple to avoid it." He lifted his glass and examined Harry through it.

Anna leveled her own gaze at Harry, lifting her chin in what amounted to a challenge. "Be not righteous overmuch; neither make thyself over wise: why shouldest thou destroy thyself?"

Harry looked at her in surprise, piqued by her misapplication of scripture but pleased at her knowledge of it. "Miss Tunstall, surely you know what comes next if we are to quote that."

She folded her arms and looked away, but he was smart enough not to continue. *Be not overmuch wicked; neither be thou foolish: why shouldest though die before thy time?*

A silence settled over them, and Hugh seemed to enjoy the tension. "Well, Miss Tunstall, I shall very much look forward to next Season, where I hope we shall be in each other's company a great deal. Henry will remain in Avebury, where he may stay 'righteous overmuch' to his heart's content."

Anna offered Hugh a polite smile, and Harry, sensing he had lost yet another encounter, made his excuses and left.

Chapter Twenty

Anna needed to get away, but physically removing herself from Avebury was impossible. She couldn't even escape her conflicted feelings by immersing herself in a good dose of shallow society. Nor could she tease and provoke some deserving subject, which always lifted her own mood. There was no one with whom she could banter. Instead, she was left alone with her thoughts and had to face the glum fact that they were not so very elevating when chasing each other around in her head. Emily had said she was tired, so Anna decided to go for a walk and headed to the cool canopy of leaves in the woods.

Anna left the bright sunlight on the path and was now stepping over the soft leaf molds. It was good to be alone with her thoughts. Lord Brookdale had been showing her preferential treatment, and she did not know what to make of it. Perhaps he found her enchanting, but she couldn't help but feel he was making her the object of his attention with the sole objective of vexing his brother. Still, there was enough charm in his address to tempt her, especially when Mr. Aston was so provokingly sober. Did he expect her to give up her pleasures just because they had formed an attachment?

She stopped short with a gasp. That was it, wasn't it? They had formed an attachment, although it had not gone all the way to a declaration.

Perhaps that was for the best. Anna started forward again, jaw set. If Mr. Aston was going to be forever moralizing, it was best she knew that now. She would certainly not have to bear such a thing with Lord Brookdale.

True, she did not feel for the marquess the same way she did for Mr. Aston—not even close—but she couldn't help but be tempted by the influence she would have as duchess. *My life would be quite comfortable if I'm being perfectly honest with myself. There would be no thought but for pleasure, and I would have the wardrobe of my desires. I would be a leader of Society, as I am meant to be. And I would not have to trouble myself with matters of my conscience.*

Even as the thoughts flitted by for her consideration, like the selection of dresses brought out at the modiste, Anna knew she could not countenance them. This was not her. She was not someone who so wholly ignored the dictums of her heart for pure status. Lord Brookdale sparked no flame of desire. And then there was that dratted Lord Brookdale's brother who did.

Anna sighed. She continued walking past a stream that she had discovered early in her walks around Durstead Manor. Emily had never begrudged her the walks, perhaps knowing how much she needed the escape. Even in her deepest moments of grief and doubt, Emily had urged Anna to them. But it had been some time since Anna had gone that far, and she was determined in the heat of the day to find the cool relief in the sound of gurgling water as it splashed over the stones.

Anna approached a bridge that crossed the stream. She did not need to reach the other side and didn't even know if the other side still belonged to the Leathams, but the rounded bridge was picturesque. It was the perfect place for contemplation. Anna walked over it, her feet making hollow echoes on the wood. In the center she leaned over the railing and let fall one of the leaves she had collected aimlessly as she made her way through the woods. One by one, she dropped a leaf into the rushing water below, and with them her confusion.

One leaf fluttered down for a life as Mrs. Aston in a quiet home where there might be love. One leaf cascaded down for a life with all the gaiety and finery she could hope for—parties and soirées and trips to the continent that would surely come if this business of war came to an end and if she married Lord Brookdale. One leaf twirled down for a life of being sustained by Mr. Aston's solid presence, to be listened to, to be kissed.

Anna shook her head. She knew which way her heart leaned, but it was too hard to let it go all the way. She just could not. *And he did not tell me the truth about who he was*, she reminded herself in an attempt to steel her heart against him.

"Miss Tunstall!"

The first flush of joy upon hearing Mr. Aston's voice was followed by a spark of anger. Did he come here to further berate her? Anna turned away from him, her gaze fixed on the water rushing under the bridge, only deigning to offer a cool nod in his direction when the sound of his boots on the wooden bridge reached her ears.

Mr. Aston broke through the feeble barrier of her cool reception by taking Anna's right hand and raising it to his lips, tugging her so that she faced him.

"Miss Tunstall, I am in your black books, and you are quite right."

He met Anna's gaze with such an earnest, rueful expression, her defenses could not stand.

"What right have I to preach you a sermon when I have had ample time to observe your generosity of spirit in assisting Mrs. Mayne with her project and your unfailing support of Mrs. Leatham in her distress. I am a blackguard."

Anna sniffed. "Well, I suppose one expects a parson to pontificate and restrict all manner of pleasure."

"Encourage restriction of vice, perhaps, but pleasure?" Mr. Aston shook his head. "I should hope not."

Anna pulled her hands free, not willing to succumb so easily. "How do you know of this place?"

Mr. Aston let her hand go and leaned on the railing next to her. "Our lands adjoin. This is not my property. It is Leatham's, but he gave me use of it for shooting and quiet walks. I come often to the stream. It is a source of soothing reflection, is it not?"

"Your brother has been a frequent visitor to our house," Anna observed. She would not add that Mr. Aston had been less so, for fear he would think that she noticed or cared about his absence. It must also be said that his last visit had not ended well.

Mr. Aston seemed to wrestle with himself before he answered. "I will not hide from you that my brother and I are not on the best of terms. Hugh can be provoking at times, and I suppose I fall into the old rhythm we established in childhood. If I'm to be perfectly frank with you, I do not like myself as well when he is near."

Anna bit her lip as she considered his words. "I suppose I can understand that. There are always people that bring out the worst in us and others who bring out the best."

There was silence except for the rushing water under their feet, and Anna realized she had missed his friendship. She stared at the trees on either side of the stream instead of at him. "I begin to fear Captain Leatham will not return, and I cannot imagine what Emily will do if he does not. I cannot stay here," she quickly added. "My brother can't spare me indefinitely as his wedding occurs within the month."

Mr. Aston straightened beside her, not answering right away.

Is he disappointed? Anna wondered.

"The news we've had has not been reassuring, it is true. But I will not completely give up hope until we receive a definite word regarding his fate."

Anna could feel his gaze on her, and she asked, "Is that what you do, then? You remain hopeful, although you have little reason to be?" She darted a glance his way. He *was* looking at her.

"Absolutely. What kind of man gives up hope so easily?"

His words began to take on a more personal meaning, and Anna's heart fluttered with his nearness, with his intent, focused gaze. She wondered if she should leave, if she should make good her escape while she still could. She had a feeling if she stayed, she would be irrevocably committing herself.

As if he read her mind, Mr. Aston said, "Anna."

She inhaled sharply and turned to him, heat filling her cheeks. He had used her Christian name.

He raised his hand to brush her cheek with the lightest of touch. "Anna, tell me I may dare to hope."

Anna was mesmerized by the intimacy of his caress and the vision of him drawing near. His hand still on her cheek, Mr. Aston leaned in and brushed his lips on hers, then pulled back as he studied her.

"I . . . I . . ." Anna's voice was nothing more than a fragment of a whisper, and she gave the tiniest shake of her head. As the sound of the rushing stream filled the silence, she lifted her eyes to his. She saw a crease form between his eyes and saw the hurt there. "Harry, I can't."

Harry took a sudden step backwards, and Anna almost fell when the air flooded the space where he had been. She saw him swallow, saw his jaw set, and wanted to call out to him. She wanted to explain, but no words came out. He gave a curt bow and turned to walk over the wooden bridge without saying anything more.

Anna had done the right thing. Of course, she could not stay in Avebury and marry a rector. The idea was unthinkable. Only look at what would await her if she did! Nothing but boring conversation and the strictest of propriety. She had put Mr. Aston back in his place.

Anna. The thought of her name on his lips came rushing back to her, and she wondered what it would be like to be on such familiar terms with him—to return his kiss instead of settling for the brief touch of his lips on hers. Anna left the bridge and began walking back to Durstead Manor. If she had done the right thing, then why did she feel like weeping?

It was only as she neared the end of the woods and her thoughts returned to the kiss she had received—the merest brush of his lips—that she gasped as realization dawned.

She had called him Harry.

Chapter Twenty-One

*H*arry reached the edge of the woods before he realized it. Seeing Anna at one of his favorite spots had been such an unexpected pleasure. From time to time, he'd wondered if she ever went that far, and today, when fate afforded him his chance, the timing felt right to declare his feelings for her.

That had not gone well. Harry continued walking at a brisk pace, attempting to bring his feelings under control before he faced his brother again. He should just slow down so he didn't arrive at the rectory before he was ready, but his heart ached too sharply, and he needed to be moving. He remembered the softness of her lips and the sweetness of her face before all the pain washed over him anew.

I can't.

He should give it up. It was clear Anna was only interested in London and all its society had to offer, and Harry had made a deal with himself never to settle for a woman like that. His wife would not be tempted by the world; she would instead be made up of the finest moral quality.

Despite Harry's best resolutions and Anna's less-than-perfect character, however, he could not help but continue to love her. Did she not respond to him when he held her face and kissed her? Had she not wrestled within before turning him away? He thought she did. And she had called him Harry. Though he might be the most foolish mortal alive, he could not abandon his pursuit until he was sure of the state of Anna's heart.

Harry was almost at his gate when the sound of a carriage caught his attention. He turned around and saw the squire. Although Harry was not interested in seeing anyone just now, he knew from experience that Mr. Mayne would come straight to the point.

"Hallo, Aston." The squire lifted his hat and gave a friendly smile as he pulled up. "I see you are just now returning. I hope my visit does not discommode you."

Harry reached up to take the bridle of the squire's lead horse. "Not at all," he said politely. "Would you like to come in? I'm sure my groom is around here somewhere."

"Very kind of you. No, I won't trouble you for long. I came with that slab of bacon my steward promised and a reminder about Mrs. Mayne's dinner party. I'm sure the invitation is mislaid, you running all over Avebury to attend to the parishioners."

"Good heavens, did I forget to respond?" Harry replied, aghast. Mrs. Mayne had at last organized a small dinner party, and Harry had meant to ask Anna if she would attend when he met her in the village with his brother and Mrs. Leatham. He'd not had the chance. "I shall certainly attend. Please extend my apologies to Mrs. Mayne. It was always my intention to come, but my brother's arrival must have thrown me out of kilter."

"Well, you know how women are sensitive creatures," Mr. Mayne said, mollified. "I was sure it was nothing more than that and told her so myself. It's not Mrs. Mayne's habit to host dinners, and she has her doubts, if I might say so. It's this school project of hers in Haggle End that has her making the push. She wishes to thank everyone personally who has helped."

The squire looked about the property to see that they were alone and then added in a low voice, "Your brother is included on the invitation, of course. I hope he won't despise a more simple supper."

Secretly Harry thought, *Probably, but he won't admit it.* Instead he said, "I am sure Lord Brookdale will be delighted to come."

"Good, good." Mr. Mayne drew a breath. "I also came to tell you a bit of news. You should know that the Bow Street Runners have settled in the village inn for the time being. They've decided it's worth looking more carefully at our inhabitants, what with the pistol being stolen from a local lord. And now, with the neckcloth they've found, they want to find its owner. Between the two pieces of evidence, they think they might piece things together."

"The pistol I understand, but I find it odd they would choose to focus their attention on the scrap of cloth. Every worker in Avebury must have one like it. However, I won't quibble with their methods." Harry was impatient to get inside, and he stepped away from the horses.

"Ay." The squire peered at Harry closely. "I must say, Aston, you look a bit peaked. I hope the duties of our parish here are not causing you to be overworked. I should not like to lose you."

Harry gave a feeble smile and shook his head as Mr. Mayne continued. "And if you don't mind my saying it, the very thing you need is a wife. A Mrs. Aston would make sure the invitations went answered and that you were getting enough food and rest. I'm sure Mrs. Mayne would oppose my plain speaking, but you know I've always been like that. I suppose I should not tell a grown man what to do."

"No, you should not." When the words were out, Harry realized he'd been harsher than he would have liked, but the squire did not take the rebuke badly. He just brought his hand to his hat and lifted it.

"Well, I shall leave you then. We'll be happy to see you at our house for dinner in two days. We've also invited those friends of yours from London, Sir Lewis and Cranfield."

"I'm sure it will be a perfect evening. Please give my respects to your wife, along with my apology."

Harry watched the squire drive off before going into the library, where Hugh was sitting in Harry's armchair. That was no surprise given how well his day had gone so far. Harry refused to be driven out of his own library and went to his desk, where he sat and pulled out his ledger.

"I am to tell you that you are invited to the squire's house for a simple dinner in two days. Let me know if I should send your regrets."

Hugh looked up from the paper he was reading. "You would like that, wouldn't you? But I think I shall go. I find there is more interesting company here in Avebury than I expected when I rode in."

Harry was too tired to rise to the bait and focused on settling his accounts. He had received tithing from more than one parishioner but had not had time to record it. A dry task like this would be just the thing he needed.

Hugh folded his newspaper and looked at Harry. "I suppose I shall pay a visit to Miss Tunstall."

Anna's name on his brother's lips was like a knife to the heart, but Harry refused to let it show. "As you wish."

Hugh did not leave the room right away, so Harry supposed it was either an empty threat to provoke him, or his brother was not so sure of his welcome at Durstead Manor—not that he usually cared about such a thing. Harry could almost wish Hugh would leave even if it meant he was going to see Anna.

He needed time to work through what he was feeling after their last meeting, and he could not do it with his brother on his heels. Harry forced himself to put his nose to the books and write his accounts. Each time his mind wandered, which was often, he forced himself back to the columns of numbers.

"How angry you look, Henry. Is anything troubling you?" Hugh had his leg crossed one over the other and was idly studying Harry.

"I cannot know what you mean." Harry kept his expression impassive, but the effort cost him. To his relief, Hugh seemed to grow tired of provoking him and soon left. Harry was alone at last.

Two days later, accompanied by his brother, Harry drove up to the squire's residence, where they were welcomed by the lights pouring through the windows. With any luck, he and Hugh would go separate ways at the entrance and would remain apart for the entirety of the party. He would need to focus on his role as rector to make it through the polite conversation and not appear as if anything was amiss. He had not seen Anna since that day on the bridge, and he did not want to be here watching his brother flirt with her. At the same time, Harry wondered whether Anna had missed him and whether she regretted her decision.

Sir Lewis and Julian came in together, and they greeted him before getting sidelined by Mrs. Rigby. Miss Rigby gave Harry a friendly smile but did not cross over to him, as she was in a conversation. Her sister appeared to be divided over whether to waylay Hugh or Jules first. Harry found he didn't care which.

When Anna walked into the room at last, Harry was hard put to keep his heart in his chest. She was as gracious in life as she was in his mind's eye and moved naturally from one conversation to the next. She shot him only a fleeting look—and perhaps it was wistful thinking on his part— but the quick regard had not been unkind. It was almost as though she harbored some regret or longing. Perhaps she had changed her mind since they'd met at the stream. At least he could still hope.

Anna had come to the party with one objective: to see how she felt about Harry after having rejected him. She wanted to see what her heart would do. Would it be troublesome and imagine itself in love with Harry? Or would it remain reliable and smart? Her thoughts had fled more than once to the memory of his lips brushing hers.

Anna made her way through the drawing room, greeting those acquaintances she knew. When she reached the end of the room, she turned to find Harry's gaze fixed on her, and she quickly looked away again. *Oh dear.* She had her answer. Her heart was causing more havoc to her peace of mind than she imagined it could.

"Why, Miss Tunstall." Mr. Cranfield was bowing before her. "It has been some time now that we have met."

Anna pasted on a polite smile. She was not fooled by his nature after having overheard him with Marianne Rigby, but she could not let him know that she had heard him, as much as it would have given her satisfaction. "How good it is to see you, Mr. Cranfield. How long will you make your stay in Avebury?"

"I could ask the same of you. I see that you are here without Mrs. Leatham," Mr. Cranfield said.

"Mrs. Leatham is unwell this evening. I have no immediate plans to leave, but I must depart by mid-September, for my brother is to be married." Anna turned as Lord Brookdale stepped in front of her.

"Cranfield. Good evening, Miss Tunstall. You look as radiant as ever." Lord Brookdale took her fingers in his and kissed them as he bowed over her hand.

"Good evening, my lord. Is this not too small of a party for you to attend? I had not thought to see you here."

Anna's mind spun as she spoke the mindless words. She had only prepared her heart to meet Harry here, not his brother. Had Harry spoken to Lord Brookdale of their encounter? Anna thought not. She sensed too much rivalry between them for Harry to have invited his brother's confidence.

"As there are no other parties proposed this evening—Avebury being but a village—I may very well attend this one, especially when there are people I particularly wish to see." Lord Brookdale's look was significant, and Anna turned a surprised gaze on him. His attentions, given as they were in public, were rather marked for what should be a harmless flirtation.

The marquess pulled his gaze from her and turned to the gentleman at her side. "Cranfield, Faure, the very men I wished to see. What say you we get up a riding party to Barbury Castle near Wroughton?"

Mr. Cranfield glanced at Sir Lewis, who had joined their party. "We had spoken of visiting Stonehenge, but that is perhaps too far for a riding party. Shall we attempt it, Lewis?"

Sir Lewis bowed before Anna. "Certainly. We could make it an al fresco picnic."

When Lord Brookdale turned his charm on Anna, she wondered what game he was playing. If she didn't know better, she would think he was organizing this for her benefit.

"Miss Tunstall, I hope you will make up one of the party, if we can persuade some of the other young ladies."

"I am quite sure Miss Rigby would be amenable to the idea," Sir Lewis murmured.

Anna smiled in his direction. "I would like that very much, and particularly if Miss Rigby can join us."

Her conversation trailed away as Harry walked over. Anna could not resist giving him a rosy smile, which Lord Brookdale did not seem to miss. Anna hoped he would not be overly stiff after their last conversation; it would be heartbreaking to see the warmth disappear from his gaze.

"Miss Tunstall, how did you do?" Harry bowed before her, and when he lifted his eyes to hers she was touched by the sincerity she saw there. He had not shut her out.

"I am very well, thank you," Anna replied. "Your brother was just proposing a ride to Barbury Castle. Will you come, too?"

Anna knew by her invitation she was giving Harry cause to hope, but she could not help herself. She *wished* for him to come. It took only one glance at Lord Brookdale's irritated expression to understand that *he* had not planned on inviting his brother. She was glad she had. As much as she was flattered by Lord Brookdale's attention, he did not set her at ease the way Harry did.

Harry's gaze swept over his brother and rested on her. "I should not like to miss it. When?"

"Friday," was Lord Brookdale's curt reply. "I would have thought your parish duties too numerous to attempt such a journey."

Harry merely smiled sweetly. "No."

They were soon called in to dinner, and Anna sat between Mr. Cranfield and Lord Brookdale. She should have been gratified to be seated between the two most eligible London bachelors, but her heart was not in it. Of the two, she favored the conversation with Lord Brookdale, knowing that at the very least she had not overheard him express any negative opinion about her. Marianne laughed loudly on the other side of the marquess in her own ploy to hold his attention.

Hester was seated on the other side of Mr. Cranfield, who, more than once, attempted to gain Anna's attention, although his own share of the conversation should have been directed at Hester. Anna admired Hester's forbearance, for even when ignored, she remained gracious. Anna resolved to spend time with Hester when the men and women separated, and she was given the chance when the ladies convened in the drawing room.

Hester drew near to Anna. "I understand you are invited to Barbury Castle. Sir Lewis spoke to me of it directly before going into dinner, and I promised I would go."

"Oh, I'm very glad." Anna's attention was caught by Marianne, who punctuated her conversation with ringing laughter. She tried to refrain from frowning at the noise. "At the moment, I was not sure who else would be invited."

Hester seemed to understand the turn of Anna's thoughts and gave a soft laugh before answering. "Mr. Cranfield invited my sister, and Sir Lewis was kind enough to invite me. We have promised to speak to our cook to contribute to the refreshments. It is easier for us, since we are not a bachelor establishment."

"Although Mr. Aston does seem to do very well with Mrs. Foucher," Anna replied.

"I believe so." Hester drew her brows together. "How is Emily faring?"

"There are times when she appears to be much improved—to bear up under the strain. Lately, I believe she's growing nearer to her confinement, however, and that must bring additional worry."

Anna glanced at Lady Allinthridge, who sat in quiet conversation with Mrs. Mayne. "Do you believe I could prevail upon Lady Allinthridge to bear Emily company while we have our picnic? She seems to be fond of her."

"I am sure she will be only too glad. We may ask her as soon as she is free," Hester said.

Lady Allinthridge agreed to the scheme just as the men were entering the room. She excused herself to attend to her husband, saying he had developed a slight cough and wished to persuade him to leave early. Lord Brookdale saw Anna standing alone and came to stand next to her.

"It seems our outing is to be successful."

"*Mm.*" Anna watched Harry deep in conversation with Lord Allinthridge while Lady Allinthridge stood patiently at her husband's side.

"What do you miss most about London?"

Lord Brookdale's question took Anna by surprise, and she faced him. "Finding Society wherever I wish, I suppose. Knowing the latest *on-dits*. Balls that go on until the early hours of the morning. The fashionable hour at Hyde Park. Gunter's lemon ices." Anna laughed. "I could easily continue. The list is quite long."

"Exactly so." Lord Brookdale gave a lazy smile, but his gaze pierced. "You will do well to keep your eye on the prize, my dear girl." He did not need to glance at his brother for his meaning to become clear: Harry was not the path that would lead her to all London's gaieties.

Anna sniffed. She would not pretend she did not grasp his nuance, although it was certainly no affair of his. She had to admit, though, there was truth to his words.

Chapter Twenty-Two

Lady Allinthridge arrived after Emily and Anna had finished their breakfast and moved to the morning room. She set down her parasol before taking a seat on the sofa next to Emily.

"You're looking a bit pinched, which sometimes happens when women grow close to confinement. I approve of your making a push to get up each day, for the routine will only strengthen you." Lady Allinthridge opened the bag she had brought with her and began pulling items out of it. "I've brought a book to read aloud from and some materials for paperwork if you'd like. I've a half-finished flower we might work on, as I know you are skilled in such things."

"I am sure we will pass a very pleasant afternoon," Emily replied in a subdued voice.

Lady Allinthridge signaled to the servant who was placing a cushion behind Emily's back. "Have that small table brought over to us so we may work with more ease. You will not mind my directing your servants," she told Emily. "After all, we will be more comfortable this way. Miss Tunstall, you must be anxious to be off."

Anna was indeed dressed and ready. She could not remember when the idea of an outing appealed to her more strongly. She needed the freedom that would come from leaving Durstead Manor for an entire day, something she had not had since her arrival. She was looking forward to Mr. Aston's company, too. Perhaps they would have time to talk.

"I shall only fetch my bonnet." She planted an affectionate kiss on Emily's cheek. "I'm happy to see you in such good hands. I have no qualms about leaving you now."

"Anna, you are a good friend to me." The words came out choked, and Anna could not resist coming back and throwing her arms around Emily's shoulders.

"You are easy to love, my dear. Thank you, Lady Allinthridge."

Anna had to stop herself from running to fetch her bonnet and appearing unladylike. With a smile and a light step, she pulled on her gloves and exited into the sunshine.

By the time the groom had assisted Anna on to her favorite horse from Emily's well-stocked stable, the party had begun to congregate on the path leading from the manor to the main road. Mr. Cranfield and Sir Lewis were present, as well as Hester and Marianne Rigby. George Mayne had also come, trailed by a childhood friend who had recently come from visiting her aunt in Cornwall. They would not be even in number, but it could not be helped because another young lady had fallen ill at the last minute. They all agreed they should not postpone their outing.

Anna's heart beat faster as soon as Mr. Aston and Lord Brookdale rode into view. She looked away, willing herself to be more natural. Although she knew of their dislike for each other, Anna could not help but admire the elegance of their person. How could she ever have thought Mr. Aston nothing more than a simple country parson?

Both men had their gazes fixed on her when they arrived, and Anna gave a nod of greeting, first to Lord Brookdale. *It is only right that I would give him preference. He is higher ranking.* But she knew her true reason was to hide her growing affection for Mr. Aston. She could not let everybody know where her preference lay.

It was becoming increasingly obvious to her that, despite the marquess's suave manner and cool poise—despite his wealth, title, and ability to speak fluidly—Lord Brookdale lacked the depth and moral fiber that Mr. Aston had in droves. Lord Brookdale could not even find it in his heart to cherish his own brother. How could he have affection for anyone else?

No, Lord Brookdale was the inferior one of the two—at least in her eyes.

"Shall we go, then?" In line with his rank, Lord Brookdale led the way. The party moved forward naturally, spreading out in the wide lane, each going at an easy pace. Lord Brookdale brought his horse alongside Anna's, leaving his brother to trail behind. She felt a pang of annoyance, but she would not bring attention to herself or him by objecting.

"Miss Tunstall, you are finally free. Are you looking forward to this ride as much as I am?"

She had difficulty imagining Lord Brookdale enjoying anything when he always projected such a languid air. It made Anna smile to think of it, and when he questioned her on her source of amusement, she told him.

"It is not fashionable to find amusement in things. Surely you know that, Miss Tunstall, for you are addicted to fashion."

"Nevertheless, I do. In fact, to answer your question, I have long been wishing for a day trip such as this. I expected more of these outings when I came to the country, but life dealt me an unexpected turn."

Or, rather, it had thrown Emily a nasty turn, and Anna went careening after her.

Lord Brookdale nodded. "Life often does that, I find, which is why I arrange all things to my satisfaction."

"A sentiment I can relate to," Anna said. Some of the riders had gone ahead of them, and she could hear the murmur of their conversations floating back. She could not see Mr. Aston, who was still trailing behind, but occasionally she heard him chime in and thought he might be talking to George Mayne.

"But I do not think we are able to choose our life at will. There are things outside our power that influence our circumstances."

"It is much easier when one decides not to care," Lord Brookdale replied. "This is why I set out in life the way I mean to go on. I will not be among those who are swept up in the current of life's passions and agonies. It is much more sensible simply to be disinterested."

It was a rational position, and normally Anna would have agreed with it. But her sentiments had started to undergo a shift. Perhaps she had led a sheltered life. If she did not concern herself with what others thought of her, perhaps that was only because her family had thought so well of her so as never to leave her in doubt of her worth. True, she did not need the approbation of others, but that did not mean earning their good opinion was of no value.

Away from the influence of home and family, Anna was discovering that her own conscience led her to the same values her family had always held. It was right to consider the needs of others, even when it was uncomfortable to do so.

"Well," she said, turning to stare at the view between her horse's bobbing ears. "I will not disagree with you, but I am not certain your path is the best course for happiness."

The road opened up before them, and Harry urged his mount around hers and galloped forward to walk abreast Sir Lewis and Hester Rigby.

She watched him go and wished he had come alongside her. Did he imagine she favored his brother? Perhaps Harry saw her *tête à tête* as a sign that her heart was indifferent to him, but it was not she who encouraged Lord Brookdale's attentions. She needed to find a way to show Harry that her affections were undergoing a change.

Heavens! The thought made her flinch. She could not be too obvious. What if others saw it? Anna could not bear to have the affairs of her heart plastered all over for everyone to see.

She renewed her focus on the marquess, but Lord Brookdale was too perceptive. He disconcerted her by saying, "I see my brother has caught your gaze. Is your attachment of long date?"

Anna felt her cheeks flush, and she offered him a bland smile. "I do not know what you mean. There is no attachment between us."

Out of the corner of her eye, she saw Lord Brookdale's cynical look. "Indeed, I should hope not. You are too alluring to settle so quickly and so soon."

Anna was flattered but irritated, and she tried to keep both out of her voice. She had to be on her guard to banter with Lord Brookdale.

"And yet, my lord, I've had two Seasons. Most would argue that I am already on the shelf and should take the first offer that is handed to me."

"You know very well they would be wrong. I urge you . . ." Anna looked at him when he didn't continue and was surprised to see the hesitation in his features. When he at last spoke, he wore his usual bland expression again. "I urge you not to rush into any engagement too quickly."

"Engagement?" Anna's laugh sounded false to her own ears. "I assure you, I have no such intention."

The ride was not overly long, although Anna had not ridden enough over the summer for it not to hurt. At last they approached the famous hill with its ancient ditches and ramparts.

"The horses will need to climb this at an easy pace," Harry announced as they formed a trail.

Anna fell into line behind Harry, and Lord Brookdale brought up the rear as they rode up the ridgeway. Anna was quiet as her mare followed the sedate pace set by Harry's horse, and Anna's eyes drank in the sight of the vast expanse of countryside before her.

Once on the summit, George Mayne pointed to the west. "Those are the Cotswolds there." He turned. "And over there is the Severn."

Anna shielded her eyes and made out the water glinting in the sun far in the distance. Others around her dismounted and began setting up the dishes they had brought to make up a picnic. Anna remained on her horse to better appreciate the remarkable view in front of her.

Harry, his eyes on her, had dismounted and reached up to help Anna from her horse. A flash of annoyance crossed his brother's face. She was grateful to be near Harry again and relieved he didn't seem to be cross with her, despite her refusal. There was hope, after all.

"Thank you," she murmured.

"My pleasure." Harry's smile reached his eyes, and he turned away to direct people where to put things. He helped set up the picnic on the grassy ridge and sent teasing replies to the other members of the party.

Lord Brookdale, his expression grim, held out his arm in a way Anna could not refuse. She placed her hand on his and followed him to where the others were seated. The marquess was tall, and she came only to his shoulder, which made her feel dwarfed. By comparison, Harry's stature always left her with the sensation that it would be easy to sink into him and have him wrap his arms around her.

What it would feel like to rest her head on his shoulder.

Anna stifled the urge to laugh. It would probably give her a pain in her neck. They were much of the same height. Lord Brookdale looked at her quizzically but did not ask to know her thoughts.

They sat on the blankets already laid out with food, and Lord Brookdale entertained Anna with questionable stories about his acquaintances with some of the actresses from Drury Lane. More than once, she peeked at Harry, who must have overheard, but he was not so improvident, she supposed, to show the disapproval he surely felt. After they had eaten, Lord Brookdale rose to refill his glass, and Harry took the opportunity to approach her.

"Miss Tunstall, would you care to walk around the full ramparts with me?"

Lord Brookdale had entered into conversion with Sir Lewis, and she took that as a sign that she was released from her role as temporary companion. At her nod, Harry helped Anna to her feet and they began walking. Her nose filled with his scent of musk with an undercurrent of cedar, and she realized this scent, which was now becoming so familiar to her, brought her a sense of calm.

"The ride has brought some color back to your cheeks," he observed.

"Yes, I fear, as a general rule, I am in sad form," she teased. "It has escaped no one's notice, I am sure."

Harry did not play the game her way because he returned a serious reply. "I only think I noticed it because I cannot help but examine your features every time I see you. I assure you, you are the most beautiful woman I have ever laid eyes on, even when sadly pulled. But when there is a light in your eyes and a bloom to your cheeks, you are unparalleled."

He turned to look at her but did not take advantage of their solitary moment by halting their progress. She almost wished he would.

"You are trying to leave me without any response," Anna said at last. "But I am made of sterner stuff than that. I will not be embarrassed. Do not forget I had always envisioned my place at the side of a political man. And someone who is destined for a life in politics must always have a snappy answer on her tongue." Leave him to think what he would of that remark.

Her comment did not seem to ruffle him at all. "You think you're destined for a life in politics, but I think you are destined for a life of love. And you may make as many snappy retorts as you wish. I shall not mind."

They were coming around the other side of the ramparts, and Anna sought to gain her bearings by giving an arch reply. "No more scolds stored up for me then, Mr. Aston?"

Harry took Anna's arm and gently pulled her to a stop. They were partially hidden from the crowd by a rise in the earth, and he glanced in the direction of their friends. He strode forward two more steps with her in tow until the terrain hid them completely from view. However, the path was open, and at any moment another person might come around the bend.

"Anna."

She looked at Harry's face, and the stern lines around his mouth revealed the gravity of what he wished to say.

"I will not press you again. Not now. And I will not hold out for a lost cause." He lifted his gloved hand to touch her cheek, freezing her in place. "But I don't think the idea of marriage between us is completely out of the question."

Harry held her captive with his gaze for a weighted moment and then turned to go, taking Anna's arm. Before she had time to digest how she felt, they reached the rest of the group.

Harry took her to Hester and stayed for a few minutes, responding to Hester's inquiries about a parish member. He then moved to join the gentlemen who were arguing whether there was not a shorter route to be had in passing over Lord Ramsworth's property. Lord Brookdale looked shrewdly at Anna.

Anna's peace had been cut up. She was not accustomed to her defenses being so easily penetrated, and although she took herself to task—*this will not do, this will not do*—her heart and her mind betrayed her.

Her defenses appeared to be crumbling.

Chapter Twenty-Three

Anna could not bear Lord Brookdale's mocking regard. He must have noticed those few minutes when she and Harry had disappeared behind the rise in the hill. *Nothing happened, I assure you,* she retorted in her mind. Indeed, the path was too open for anything of a clandestine nature to have occurred.

She was too unsure of how she felt about Harry's words to bear up under the scrutiny of another, especially one as cynical and knowing as Lord Brookdale. Of course, it was perhaps only her own imagination that led her to think Lord Brookdale thought anything of the matter at all.

And then there was the uncomfortable fact that something *had* happened. Harry told her he had not yet given up, essentially reassuring her of his feelings for her and letting her know the burden of decision fell now on her, which made her writhe internally. How ever could she decide? How could he expect it of her?

Uncomfortable was a word she was coming to associate too closely with Harry Aston. *And love should not be uncomfortable!*

Anna spent the remainder of the afternoon in conversation with various members of the party but not Lord Brookdale or Harry, who seemed to have no desire to converse with her. When it was time to leave, Lord Brookdale assisted her onto her horse. He did this with his usual polished address and let his fingers rest on her boot once she was hoisted in the saddle. He mounted his own horse in silence and followed Anna as she trailed Sir Lewis and Mr. Cranfield, who had taken the lead.

They rode like that in silence for nearly a quarter of an hour, and Anna was relieved to have some respite from conversation. She was content to listen to the wisps of conversation around her and feel the fresh air lift the small tendrils of hair that had come loose from her chignon. They had chosen their day well for their ride.

"Will you attend Sunday's service?"

Anna was pulled out of her thoughts by Lord Brookdale, who was still riding at her side, apparently undeterred by her lack of conversation.

"Of course. How can you ask such a thing?" Even the most indifferent members of society would not risk the scandal of eschewing church on Sunday.

Lord Brookdale sniffed. "Your faith is important to you, then."

She didn't understand his meaning but felt its criticism and was stung into a retort. "You are quite provoking. Surely you know one cannot miss Sunday service without raising severe criticism."

"And that is the only reason you attend?"

Anna did not like being backed into a corner. There was more to it than obligation. She was touched by the purity of the most sincere worshippers and longed for what they had. But that was not something she would ever admit, especially to one as cynical as Lord Brookdale.

She gave a tight smile and kept her gaze fixed on the path before them. "Are you leading us through this meandering conversation with any sort of destination in mind?"

Lord Brookdale laughed. "I am simply wondering how you find Henry's discourse on the Scriptures. Perhaps I am wondering how you stay awake."

She should not have been, but Anna was surprised by this cynical observation. Even the biggest skeptic had to admit Mr. Aston was born to his profession. He brought a dusty religion to life. Perhaps Lord Brookdale was worse than a skeptic. Perhaps he had no heart.

Anna's mare picked up the pace as the others in front of her did, and she let the horse have her way. It gave Anna time to put order to her thoughts. Finally, she decided to risk telling the marquess what she thought. After all, this was not the first time she had done such a thing.

"The continual aspersions you cast on your brother do not harm his reputation, which remains true to the life he leads. But they do your own character no good. I would never be so presumptuous as to recommend you to a different comportment, but neither will I join you in defaming the character of one whom you should hold dear."

The path narrowed and brought their horses together until her legs were almost touching his. She glanced at Lord Brookdale and noticed a muscle twitch in his cheek.

"Far be it from me to cause you any compunction, but I wonder if this is not merely a passing fancy, and that when you return to more reasonable society, you will have cause to rethink things. You may yet determine I have the right of it. But never fear, I shall not change. You and I are well suited, I believe."

Any witty retort that might have flown from her dried up. Lord Brookdale's words left no doubt as to his meaning, but she was far from wishing for them. However, how could she say she did not wish for them when he had not made a more specific offer?

Anna strove for a level voice. "Surely. As equally suited as any members of the ton who enjoy the same parties."

Lord Brookdale laughed once again and rode ahead, apparently certain of his conquest.

The next day, Emily claimed a need for rest. It seemed she had been feeling pains, although Anna only knew of it after she pressed Emily for information. Even then she had been fobbed off. Emily appeared to think the pains were nothing to worry about, and Anna had to be content with that.

Left alone, Anna escaped to the sanctuary of the outdoors and sought out the gardener for a cutting tool, having decided to replace some of the wilting flowers indoors with freshly cut blooms. She was thus employed when Lord Brookdale strode up to where she was kneeling.

"Come, walk with me," he said, as soon as he had made his arrival known. "I have a proposition to make you."

Anna handed the selection of flowers and clippers to a waiting footman, unnerved by the direct request coming on the heels of yesterday's comment. Lord Brookdale usually seemed to glory in being circumspect. Anna supposed it was a conversation that needed to be had and took her place at his side.

"I believe I owe you an apology for my words," he began, taking her by surprise. "They did not please you. That I noticed right away."

Which words? she thought. *Your cutting words regarding your brother or your insinuation that we are well suited?* She decided she would not ask.

"You are very astute, my lord."

"You do have affection for my brother, then, if you are to defend him in such a manner?" The last bit was spoken in a question, which would have made the marquess seem human if it were not spoken in such a chilling tone.

"Your brother and I are nothing to each other," Anna replied quietly. *Not in any kind of formal way.*

"I am happy to hear you say it," Lord Brookdale said. "Henry is a good sort of fellow, but . . . Let us just say that I have been coming to appreciate your worth in these short weeks. It is not the life of a parson's wife for you. You belong to the kind of society I keep."

Anna continued walking, not knowing how she could turn the discourse, only that she must. His parlance spoke of intimacy, but he'd said nothing she could refute or give an answer to.

It did not appear as if Lord Brookdale needed her response, for he continued the walk, leading her, whether on purpose or aimlessly in the direction of the rectory. They would soon be on the public road that joined the two houses.

"As for myself," he said at last, "I have never seriously considered marriage. I knew I would one day have to contemplate the idea, but it seemed only natural to push such a thing off as long as possible, inasmuch as I did not find anyone I could admire."

Oh dear. If there was any doubt before, there was none now about where this conversation was headed, but he had not, before yesterday, given her any great warning that it was to come. Or perhaps she had purposefully turned a blind eye to his hints.

Had he made a cold-hearted decision that precluded personal feelings, or did his feelings simply not run very deep? Anna could not imagine how to put a stop to what she was sure was to be a declaration before he made one. It would be presumptuous to assume and humiliating to be caught cold at it.

"I have never envied my brother a single thing. If anything, it should be the contrary, but if I say something in Henry's praise, he does not appear to be prone to jealousy. I am credited with the better looks."

I'm sorry to contradict one so sure of himself, but despite what you are credited with, it is Harry . . .

Anna could not finish her thought. It still frightened her to admit it. She was now convinced she loved Harry, but she still did not love everything that came with him. She did not love his life.

"And I will inherit the dukedom," he continued. "I am not required to earn my keep or try out life as a simple country parson as a way of gaining a sense of worth. If Henry had more sense, he would have taken the living my parents gave him. He would be much better off than he is now."

For one who seems to despise men who prose on and on, you need to get to the point, sir, so I may reject you and be comfortable again.

Lord Brookdale moved forward, halting neither his steps nor his suit. "Imagine my shock when I found for the first time something of his I might be jealous of." Lord Brookdale stopped and turned to face Anna, whose sense of alarm flew up into the boughs, along with all rational thought, apparently.

"Your regard!"

This she had not expected. It was equally impossible to confirm her regard for Harry as it was to deny it. "No . . . rather . . . I must say . . ."

"You need say no more, Anna. How much you relieve my mind that he has not permanently engaged your affections. It means I have a chance to win them for myself."

Without wasting another word, the marquess wrapped his arm around her, pulling her flush against him. In one gesture, he leaned down to take possession of her mouth. With his other hand, he held the back of her neck in a firm grip, and Anna remained stock-still, too shocked to do anything but stand rigidly while his lips covered hers and then traveled over the rest of her face. Lord Brookdale pulled away only enough to murmur, "We'll thaw that ice soon enough, my dear."

Those words were all that were needed for Anna to draw breath and for the shock to turn to a burning rage. On a shuddering exhale, she pulled back to slap the marquess, but he caught her hand mid-air with a vice-like grip.

"*What the deuce!* Lord Brookdale's face was white as he held her wrist in a tight grasp that brought tears to her eyes. She blinked them back.

"Have the goodness"—Anna's voice trembled, and she controlled it, along with her tears, with every ounce of her being—"to unhand me, my lord."

The marquess finally loosened his punishing grip, and she dropped her hand to her side, refusing to rub where he had hurt her or drop her gaze from his.

"Have you gone mad?" he spat out.

"Mad—me? I did not give you leave to do something so wholly inappropriate as to kiss me without even stopping to learn whether I returned your regard. Had you addressed your intentions in a more proper manner, you would have been undeceived in short order. Traditionally, a kiss follows an acceptance and does not precede it."

Lord Brookdale's eyes flashed in anger before his mask of cynicism was back in place. He laughed harshly and pinched her chin between his fingers, forcing her to face him. Anna could not control the heaving breaths, but she refused to give him the satisfaction of looking away. He kept his face inches from hers as he studied her, a glint in his eyes.

At last he released her. "I was mistaken in you. Did Henry try to steal a march on me, then? Those minutes you were hidden from view at Barbury? Don't think I didn't see that."

Lord Brookdale scanned her face, his mouth set in hard lines. "Whether you live to regret having refused me or I live to regret having been turned off remains to be seen. But somehow I don't think the regret will come from me," he said softly.

He took a step back. "Henry might have captured your fancy, but he has not ignited your passion, and you know it."

With that, he left.

Chapter Twenty-Four

*H*arry strode toward Durstead Manor with purposeful steps. After witnessing Anna's flushed cheeks yesterday, as she rode alongside his brother from Wroughton, Harry decided it was time he made things clear. His brother was dallying with Anna. Harry could see that for himself even if she could not. He had witnessed such an exchange with a hopeful female, time and again, and did it result in a proposal? No. A proposition, more like.

Harry was coming to Anna with honorable intentions. No. He halted his progress with the force of his feelings. He was coming to her with his heart in his hand. Even if Anna was not ready to commit to him, she should know what Hugh was, lest she be swayed by a wolf who hid under the veneer of his title. *She may not choose me, but let her know Hugh for what he is.* Harry's heart quickened as he remembered how she had stilled at his touch at the ramparts.

I don't think she is entirely decided against me.

He left the main road and branched out in the direction of Leatham's estate. After the fork in the road was a large sycamore tree, whose trunk was split in two, forming a nature-hewn seat. Harry stopped to catch his breath and meditate on what he should say and how he should say it so he could best persuade Anna. She must not imagine he had ulterior motives for maligning his brother.

Harry leaned his hand against the trunk of the sycamore. When he looked up, his breath froze in his chest. There, at some distance on the path interceding his, Hugh was walking with Anna. In another moment they would see him. Harry clenched his fists. *When will Hugh take himself off? How can I get a minute alone with her with him here?*

Harry knew he was spying, but he could not help but watch her every movement as Hugh turned to address Anna. Would she respond to Hugh the same way she did to him? She did not look entirely pleased, which gave him heart. But his brother's face was worrisome. He had never seen Hugh look so intent with one of his flirts.

Without warning, Hugh seized Anna in his arms and kissed her. Harry's blood went cold. In one masterful movement, Hugh had made Anna his, and Harry had been too late. He did not need further proof that his hopes were dashed, and in that instant, grief and fury tore at his soul. There was no mistaking it. Anna did not resist. She did not turn away.

Harry did.

Without pause, he retraced his steps to the rectory and slashed with his cane at the weeping grass, brown from two weeks without rain. Harry jammed his hat further down on his head and from the recesses of his brain formed the desperate hope he would not meet anyone just now. He could not face another soul when his shoulders were hunched by the crushing blow, and it took everything in him to blink away the tears that threatened to fall. Anyone could see at a glance he had just met with the most severe disappointment.

Harry tried to slow his breathing as he marched forward. Anna loved Hugh, did she? Of course she did. He had seen it with his own eyes that she stood, frozen, while his brother pulled her into a passionate embrace and claimed her for his own. Clenching his fists, Harry felt, rather than heard, the strangled sob that emitted from his throat. Now it all became clear. Anna had smiled upon Hugh's suit from the first time they met. At least Hugh was honest about who he was, not trying to hide his parentage in a misguided attempt at humility. And Hugh had been persistent in his courtship. Harry had seen the display for himself, and who knew how many times they had met without Harry even being aware of it.

Suddenly her blushes on the ride back from Wroughton lent a different hue. She was not uncomfortable from the attention. She was smitten.

He had been a fool. How could she *not* love his brother? Hugh was a full head taller than he was, he did everything *comme il faut*, and he would inherit. This had been drummed into Harry's head from his earliest memory. Hugh also had the tongue of a viper and could deceive anyone in the turn of a phrase. *How could she have been blind to it?* Harry lashed out at the tree bordering the path and felt a crack form in his cane. He cut across the meadow and into the privacy of the woods, where he stopped and gulped for air. His knees went weak, and he fell against a tree. He sank to the ground, moaning, and put his head in his hands. He had lost Anna forever.

Before entering the house, Anna needed to recover from the shock and disgust at being kissed against her will. She set out in the opposite direction of the house and walked on the paths that bordered the winter garden, her mind in a tumult. Before she realized where she was going, Anna was at the stream—the place she now associated with Harry. She knelt beside the rushing water, not caring about the stains to her dress, and dipped her hands in the frigid water to cool her face. That was not enough. She scrubbed her face furiously with the water before standing and walking to the bridge.

What if Harry came here? Would she confess all, including the feelings she harbored for him that she could no longer deny? If anything had made that clear, it was receiving the unwelcome advances of a man she did not desire. Anna did not know if she would be bold enough to tell Harry, but in the end she was not given the chance. The bridge was empty, save for a tiny sparrow that settled on the tip of the bridge's railing before taking flight when she made a sudden movement. She leaned against the wood and listened to the rushing water. As the minutes ticked by, the source and movement of the stream calmed her.

When I see Harry, I will know. At least I think I will know where my heart stands and whether I welcome his suit. I am now only certain I do not want Lord Brookdale.

Anna looked around with the vague hope of seeing Harry, but the only thing that met her gaze was water and woods and the occasional rustling in the leaves of some woodland creature.

After a half-hour, Anna's mind was more settled. She returned to Durstead Manor, where she was met with silence. Emily must have been resting. Anna had come to the overwhelming conclusion on her walk home that she needed to see Harry without delay. That would set everything else at rest. Perhaps he would come and visit without his brother so they might establish things more clearly between them. At Barbury, he had made his continued interest perfectly clear. It was only she who had held back from revealing her heart.

As another day passed, Anna's own feelings became clearer. She longed for him, but still Harry did not come. In his absence, and in the excess of solitude with Emily resting more than she had been, Anna was left to reexamine her own behavior. She had to admit it was not exemplary. Initially, she thought only to punish Harry by engaging in a harmless flirtation with Lord Brookdale. She had played with fire and had been burned, and she now realized she'd made a mistake. Anna hoped it was not an irrevocable one.

The next time she saw Harry was at church two days later. Emily accompanied her, although her pains had increased, leaving Anna with some misgivings about the wisdom of setting out. Emily insisted they were nothing to worry about yet, but her increased need for rest and quiet belied her protests. Anna had told Emily nothing of what had transpired for fear of troubling her and was too glad of Emily's comforting presence at church to insist she stay home. As they took their seat in the pew midway back, Anna could see that Emily looked pinched. *I have been selfish, but I need her. I cannot face Harry alone.*

Suddenly, there he was sweeping in from the side door in the front of the church. Anna felt faint. Even in his clerical robes, she found Harry overwhelmingly appealing, a thought that she banished quickly. This was not the place to entertain such thoughts. She kept her eyes trained on him, willing him to look at her, which he did not do in the flurry of activity as people took their seats. When he finally came to the center of the aisle, his gaze at last swept over the crowd and settled on her. Anna's heart sank. His was but a cold glance, which he quickly withdrew as Mrs. Banbury came forward to greet him.

Anna continued to watch him as he conversed, but she thought it was an effort for him to train his features to appear interested. Harry was not an actor. He could not easily hide what he was feeling, so he must be trying to banish her from his mind. *His brother must have told him some falsehood.*

The congregation was called to order by the altar boys carrying candles to the front to light the larger ones there. Numb, Anna sat beside Emily and listened to the entire service, repeating the liturgy by rote. She did not know if it was her imagination, but she found less passion in Mr. Aston's voice. There was certainly less laughter in the church, but she supposed it would be ridiculous to assume *that* was a weekly occurrence.

Emily leaned over to whisper, "Our parson looks quite glum. I don't suppose you know the reason for it." Although her brow was clouded with concern, Emily sounded more like her old self.

Anna kept her eyes trained ahead and shook her head. *I can only assume Lord Brookdale has lied to him. He should know better than to believe anything his brother tells him.*

At the end of the service, she and Emily made their way to the back, and Anna didn't know whether she welcomed the encounter with Harry or dreaded it. The line felt interminable as Harry shook hands with everyone and shared a few words with each member of the congregation, as was proper for a rector. Then it was their turn.

Harry trained his eyes on Emily. "I may have some news for you, Mrs. Leatham. I hope I may call on you tomorrow. This afternoon I am unfortunately otherwise engaged." By carefully avoiding her gaze, Harry managed to make Anna feel like a stranger to their conversation.

At his words, Emily's face grew pale. She reached for Anna's hand and squeezed it. "This does not appear to be good news, Mr. Aston. I hope my husband . . . you have not received definite word?"

"No, not that," Harry was quick to reassure her, as he must have realized what his words implied.

Emily squeezed her hands tightly in front of her. "Please come, then, as soon as you are able that I might be put out of suspense."

He nodded. "I will be sure to come." Then he gave another nod in Anna's direction.

"Miss Tunstall."

So that was all she was to have. Anna raised her head slightly and then lifted her chin and turned before she revealed any of the hurt that washed over her. She took Emily's arm, and as they walked out of the church, she heard a whispered giggle behind her. Someone had noticed her fall from favor.

She knew she must support Emily, for it did not seem as though her friend would be given much encouragement tomorrow, but Anna's own heart was broken. He blamed her! He blamed Anna for whatever he imagined had transpired between her and his brother without even taking the time to find out what had truly happened. That was the height of unfairness. Even if his brother had falsely accused her, Harry should have trusted her enough to come and find out what happened for himself.

Anna pushed aside the hurt feelings that pierced much more deeply than she could have imagined and clenched her jaw. *Fine.* It was not as if she had ever seriously considered marriage with a mere country parson. A wave of chagrin hit next, and she had to own to herself it was not true. However, if the deeper feelings hurt this badly, she would have been better off never to have experienced them.

They were soon in the carriage, where Emily was too distracted by Harry's disclosure to notice that anything was amiss with Anna.

"What do you think it could be?" Emily asked in a breathless whisper. She noticed Anna's tears that threatened to fall and seized Anna's hands. "So you are as afraid as I am? It must be dreadful news."

Anna swallowed and blinked away the tears, taking hold of her emotions by sheer force. "No, do not think the worst before you know what it is. I assure you, I do not." She attempted a smile. "After all, Mr. Aston said there was no definitive news, so all hope is not lost. We shall find out tomorrow, and today let us occupy ourselves well so we are not overset by worry. Perhaps I will write to Phoebe and you can tell your mother about the exceptional harvest of plums. Then we will play backgammon. I think it was Mr. Aston"—Anna gulped—"Mr. Aston who said, 'Do not borrow trouble from tomorrow. Each day has enough trouble of its own.'"

The afternoon repast was for mere form's sake as each was lost in her own thoughts. The friendship was of long enough date they did not feel themselves obliged to make idle talk. And when Anna was at last alone in her room, she sat at the escritoire tucked in the corner and pulled out a cream sheet of paper.

Dear Phoebe,

Oh, how I miss you. I have needed you and have never felt your absence more keenly. You will notice that for once I am not jesting. I cannot, for you will never believe what has happened to me. Mr. Aston, whom I have written about—Avebury's rector—is none other than the brother to the Marquess of Brookdale and the son of the Duke of Kirby. You may imagine my surprise when I discovered that, for he is no simple country parson. In all the time I have known him, he did not once give me a hint as to who he was. I own I did not like being deceived, and I did not open my heart as readily as I had done before, causing Mr. Aston to withdraw his suit to some degree. I did not know how to take that, for you see, I had found myself quite attached to him.

Wisdom and I have apparently parted ways, though, for Lord Brookdale was ready to step in where Mr. Aston had not. You may guess what occurred next. In my usual folly, I encouraged Brookdale's advances, although my heart did not follow. I was indeed foolish, my dear Phoebe, for it led to a proposal I did not want—or, at least I think it was meant for a proposal. I do not believe he has sunk so low as to offer me a carte blanche.

And instead of asking me like a gentleman so that I might refuse him, he took me in his arms and kissed me by force. It was the most disagreeable thing I have ever experienced. Do not tell Stratford, I beseech you. I do not want him to feel obliged to challenge Lord Brookdale and possibly make Eleanor a widow before she is a wife. You will tell me such a thing is impossible, of course, but you see, when you love someone, you begin to imagine your life with them. So it's no use saying Eleanor won't be widowed, even if it's not in the proper sense. I am rambling, and you will be hard pressed to understand my letter, but do not speak of it with Stratford, for I am perfectly able to handle the affair myself.

And now I shall contradict myself. I feel tainted, my dear Phoebe, and I wish you were here to console me with your calm, good sense. You have always been a steadying force for me. And you see what happens when we are separated. I lose all common sense. I saw Mr. Aston at church, and he must have known. Oh, Phoebe, you could not imagine the look he gave me. I did not think such warm brown eyes could hold such a wintry look. I am distraught. And I fear you will have to pay the postage for a letter that is illegible because of the tears. I do not know how to fix this, and I only wish I might return home. However, even if Aunt Shae were well, I still couldn't leave Emily, as the scarlet fever has continued its way around Emily's sister's household, and her mother is held prisoner to its invalids. So I must stay and face what I have done.

You would encourage me to be stout of heart, I am sure. I will endeavor to be so. But the heart is a fragile, weak sort of thing, and I do not believe my own has ever ached so much. Since I had begun to believe I had no heart, I suppose this is excellent news to find that I do indeed. I will leave you only with this short missive, for I have not the energy to laugh over the folly of Avebury's villagers or write any other inane bit of news. Emily is much the same. She is moving about and determined to be strong, but there is this air of melancholy that is settled over the house, and it suffocates. I am not sure I will ever recover from this.

I will need to get into Society again to regain my equilibrium, I believe.

Yours miserably,
Anna

Chapter Twenty-Five

*H*arry had not seen Hugh since the ill-fated moment when he spied him kissing Anna. The first day, he thought himself lucky because he was not prepared to see his brother. The hurt was too fresh, the anger would be uncontrolled, and he would be a target for mockery, especially when his brother announced his betrothal.

The second day, he was confused. He wondered if his brother had cast off restraint and had ridden off to the hunting boxes of one of his cronies for a weekend's debauch. Was it a celebration of his betrothal? Harry paused as all breath fled. Was it to console himself after a rejection?

The third day, he was anxious. Would Hugh have gone off to London to have their betrothal announced in the *Gazette* without even so much as a by-your-leave for his brother? Of course he would. Harry didn't know if he preferred not having to see his brother's gloating face or the chance to have it out in proper style. *Not that I could demand satisfaction or anything,* Harry thought glumly. One couldn't exactly call one's own brother out for pistols at dawn. Especially when one was a rector.

In the end, Harry entered the breakfast room on the fourth morning to find Hugh sitting at the table, looking very much the worse for wear. So it had been the debauch.

"Where have you been?" he asked. *And why did you come back?*

Hugh drained the contents of his coffee, his eyes trained on Harry, and set the cup on its saucer. He answered in a voice weary from exhaustion. "Bromley's. I've only just returned, but I shall be leaving as soon as I've had a hot bath and this breakfast. I've been away from London too long as it is."

"You could have returned there at any time. There was nothing hindering you." Harry's black looks and irony bounced off his brother's disinterested mien.

Hugh said nothing further, and Harry waited. His brother split a roll and spread a generous slab of butter on it before gesturing to the chair across from him. "By all means, sit."

Harry refused to be goaded—or sidetracked. "Have you an announcement to make?"

Hugh paused, food midway to his mouth, and raised a brow. "Are you, perhaps, better informed than I about some cause for celebration?"

His confusion appeared genuine, which was maddening, and Harry lost all desire to fence. "I am speaking of Miss Tunstall. I assume you are not so depraved as to kiss a lady and do anything other than propose marriage. You have never shown much signs of possessing a conscience, but you have not stooped so low as that, I believe. I have daily been in expectation of your news, as—is generally the case in matters of alliance—the family is informed ahead of the ton."

An unidentifiable flash of emotion came over Hugh's face. Before Harry could decipher its meaning, it transformed to amusement.

"You saw the kiss, did you, brother?" Hugh laughed softly, and the urge to throttle him became nearly impossible for Harry to resist.

"May I remind you that you have yet to answer the question. Have you an announcement to make?" Harry was having trouble breathing from the suppressed emotion.

"Why?" Hugh shot back. "Do you plan to perform the ceremony?" When that received no reaction, Hugh brushed the crumbs off his hands. "You are mistaken. There is no announcement. There is to be no wedding. How can there be when there has been no proposal?"

Harry strode around the table with one purpose in mind. "You really have lost all decency."

Hugh got to his feet and put one hand up to Harry's chest, blocking his progress. When Harry swung his fist, Hugh brought his other hand around to grab it.

"Don't do something you will regret, Henry," Hugh muttered in chilly accents before pushing Harry away.

Harry wrenched free and put his fists up, but Hugh's next words stopped him cold.

"Miss Tunstall does not intend to marry."

"You kissed her against her will, then," Harry said, dropping his arms with effort. "If you knew she would not marry, you took from her what did not belong to you."

"Oh no. You mistake the situation." Hugh eyed Harry, then returned to his seat and picked up his butter knife. "Sit, Henry. Let us not enact a Cheltenham tragedy before breakfast."

When Harry remained standing, Hugh said, "Very well. Your Miss Tunstall informed me she does not wish to marry and has sufficient means for this not to be a necessity. She asked only to know what a kiss would feel like since she is to remain a spinster, and I obliged her. That is all. There is to be no wedding through no fault of my own, so you can stop coming the ugly."

Harry's mind spun. *Is it true?* He remembered her words when he asked her. She'd said, "I can't." She did not say no, only that she couldn't. Was it because she had made up her mind not to marry at all? The rage left him, and Harry felt only emptiness. He slid into a chair some ways from his brother.

"That's better," Hugh said. "I much prefer my breakfast company to be seated. Perhaps you have not yet eaten. May I serve you?" Harry shook his head, his arms on the table.

"I advise you to try some of Mrs. Foucher's kippers. She makes them in such a delightful way, I may ask her to share her secret with Peterson if she is learned enough to write it down. No? Never mind. I shall remove myself, as I said, and you may return to your comfortably tedious existence."

Something in Harry snapped, and he raised his head to meet Hugh's gaze directly. "I will be glad to return to it, for I find it to my liking." He took a breath and straightened. He'd had enough of being made to feel his brother's inferior. "Just know that this 'comfortably tedious existence' of mine, as you term it—when stacked, minute upon minute, hour upon hour, and year upon year—is the richest, most vibrant existence one could hope for on this earth. And if there were some way you could truly taste it for yourself—if only you would humble yourself enough to question the manner of your own existence—you would see your life for what it is: shallow, vainglorious, solitary, and destitute."

As Harry punctuated the last four words, a look of pain swept over Hugh's face before he could mask it. He reached for the coffeepot and served himself, marring the pristine white tablecloth with the liquid that sloshed over the side of his cup. The silence stretched as he drank the coffee.

When at last Hugh replied, it was in a bored voice. "You move me, dear brother."

Harry had no appetite, and he left the room. He had promised to call at Durstead Manor today, and it took everything in him to still go after what he had learned. But he had given his word to Mrs. Leatham, so he would go. By the time he was finally ready to set out, his servant informed him that the marquess was gone.

Anna and Emily were in the drawing room when Harry was announced. He gave Anna a formal bow before taking a seat across from Emily and infusing more warmth in his gaze for her benefit.

"I won't delay my news, for I know you have been wanting it. I've had a second letter from the Admiralty. My father's contact wrote to say they found pieces of the mast and stern from the frigate your husband sailed upon caught on the rocks and washed up on shore. There were also wooden planks that had been burnt in a fire, perhaps from an explosion of some sort on board."

Emily gasped, and Harry, in all readiness, pulled out his handkerchief and pressed it into her hands.

"The generally held belief," he continued after a pause, "is that an enemy ship towed the remains of the HMS *Cornwallis* to salvage for their own use, which is why we had nothing more than the broken masts and some planks. However, the Admiralty's greatest concern is over the fact that there has been no letter from the French. Whether it was a man-of-war or privateer that found your husband's frigate, the fact that they did not ask for an exchange of prisoners is not encouraging."

Although Mr. Aston's face showed nothing but gentleness, Anna felt all the horror of the situation and sought Emily's gaze. She had gone white.

Harry leaned forward. "Mrs. Leatham, this is very distressing news I am delivering. I will do everything in my power to assist you through this trial, but I am also here to say that you are much loved in Avebury. I have full confidence the village will stand with you. You will not be alone."

Emily's eyes were bright with tears, and when she spoke, it was as if the words were wrenched out of her. "I cannot see my way forward. I do not know how I will go on. I know only that I must do what I can to see that this baby makes it safely into this world."

Emily's defenses broke then, and she finished her sentence on a wail, rocking back and forth.

"You do not need to know the path before you and how it ends. That knowledge is reserved for Someone Greater. You need only fix your eyes on the next step before you." With Harry's focus entirely on Emily, Anna again felt like an outsider. She did not know if she should rush to Emily's side with Harry there in his official capacity. She stayed in her place.

"Do you have someone to see to your material needs?" he asked her. "I do not wish to intrude upon your affairs, but I want to ensure that your physical needs are taken care of. Who is overseeing your interests, if I might be so bold as to ask?"

It was some time before Emily was able to answer, but she struggled to do so. "I . . . I have a large portion left to me from my mother's side, and John has said he has made ample provision for me should anything happen to him." She took a deep breath, forcing her voice to be more composed. "My father's solicitor in London is still involved in my affairs, so I will not be cast out of my home."

"I am glad to hear of it." Mr. Aston exhaled and sat back in his seat, giving Anna the fleetest glance before rising to his feet. "I will bid you farewell and pledge my word that I will return to see how you go on. Now, if you'll excuse me . . ."

Anna stood, too. "Emily, please spare me for a moment as well. Mr. Aston, I hope you will accord me a few minutes of your time. If so, I will see you to the door."

Harry hesitated, and Anna went still with fear and embarrassment until he at last gestured forward. "Of course."

Anna followed him out the front door and began walking at his side, which made her suddenly long to weep. It was just in that comfortable way they often had when together. Was it not the basis for their friendship from the beginning—always meeting out of doors, always walking together and speaking on various topics, whether general or intimate? Anna supposed it didn't do to think of that now. *He* apparently had no such thought in his head.

She took a fortifying breath. "I see you are determined on a course of rigid formality, so let us handle the matter without gloves, shall we? I assume your brother told you something about me that has caused your regard to suffer a change. I did not see him at church yesterday, so I must suppose he has left Avebury."

They had not walked far from the house and were in full view of every window from which any servant might happen to look. But Anna had no thought for that when Harry took a step toward her until they were mere inches away. With barely suppressed anguish, he ground out through his teeth, "Yes, my brother is gone, but he did not need to tell me anything. I saw it with my own eyes."

He was close to her now, and his eyes bored into hers, his lips a mere breath from her own. She saw the stirrings of anger and desire battling in his regard.

Her knees weak, Anna could barely form her words. "You saw what, exactly?"

"I saw the *kiss*." He let the words sink in as they stood toe-to-toe, their gazes locked.

Anna's mouth dropped. "*And?* Did your brother not have more to say about *this kiss* before he left?" She was stunned. Did Harry believe she would engage willingly in such an act?

"Oh, believe me, he did, Miss Tunstall. Brookdale told me you had no interest in entering into the married state and wished only to know what it was to be kissed before you embarked on a life of spinsterhood. He was only too happy to oblige, as I am sure you must have known."

Harry's words were heavily tinged with irony, and the anguish that had been building in her ever since his cold reception at church was replaced with icy disdain. Lord Brookdale's falsehood surely explained why Harry wanted nothing to do with her, but *merciful heavens* he should have asked her. He should have given her the benefit of the doubt. Wasn't that what one did if one's affections were engaged to the point of making an offer? Anna squared her shoulders as the shallowness of his trust sank in. How dare he levy such accusations against her!

They had not moved from their close proximity when Harry's expression softened. He searched her eyes, perhaps looking for a sign from her that he had been misled. Several seconds passed with their gazes locked, and it seemed to Anna he was warring within himself. Was he to trust her or not? Should he try to win her or give her up?

Anna was too incensed to help him with his decision. "Well, if you've seen our kiss, I suppose you know all there is to know."

She saw the change in his eyes—the dagger look of hurt that swept through him before his regard turned to ice again. He took a step back, his gaze still fixed on hers.

"I suppose I do."

Harry had his hat in his hand, and he shoved it on his head and turned. The sight of his proud form walking away from her nearly crumbled her defenses. Anna almost called out after him to say he had been wrong. That she had never been interested in his brother and that her heart belonged to him. But Harry had been too quick to believe the worst of her, and Anna had her pride after all.

A servant called out after Anna as she entered the house. "Miss, if you please. Mrs. Leatham is requesting that you come to the drawing room as soon as you are able."

Anna let her arms fall to her sides and turned to the servant, her smile surely a pitiable effort. "Tell her I will come soon. I must fetch something in my room first."

As she climbed the stairs, she forced her steps to be measured, her heaving breaths to slow. Mr. Aston had proven unworthy of her more tender emotions, and she had done well to hold off from accepting him.

Chapter Twenty-Six

ell, I suppose that is the end of that, Harry thought, as he sat in his library at the close of day. Despite the raw pain of having been betrayed by Anna, he took solace in the fact that his brother was gone from the rectory. Never before had he been so thankful to have his house to himself.

When Harry had arrived from Durstead Manor that afternoon, Tom had taken one look at him as he entered the gate, then turned away as if the pain he saw there was too personal to look upon. Mrs. Foucher was equally as perceptive, and she brought him a hot drink without saying a word shortly after he sank into his favorite chair. He had not stirred from it since.

He had stood close to Anna, torturing himself in their nearness. A strange compulsion had come over him in that moment. He had wanted to see if she would turn to him the way she had to Hugh. He, too, wanted to know what it was to hold her.

Anna's words came back then unbidden, her face resolute in her disdain. *Then you know everything.* She had not chosen Harry. Even if she had decided to remain a spinster—or perhaps that was just a way of letting Hugh down in a civil way—she had still made it clear she did not want Harry.

Harry got up and began to pace. Why did she have such a look of despair on her face when he confronted her? He had seen it. No matter how quickly she put up a mask of cold unconcern, he had seen her misery. And it closely resembled his own.

He could almost smell her fragrant notes of lilac, a light scent that didn't seem to match such a remarkable force as Anna Tunstall. One would expect her to wear something more heady. He could see the pert line of her lips and the nose that turned up, her blue eyes that opened with large innocence but that held such a look of comprehension. Those eyes pierced. They saw folly and mocked it. They saw pain and filled with compassion over it.

They've seen me and made me want to be someone better. Harry sat again and covered his face with his hands, remaining in that posture as if it could block the pain. The shadows lengthened, and he no longer knew the hour.

At last he stood. He would not accomplish anything tonight. It had been torturous enough to try to prepare a Holy Communion last Sunday, and he wasn't sure if he would find the passion to prepare one in the same manner again. He would become one of those dry preachers that everyone tolerates but no one admires. Despite himself, Harry smiled somewhat mournfully at the thought of himself as an old, celibate clergyman boring his congregation at great length, week after week. His smile just as quickly fell.

Someone knocked softly on the door, and Mrs. Foucher entered. Her expression revealed without words that she, at least, knew of his dejection—if not the entire household of servants.

"I will bring you your dinner, Mr. Aston," she said.

Harry was about to decline but then thought how nonsensical it would be, particularly after she had likely put herself out to prepare something for him. "Just the lightest fare, if you please." He gave her a weak smile, and she did not comment on his subdued tone.

He ate in silence, determined to end his day early. Sleep cured all manners of things, he had found, although sleep had not healed his heart in the four days since it had been broken. When he exited into the corridor, he was startled by Tom stepping out of the shadows.

"Tom." Harry didn't have the strength to ask what he wanted.

"I came to tell ye I be vamping. I don't want 'ee to be thinking I won't be back, 'cause I will." Tom's hat was a worn lump in his hands as he massaged the brim. "If 'ee'd be taking me back, 'tis to say."

Harry was surprised, and it pulled his attention from his own pain, if only for a moment. "You're leaving? Where are you going?"

"I can't say, sir, begging your pardon. Leastwise 'tis a duty I hev, but I'll come hwome."

Tom's look was pleading. Harry knew as his employer and as his guide in the faith he should ask for more details, but he could not bring himself to do it.

"All right, Tom. You may go then. I know you'll come back as soon as you are able."

Harry gave him a quick smile, and Tom looked torn between guilt and relief. Tom bobbed his head and disappeared back into the shadows as Harry went on his way, wondering whether he had just laid one of his flock open to temptation.

Lord, he prayed silently, *you will just have to take watch over this one. I don't have enough left in me to do it this time.*

A good night's sleep did nothing to dull the ache in Harry's chest, but he woke up resolute to perform his role as rector to satisfaction. No one could accuse him of shirking those duties at the very least. It was all that was left to him now. He hitched the cart to his dray horse and set out for the dwellings that lay on the other side of the village. He considered looking in on the squire. His house was situated not far beyond the stone circle, but Harry wasn't sure he was ready for any visit that wasn't strictly clerical in nature.

As he drove into the village, he passed a couple walking, their heads bent together. They looked up as he approached.

"Aston," the gentleman called, and Harry reined in. It was Sir Lewis walking with Hester Rigby. Harry directed his cart to the side of the road to avoid hindering other carriages.

He plastered on a smile that he hoped would fool his friend. "Hallo, Lewis. Miss Rigby." He tipped his hat. "How do you do?"

"You're looking mighty somber," Sir Lewis said lightly. It hadn't fooled him. "Step down a bit. I've something to tell you. Here, you," Lewis called out to a boy that Harry recognized from Haggle End. *He's probably here to pilfer something from one of the shopkeepers*, Harry thought before recoiling from his own cynicism. When had that happened? *I must not turn bitter.*

"Take the reins and tie them to that post," Lewis told the boy.

Harry handed the reins over, giving the boy a smile to make up for his unkind prejudice. He then turned to Lewis. "Well?"

Sir Lewis pulled back and studied Harry, who was not ready for the scrutiny. When at last Sir Lewis spoke, his smile was self-conscious. "Wish me happy, if you will."

Harry watched two bright pink spots appear on Miss Rigby's face and understood immediately.

"Willingly. I wish you very happy." His smile came naturally, but this time it was not without a pang. He shook his friend's hand and bowed over Miss Hester's. "When is the joyful event to be?"

"Hester's parents think it best to wait until Christmas, and so we shall." Lewis pulled his betrothed closer. His eyes on her, he added, "I would wait as long as it took, but Christmas will do very well. It shall be a festive wedding breakfast."

Harry thought Miss Rigby never looked better. *Love must do that to you.*

She and Sir Lewis were looking at him curiously, and he realized after a moment that he had forgotten to respond. "I am delighted for you. And Jules? Will he assist in the preparations?" Harry asked, already suspecting the answer.

Sir Lewis gave a wry face. "Jules is gone. He said now that I am getting leg-shackled it would be too much of a bore to remain, which must surprise no one, I suppose. But that's neither here nor there. The thing is . . ." Sir Lewis glanced at Miss Hester who gave him a small nod. "We would very much like for you to perform the ceremony—that is, if you would be so obliging."

"Oh." The request should not have been unexpected, but it was. He had been trying *not* to think about weddings for the past week.

Harry gave himself a mental shake. "Why, of course. You may depend upon me."

The three stood in awkward silence for a moment. "Well . . ." Harry was desperate to get away, and he was about to make his excuses when two gentlemen exited the village inn and stopped short at the sight of him.

"M'lord. Just the wery man we was wishing to see." Mr. Meade raised his hat in Harry's direction.

Harry faced them slowly. He hadn't seen the Bow Street Runners since they'd come to his house. They were the last people he felt like talking to, but to refuse was impossible.

"Well, I shall leave you then." Sir Lewis gave him a sympathetic smile and led Miss Rigby away, handing Harry over to his fate. At least that's what it felt like.

"Why don't we jest sit right inside the inn. 'Tis nice and snug—the wery thing for a chin-wag." Mr. Meade gestured forward in a way that Harry took immediate offense to. It was as if he were a suspect.

Mr. Howe must have noticed his expression of discontent because he soothed, "We won't take but a moment of your time, my lord."

Harry nodded curtly and led the way into the inn. When they were seated, he came straight to the point. "I have a number of parishioners yet to visit, so if you please, do let me know how I may be of assistance."

Mr. Meade sat back and eyed Harry with scrutiny. "We was wondering where we might find Tom Wardle."

"Tom?" Harry suffered a sinking feeling in his stomach. They were after Tom. He had been afraid of this—that they would falsely accuse Tom because of his past. Harry's sense of dread grew as the next thought assailed him. *Or perhaps their accusations are founded on truth.*

Mr. Howe nodded. "We have been watching Tom as a person of interest, and as such it might signify you to know that we have proof he was with the high pads that day."

"If you're talking about the handkerchief," Harry interrupted, "this kind of evidence cannot stand. There are too many articles like it, especially among the laborers."

"It's not just that," Mr. Howe continued. "The pistol we found on the scene? The one that belonged to the Lord Ramsworth? It was nicked by Mr. Wardle back in the day when he didn't have such an honest position. Oh yes, my lord. Perhaps you didn't know Tom Wardle wasn't always the upstanding servant he now appears to be." Mr. Howe looked down at the careful notes he had taken.

"But we know this because we tracked him to where he used to live, above an old pub clear over by Bishops Cannings. We looked into his things, though the room has not been used as of late, and we found the pistol's match. A set of dueling pistols."

Mr. Howe paused to see the effect that had on Harry. Truthfully, it came as a great blow. He knew Tom had not led an exemplary life, but what evil had he wrought with those pistols? And the fact that one of the guns was at the scene of the robbery and with Tom so near it. Was he involved?

"You hinted to Tom's past sins. I am not unaware of them," Harry said shortly, preferring to say as little on the subject as possible. "I have absolved him of them and have given him a new start."

Mr. Meade turned wide eyes on Harry, his strong accent showing his shock. "You'd better 'ave turned 'im in, m'lord."

"You answer to your authority, and I answer to mine," Harry replied. "Every man deserves a new beginning, and Tom has not been undeserving of his. In fact, since he has been with me, his ways have been faultless."

"Faultless until the temptation was too great mayhaps," Mr. Howe said. "He was there. And his intentions were not honorable."

"*Tsk.* Speculation," Harry said with an impatient shake of his head. He spoke the words with confidence, but the truth was, with all the evidence pointing to Tom, Harry's faith in humanity had never been weaker. The next words destroyed it completely.

"Then mebbe you ken explain what he 'us about when he stole the pistol right from my room?" Mr. Meade folded his arms and raised his chin in a direct challenge.

"What's this?" Harry asked, now seriously alarmed. "What proof have you?"

"Seen 'im with me own ogles." Mr. Meade shared a look with Mr. Howe. "I 'us sleepin' when a noise woke me up. I looked up and who should be creepin' out my window but Tom Wardle? I went arter him but he 'us too quick, he was. And me in me night shift."

Mr. Meade looked conscious then. Under different circumstances, Harry would have laughed at the vision it presented.

Mr. Howe put the final seal on the depressing news. "And the evidence was gone. We went out early this morning to his lodging, but he wasn't there. The people at Haggle End have been mighty closed about Tom, though he comes from these parts. Thought p'raps you might know where he'd gone. Or be willing to talk to the people."

Harry's mind raced over all the facts, and he shook his head. He could no longer turn a blind eye. Tom was guilty. He couldn't have been guilty of everything because he was too often present at the rectory, but his was not the behavior of the innocent. It should have made Harry sad, but he felt only numb.

"I haven't seen him. He asked for a few days to take care of business, and I granted it to him. He promised he would return."

The Runners exchanged a look full of skepticism.

"I will talk to the people at Haggle End right after I leave here." It was the only thing Harry could do. He, too, had a responsibility in this. "They may trust me enough to open up to me, but I won't make a secret of the fact that I've spoken to you. And I won't abandon Tom to his fate without attempting to see whether there was some coercion, or perhaps some other reason."

"Generally speaking, my lord," Mr. Howe said with an expression of sympathy bordering on pity, "a man don't change his colors."

True to his word, Harry rode directly to Haggle End after exchanging his cart at the rectory for his roan stallion. All thought of his other morning visits fled his mind. He wouldn't be fit for conversation after such news as this. When he arrived at the school, he was hailed by the laborer and then by the overseer, but one look at Harry's face and their salutations fell short.

"Good afternoon," Harry said. "I'm trying to find Tom. Have you seen him?"

They exchanged a furtive look, Harry thought, and he wondered whether he was suddenly seeing things in a more accurate light or whether he was now jaded.

"He's not been this way? You've not seen him?" Harry tried again.

"No, sir," the overseer said. "He be heving some trouble?"

Harry paused before answering, and it was so long his horse gave an impatient start. "Yes, you might say that. If you see him, please tell him I am searching for him. But let him know, if you will, that the Runners paid me a visit so he understands the purpose of my request."

The two men shared another look. The overseer examined his boot and scraped the mud from it on the edge of the wall. "Ay. If I see 'im I'll tell him."

Harry had to be content with that, and since he lacked the courage to continue the search, he turned his horse homeward. Anna did not love him. Tom was guilty. The parishioners no longer saw Harry as shepherd in good faith but as a nobleman. His brother was a rake of the worst order and would likely never change.

Harry kept his eyes straight ahead as the horse traced the familiar path to its comfortable stable. He was twenty-eight years old and already a failure.

Chapter Twenty-Seven

*T*he first of September had arrived, and Emily was growing rounder. Her pains continued, but Anna had begun to accept they were false pains, as Mrs. Foucher had assured Emily was the case, and that there was no imminent need to run for the doctor.

After another week without seeing Harry, although he had promised Emily he would come, Anna had begun to accept that this interlude—the brief spell of what she had come to own was love, at least on her part—was over. Perhaps it was for the best. She had not been true to herself when she considered the idea of leaving the life she was born to in order to bury herself in the country. As she stood before the window, watching the road that led to the rectory, empty as usual these days, the raw pain in her heart filled her being until it stole her breath.

Emily came to the doorway of the morning room, her bonnet tied and her gloves in hand. "Shall we?" she asked.

Anna nodded and turned to accompany her outdoors. *What a pair we make*, she thought. *We could cause a child to cry at the Twelfth Night festival between our two long faces.*

In the brilliance of the outdoors, they set out slowly on the path that wound around Durstead Manor's gardens. Anna took a deep breath and decided to shove away the pain that was eating up her heart and soul. What could she do? Go and beg at Harry's feet? Would she want him on such terms?

They rounded the house in silence, and Anna thought that Emily suffered under reflections that were even more somber. Her face was pinched more than usual, and her steps were halting. They were nearly at the hedge that enclosed the French garden when Emily cried out in pain and put her hand to her abdomen.

"Anna," she gasped. "I do not believe this is quite like the pain I have been experiencing before. I believe this is new."

It took only a second for Anna to recover from her surprise, but the sensation was quickly replaced by fear. She said in what she hoped was a bracing tone, "Let us go to the house, where I will see that you are settled before sending for Dr. Carson."

She put her arm around Emily. Then, when Emily had difficulty walking, Anna took Emily's arm and put it over her own shoulders so she could support more of her weight.

"I do not think I can walk," Emily said.

"I cannot leave you here, dearest, and there is no place to sit. Come. If I let you lie down, you will never be able to get up again." Anna was trying for levity, but it fell far short. "You see the house is not far. Let us take one step after another, and we will reach it. You need only a little strength. You have more than you think."

Emily did not respond, but she obeyed and began to walk forward, one step after the other, stopping as the pains came on. Anna held her tightly and bore as much of the weight as she could. When they were still some ways away, a scullery maid came rushing out the back door, bringing a wave of fresh relief to Anna. The servants had spotted them through the window.

Anna called out, "Go get Albin. No, wait. Get Forrester, too. Albin will be strong enough to carry Mrs. Leatham, and Forrester can send for Dr. Carson."

The maid darted back inside. Shortly afterwards Albin appeared, running as fast as his stocky frame would allow, while another footman sprinted toward the stable. Albin took Emily from Anna, hoisted her into his arms, and set out at a brisk pace with Anna trailing behind. He carried Emily up the stairs, his breathing labored, and set her gently into her own bed in the main room.

Anna felt helpless. She knew absolutely nothing about childbirth, and when Emily cried out in pain, Anna forced herself to sit at Emily's side rather than follow her own inclination and run. *You said you were joking, Emily. But you have indeed required me to hold your hand, and here I am to do it.*

Another wave of contractions came over Emily, and again she released a groan that sounded other-worldly. It chilled Anna to her marrow. All thought fled, and she could do nothing but accept the basin of lavender water the maid had brought without being asked and dampen Emily's brow.

An hour passed, then two, and Anna began to be filled with dread. She could not do this without help. When the sound of wheels crunching over the gravel met her ears, she rushed to the window. Dr. Carson!

She was faint with relief and turned to Emily. "Dr. Carson is here. You need not fear. All will be well." Emily's eyes were shut in pain and concentration, and she did not answer.

It seemed to take forever for the doctor to climb the stairs and enter their room. After a bow to Anna, he asked her to turn aside while he examined Emily. Anna obeyed, thinking at that moment just how vulnerable women were. Whatever could possess a woman to wish for such turmoil?

A vision hit her, and with it a bolt of desire—Anna holding Harry's child against her chest, while he looked at her in that way that seemed to pierce straight through to her soul, cherishing and loving what he found there. It was too much, and she wiped the tears from her eyes.

Dr. Carson's voice was steady when he said, "Miss Tunstall, I will ask you to fetch Mrs. Foucher. She is a skilled midwife, and I believe I will need her help." It took a second for the urgency to reach Anna's conscience, and the doctor did not look again in Anna's direction.

She quickly exited the room and left Durstead Manor, hurrying toward the rectory. Anna was a third of the way there when she realized she had forgotten to put on her bonnet. She should have sent a servant or asked for a carriage to reach the rectory more quickly. She wasn't sure if it was the fright of having been with Emily while she suffered for those hours, or if it was a deeply buried need to set her eyes on Harry again, but she wasn't thinking at all. Throwing away all propriety, Anna began to run in fear that her delay would cause some harm to her friend.

She rounded the gate of the rectory and ran to the front, where she pounded on the door. It opened quickly, and Harry stepped out, his eyes wide with concern. "Anna, what is it?" Despite her panic, she heard it. He had called her Anna.

She struggled to speak through her wildly beating heart and breathlessness. "Dr. Carson said he requires Mrs. Foucher's help. Emily is having her baby."

Harry spun at once and strode to the kitchen, calling for Mrs. Foucher. Anna leaned against the wall to catch her breath and found that her knees were weak. In minutes, Harry came out the door with Mrs. Foucher, a basket in her arm and a martial look in her eye. She was ready to bring a baby into the world.

"I will have the curricle harnessed." Harry stopped short. Although he did not address Anna directly, the hard look in his eyes was gone. "No, I will harness the wagon, and we can all three of us go."

"No, no. Take Mrs. Foucher without delay. I will walk back," Anna urged.

Harry hesitated only a moment and then turned to where the groom was leading the horses out of the stable. Mrs. Foucher took a moment to squeeze Anna's hand, and the sisterly touch brought her comfort. The curricle was harnessed, and in another moment, they were gone.

Anna began walking, this time at a much slower pace because her legs would not carry her any faster. She followed the country path and came to the fork in the road before finally giving up. Her trembling legs were not willing to carry her anymore until she had rested, and she sat on the deformed trunk of a sycamore on the side of the road. The sound of crickets reached her ears over the sound of her beating heart and the anomalous expression of the turtle dove cooing in the heat of the day.

She thought about Harry. It was the first time they had seen each other since that ill-fated day, and he had used her Christian name. Surely that should mean something, should it not? Yet after his cold reception of her at church and Durstead Manor, she must consider their connection to be at an end. He had probably spoken without thinking when he had seen she was distraught. Harry had touched her heart more than anyone else, but after all, what was that to him? The prize of having won her affection evidently held little value for him now. What agonized her the most was that it was *her* folly—her flirtatious nature—that had ruined it all.

After some time had passed, Anna got to her feet and began walking with a bit more strength. She needed to return to Emily. *I am young, after all. I will find someone new.*

She wiped the tears from her eyes, as the sound of carriage wheels traveling over the road reached her ears. An errant temptation to dive for cover behind a bush nearly overcame her, but Anna would not stoop to that no matter how little she wished to meet anyone just now, especially so inappropriately attired. When the vehicle came into view, the sight of Mr. Aston's caramel-colored horses sent her already tumultuous emotions spinning.

"Miss Tunstall," he called out to her when he had pulled up. He alighted from the carriage and kept the reins in hand, as he extended his other hand to assist her to climb up. "When you did not return right away, I thought the short journey might be too much for you, and I came in search of you."

She put her hand in his, thankful for the assistance. "I believe it is the shock, but my knees would not permit me to walk." Anna turned forward and allowed him to concentrate on maneuvering the curricle to turn the other way.

"Leatham's baby will make his appearance sooner than expected," Harry said, now setting the horses to walk. "Mrs. Foucher only came out briefly to give some orders to one of the maids and told me the arrival is imminent. I did not stay afterwards."

Anna was profoundly grateful for the slow pace, for not only did it permit her to delay returning to a home where she would be of no use and would only suffer from hearing her friend's cries, but she also hoped it permitted her a chance to explain. Perhaps Harry would seek to know more about what had happened between her and Lord Brookdale.

"I am glad if her pains will soon be over."

"Pain must run its full course," Harry replied, his voice grave. "It is the natural order of things."

Those were daunting words. He was referring to her feelings, she was sure of it. Anna felt her heart plunge and wished he would pick up the pace after all so she could exchange one suffering for the other.

What am I saying? Harry clicked on the reins to urge his horses to a trot. Setting his gaze on Anna's enchanting face after a week's privation had clearly disordered his senses. *Pain must run its full course.* Good heavens! He was thinking, of course, of the mourning period he must go through to rid his heart of any feelings he once had for Anna. *Anna.* No, she must be Miss Tunstall now.

But then a glance at Anna's expression showed, not a hardened flirt who wished to throw one brother over for another. One glance at her face, and he saw his own suffering mirrored in hers. She had not answered, but then how could one answer such an inane utterance?

"How much longer is your stay in Avebury?"

"Emily received a letter yesterday that her mother would surely arrive within the fortnight. It is not too soon, for I must go to my brother's estate as soon as might be arranged."

To an untrained ear, Anna appeared to carry the conversation with civility—almost indifference—but to Harry, she sounded dull. It confused him. *Was* she suffering?

"That is good news then. You will not wish to miss the wedding preparations. And then you will be in London for the Season?"

"Where else?" she said with a small shrug.

A silence settled over them as the wheels of the curricle crunched over the ground and the clip-clop of the horses carried them to their separation. A spirit of rebellion overtook Harry. He *would* mention Hugh's name. She would be made to feel his grief for the choice she had made.

"My brother left this week. I suppose you have plans to see him again in London."

Anna set her jaw. "I cannot imagine why you would suppose it. We have made no such plans."

Harry turned to her, stunned, but the curve in the path brought his eyes forward again as quickly. *What? So Hugh had been right, and she refused to marry. But what woman will kiss a gentleman and then not marry him?* He could not marshall his thoughts to make sense of what he was hearing. They had reached the front of Durstead Manor, and he pulled on the reins to bring the carriage to a halt. He turned to look at her fully.

"No plans to see Hugh? Had he made you an offer? Did you truly refuse after . . ." *Good heavens.* How could he complete the phrase? Anna seemed to be waiting for him to do just that, for she did not fill in the rest for him. "The kiss?" Harry said at last, his voice sounding weak in his own ears.

Anna's face was rigid, all traces of hurt replaced by colored indignation. "As you have already seen fit to remind me, you saw the kiss. What more is there to say?"

Their gazes remained locked when the door opened and the maid rushed out, her face wreathed in smiles.

"Mr. Aston, Miss Tunstall, the very best news. It is a boy!"

Chapter Twenty-Eight

Anna was thoroughly charmed by Master George Leatham, but she could not stay another minute in the house and left Emily cooing over her little miracle and softly caressing his cheek—even if it was only to wipe the tears that fell from her own face. Her friend did not have an easy road ahead of her, Anna thought, as she asked the groom to harness the curricle and accompany her to the Rigby house. It had been an impetuous request, and it wasn't until they were in motion that she decided what she was going to say upon their arrival.

Hester was kneeling outside the rose bush, cutting perfect blooms and placing them in a basket. When she saw Anna, she set the shearers on top of the stems, her face a look of concern.

"Anna, what a pleasant surprise. Is all well with Emily?"

Anna quickly reassured her. "All is well with Emily. And with Master George." She smiled as she saw comprehension dawn on Hester's features.

"She's had her baby, then." Hester wiped her hands on the apron that covered her morning dress and walked toward Anna. "And it's a boy, you say? I will come visit her without delay if you believe I will not be an intrusion." Anna shook her head, and Hester's expressive face turned wistful. It was in a somber voice she added, "Her joy will not be without a mark of sorrow."

"No." After a pause, Anna said, "I came on quite a different mission. Tom Wardle is being suspected of having a hand in the robbery, and I know this is a blow for Mr. Aston, who trusted him. Mrs. Foucher visited us to see how the baby was and said Mr. Aston has looked quite careworn as of late."

Anna paused, suddenly finding it difficult to breathe. Mrs. Foucher couldn't know Tom wasn't the only cause for Harry's careworn expression. It was unthinkable that he would have confided in her given their different stations.

"I would like to go to Haggle End, where he is from, and see if I might find someone who can lead me to his whereabouts. Do you know who might take me there?"

"I had heard of Tom's involvement from the squire—a most surprising and distressing development," Hester apprised Anna. "Haggle End is not at all considered safe for a woman of gentle breeding, but then, I suppose you must know that. We might prevail upon Sir Lewis to accompany us. Perhaps the desire to assist Harry will make him consider the idea."

A faint blush stole over Hester's features as she added, "However, I believe it best to wait until he calls upon me to propose it, which I suspect he will do today or tomorrow. I would not wish to be forward by sending him a message."

Anna studied Hester, and her lips curved upwards. "You seem to be upon terms with Sir Lewis."

"I . . . that is to say . . . " Hester turned her face toward the house. "Would you come in to have some tea?"

It seemed Hester was not ready to confide in Anna. Perhaps that was just as well. As much as Anna was ready to wish her happy, she was not interested in more talk of weddings, especially since her two months before Avebury were spent discussing Stratford's wedding.

"I should not like to disturb you," she said. "Are your mother and sister in?"

"They have gone calling. It will just be the two of us." Hester's smile held some mischief as if to say she knew her mother and sister could be a trial.

Anna did not dissemble. "Then I shall be delighted. It is not often I'm able to leave Emily, and now that George has arrived, he gains her undivided attention, if you can imagine."

Hester gave a soft chuckle and called for tea to be brought as they entered the morning room. When it had been steeped, she poured two cups and handed one to Anna.

"Sir Lewis and I have reached an understanding." Hester glanced up, her eyes bright and happy. "It will perhaps come as a surprise to you that such a distinguished gentleman would spare a thought for one as plain and inconsequential as I."

"Perhaps not as much surprise as you might think," Anna said, accepting her tea and taking a sip. "I've seen his attention directed your way, although it was subtly done. I like Sir Lewis. He is a discreet man. Had you made each other's acquaintance in London previously?"

"No, we had not. It must seem rather sudden," Hester said. "Perhaps on his side, he is simply ready for a wife, and my family's standing is credible enough. On my side, I find him to be a man of excellent understanding, and his compassion for the poor coincides with my own. I expect to have every sort of happiness."

Anna suffered a small pang of envy, although she would not have admitted it for the world. It was true that, at first glance, Sir Lewis and Hester did not seem to have much in common, but Hester would undoubtedly make the man happy. She had good sense, and her beauty grew upon one, Anna decided. She had no doubt that Sir Lewis had made his choice willingly and not simply because he was ready to take a wife.

"I have every expectation that Sir Lewis will be equally happy in his choice," Anna assured her.

When they had finished their tea and discussed in what ways certain villagers might be of service to Emily, Anna took her leave of Hester. She had accomplished her principal mission and found her time away from Durstead Manor to be restorative. She hoped Hester would be able to prevail upon Sir Lewis to accompany them.

Anna was not to be disappointed, for the very next day Sir Lewis arrived in a barouche, accompanied solely by Hester. She supposed there were advantages to being engaged, such as riding alone together without giving rise to speculation.

Sir Lewis handed the reins to a waiting footman and bowed before Anna. "I am to understand that you wish to visit Haggle End, although I am not overly confident about the success of your endeavor. However, I believe I may put my mind at ease regarding your safety, for there are men working on the new school, and I have come to know some of them. I will ask for their assistance to see to Hester's and your protection. Are you able to leave now?"

Anna looked back toward the house. "I believe so, only let me get my bonnet. Emily is resting, and the nurse is caring for Master George. I will just let the servants know so that she does not worry when she wakes up."

With this accomplished, Anna returned and found Sir Lewis standing near the door to the carriage.

"You did not tell Mr. Aston of my proposal?" This was something that had been worrying her, for she would not have liked him to know the efforts she was making on his behalf. He might think she was attempting to regain his favor.

Sir Lewis shook his head. "Hester did not think you would want the project generally known." He and Hester shared a look that was filled with tenderness, and a lump rose to Anna's throat. She climbed into the barouche, and Sir Lewis climbed up on the driver's seat and took the reins.

Anna turned to Hester with a look of confusion. "No groom?"

Hester smiled and shook her head. "One of his mares is foaling, and Sir Lewis preferred him to remain behind."

They rode for nearly a mile, and Sir Lewis explained that he would show her the school that was being built before going further in to make inquiries. Anna could hear the excitement in his voice as he described his recent involvement.

Upon first view, Anna was surprised by the size and elaborateness of the school. If she pictured this charitable project at all, she thought it would be a mean building with just one room. No such thing! This school had several rooms, and each one was of considerable size. She wasn't sure there was such a school for the disadvantaged, even in the wealthier parts of the country.

As she picked her way around the mounds of building material, she asked, "Whose concept was all this?"

A worker came and doffed his hat, and Sir Lewis greeted him before responding. "There have been several who contributed ideas and funds, but I believe you must already know that the Maynes play the largest role in founding the school, with Aston lending his assistance to no small degree."

Anna crossed the stone floor that had been laid, with the interior walls just knee-high. The school room would be solid, and it would provide some warmth in the winter, which might be the best way to entice some of the children to attend. She turned to Hester. "Will there be any breakfast provided for the schoolchildren?"

"We have thought of that, and the Maynes are considering ways to bring that about with the help of Mrs. Foucher and some of the local farmers and their wives. Here, in this room, is where the girls will learn to sew."

Hester had taken over the tour, and Anna saw with some surprise that she was not discovering the school for the first time. Apparently her concern for Anna's safety did not extend to herself.

"There are more windows here so they will have enough light. And here we have the room where the boys will learn. We hope one day to get them established in trade."

Anna could see there was a great deal of pride in Hester's eyes, and she knew that Hester had more than a casual hand in the project. This was one close to her heart. Another pang of envy struck Anna, one that had nothing to do with unrequited love. The budding desire was foreign, but Anna wished her life could mean something in the way Hester's did—that through her good deeds, Anna, too, might bring about real change in society and not simply by hosting political parties.

Anna walked outside to study the exterior walls, which were now chest high. One of the men removed his cap as she walked by.

"Good day, miss." She nodded in return, wondering how she would broach the topic of Tom's whereabouts and with whom.

Sir Lewis approached the foreman to discuss the delivery of additional stones, and Anna cast her gaze around the opening in the trees that had been cleared for the new school. A crowd had gathered, perhaps owing to the presence of visitors, and Anna saw it was some of Avebury's poorest who must live in Haggle End.

Here was her chance to see what she was made of. Would she be fearful and wish for them to keep their distance? Or would she be filled with philanthropic impulses? On their faces were various expressions of mistrust—of hope, she thought—and of speculation in some. She scanned the crowd, her gaze resting on one whose profile seemed familiar. When the woman turned, Anna gasped.

"Beatrice!"

Anna darted after her without any thought as to the wisdom of her actions. Through the barely visible opening in the trees, Anna kept her eyes on Beatrice and managed to keep pace, although Beatrice did not turn back or respond to her call. Anna was determined not to let her out of her sight as Beatrice continued to dart down the narrow path.

What had happened to Beatrice? She had remained a mystery, and Anna's mind had been so filled with other things, she had not even given her a thought for weeks. She supposed it made sense that Beatrice was in Haggle End since she was from here, but the Runners had said they were unable to find her. How had she managed to remain hidden?

Without giving any thought to her own safety, Anna trailed Beatrice at a near run. *This is probably the most foolish thing I have done,* Anna thought. Yet she hurried on. She wasn't even sure if Sir Lewis and Hester had seen where she'd gone, but she knew there was no one immediately behind her.

Beatrice left the path and began to dodge through the trees. Anna followed her, although she was regretting her choice at every step. She could not turn back now. In fact, she was not even sure she would know how to find her way back. Anna followed Beatrice still, calling to her once again, until she reached a small opening that held a dwelling of extreme poverty. Beatrice disappeared into the house, and Anna rounded the side to go in after her.

"Miss!" The astonished voice belonged to Tom Wardle.

"Whatever are you doing here?" Anna's breath came fast, and her eyes took in everything at once—the woodpile and small vegetable garden, the patched roof. "Do you know Beatrice? But how?"

Tom rubbed the back of his neck, his gaze darting from Anna's bonnet to the ground, anywhere but directly meeting her eyes.

"Ay, miss. Beatrice be my sister. P'raps ye mid sit."

He led the way into the house, and Anna suffered a shock at his admission. She fell into a roughly hewn chair set in front of the simple table and tried to regain her bearings. There was something about the woods and the sound of this voice in the midst of the trees. Perhaps it was that plus the woodsy smoke smell mixed with earth and sweat, but it took her back to her attack, and she began trembling.

Mustering her courage, Anna said in a low voice, "Tom, I'm trusting you as someone who has been a servant and even a friend to Mr. Aston, that you will bear me no harm, and that after I speak with Beatrice, you will take me back to Sir Lewis and Miss Rigby, who must surely be worried about me now."

"I give ye my oath, miss." Anna kept her gaze on his, and he met it unflinchingly. Despite her trepidation, she could see something honorable in Tom, and she understood why Harry thought he was trustworthy.

Beatrice had been hovering in the corner by the fireplace, looking defiant, and Anna took her in at a glance. There were no outward signs that Beatrice had been harmed, but then it had been several weeks. Anna was startled to hear a baby crying in the corner, and when she peered over the cradle, she saw the baby was old enough to be teething. "Is he yours?" Anna addressed Beatrice, but Beatrice shrugged and folded her arms. More defiance.

"Aw, Bea. Best ye answer now." Tom walked over to Beatrice and nudged her in a firm, brotherly way. "She ain't going to do thee harm. Nor, will you, miss?"

"I am not here to cause mischief," Anna said. "I am here to get answers."

Beatrice's expression remained closed, so Anna urged, "Please tell me what happened at the robbery. Where did you go, Beatrice? I assume you came here since you appear to live here. But why did you not come forward?"

When Beatrice remained silent, Anna clasped her hands. "Perhaps I should ask, what part did you have in the robbery, and did you steal my jewels?"

Beatrice glowered at Anna and shot a look at her brother. "Ye ought to have taken her away. She'll do naught but ill here."

"I can't let the pa'son down, Bea. Ye do what miss says, and 'ee answer her." Tom folded his arms, looking very much like a male version of his rebellious sister.

"I will begin again." Anna fought to keep her voice neutral. It would do no good to raise the girl's ire. "Did you know the robbery would take place?"

"I had my suspicions. I warned ye, miss."

"Were you a participant in the robbery?" Anna studied Beatrice carefully, who lifted her chin and set her mouth.

"Ye won't believe me, but no I 'twaddn'."

"Did you take my pouch of coins and jewels?" Anna folded her own arms. Despite the fact that she was entirely out of her element and probably in more danger than she'd ever been in her life, the robbery aside, Anna could be equally as stubborn as Beatrice.

"Jest a coupl'a shillings, miss," Beatrice said at last with a mutinous look at Tom, who was silently urging her confession. "I had naught to pay for my baby's nurse, but ye came 'afore I could put them back in the trunk."

"And when you could not put them back, you did what?" Anna asked, her gaze not leaving Beatrice's face. "How did they get returned to our carriage the night of the Rigby ball?"

"'Twas me, miss." Tom spoke quietly. "I told my sissy we'd be heving no more o't. Our thieving days be done after what the pa'son did for me." His voice became gruff, and he dropped his gaze to the ground.

There was still part of the puzzle that didn't make sense. "Tell me truly, Tom. Were you there that day? I have the oddest notion you were. I didn't see you, but I . . . I *felt* you were there. Were you there to cause harm? And if you weren't, why did you steal the pistol from the Runners?" Anna stopped short then. Too many questions and she would overwhelm him.

Tom hesitated for a long moment before responding. "Ay. I was there, jest as ye say. I be sorry you was hurt. 'Twas to rescue my sister, and ye, too. I knowed 'twas Ambrose hwolding ye, and I was afeared of what he and Jerry would do."

He turned his pleading gaze to Anna. "'Twas *his* head I meant to hit, but he turned and you got milled as well. I hev been worritin' about that ever since."

"Why did you steal from the Runners? It was a foolish thing to do because they caught you, and now they know you were there, even if it was not with ill intent." An idea struck Anna, and she took a sharp breath. "Tom, come and talk to them. I will vouch for you. You know who the guilty party is, and you can clear your name."

Tom was already shaking his head. "I can't squeak beef on them. We was friends 'afore."

How ludicrous to give up one's freedom out of misplaced loyalty. Anna was about to apply her most persuasive reasoning when Tom shot his head up at a noise outside.

"Anna!"

The sound of Hester's frantic plea from outside reached them, and Anna called out, "I'm in here. I am unharmed." She turned toward Tom, but he was gone. Beatrice moved closer to the baby and stood in front of the cradle.

Sir Lewis broke into the room first, followed by Hester, who was holding her side and breathing hard.

"You are here," Sir Lewis said. "Why ever did you dash off like that? We had the hardest time getting the carriage close enough, and I had to abandon it to that Smith fellow." He looked doubtful. "Well, I hope the man's honest enough. I greased him in the fist and promised him more. This was not my best idea. When I brought Hester, I had Julian with me at least."

Anna barely lent him an ear. The relief of having been found and of no longer having to hide her fear stole over Anna and left her weak. "I will explain as we ride home," she said.

She followed Hester and Sir Lewis out of the hovel but turned back at the doorway and met Beatrice's sullen gaze. "I harbor you no ill will, Beatrice, and I will not add to your burden by starting a process against you. I hope you will not carry any guilt of your own over this incident."

With one last glance at the baby, Anna followed Sir Lewis to the path, where Hester hugged Anna. "I don't believe I've ever been so worried."

Anna hugged her back. It felt odd since she was not of an overly affectionate disposition. However, at that moment she found it a comfort. "I suppose I deserved anything that might have happened to me after running off that way, but I was fortunate. How did you find me?"

"Eli Smith saw that you had set off after Beatrice, and he showed us where she lived. He said she is Tom's sister. Why did you follow her?"

They had reached the barouche on the road, where Smith was faithfully standing by the horses' heads. Sir Lewis's shoulders relaxed visibly to see his horses and carriage intact, and he helped the women into the barouche before going to exchange words with Eli.

"Beatrice was the maid who accompanied me from London. She is cousin to one of Emily's scullery maids, and she was attacked when our carriage was held up."

"Oh, yes," Hester said. "Emily told me a little about this in the strictest of confidence—which I kept," she was quick to reassure Anna. "It was only to explain why you were unwell at the beginning of your stay and could not receive visitors."

"So you know who Beatrice is, then, and you'll understand why I followed her."

Anna was not sure if she should discuss having seen Tom. Her responsibility in disclosing Tom's whereabouts after she found him had not occurred to her, but she did believe in his innocence. She was not given the chance because Sir Lewis came to the door of the carriage.

"Dearest, you've muddied your pantaloons," Hester said.

"It does not signify." Sir Lewis put his hand on the side of the carriage. "I do not know what possessed me to come without even a groom to ride on the back. I am only lucky I did not live to regret this day's work."

He was about to climb up on the front to drive, but Anna put her hand on his arm.

"Thank you, Sir Lewis. All has ended well. I have no regrets, for I have some of the answers I came for."

She smiled and released his arm, thankful to be going home.

Chapter Twenty-Nine

The demanding shrieks of Durstead Manor's newest occupant were quieted, and Anna left Emily nursing her son. It was such a look of maternal bliss, unhindered by fear or worry for the future, and Anna thought that only a baby could do that to a person. There was something so hopeful about a baby, such perfect promise for the future. It created an undeniable longing in Anna's heart, although she had long thought she would only become a mother to fulfill a duty rather than a desire.

Once outdoors, she began to follow the garden path toward the main road. Her steps frequently went this way. Although she tried to tell herself it was just to get air or that it was because the public road was the prettiest of all, lined the way it was with trees, she knew deep in her heart that it was in hopes of meeting Harry. Stratford was getting married, and Emily's mother was finally set to come. Anna would leave soon. There had not been any kind of grand farewell, just a fizzling out of feelings that ran too deep for farewells.

A figure approached from the rectory, but it was not Harry. Anna went to greet Mrs. Foucher, slipping her hands into Mrs. Foucher's outstretched ones as if greeting a friend. It certainly felt like it with the time they had spent lately caring for Emily.

"I feel I am delinquent in my duties to Mr. Aston, but I cannot help but come and see how Mrs. Leatham goes on, and her son as well," Mrs. Foucher said as they turned to walk toward the manor.

"I will take you to her myself," Anna replied. "I had thought to go for a walk, but I will gladly bear you company. I can always walk afterwards."

Perhaps accompany you home? But no. I must let go of such a foolish dream. It will not happen.

"Mr. Aston has been keeping busy." Mrs. Foucher pulled Anna out of her own thoughts as they walked unhurried. "I did not know him many months before you arrived, but I have never seen him so busy . . . and so unhappy."

Anna did not respond, and Mrs. Foucher paused as though to weigh her words. "I am not one to meddle in the affairs of another. But I thought that perhaps there is no fault in making an observation about someone to whom one is particularly attached and to whom one wishes the very best."

Anna could not resent the intrusion of this pointed observation. In fact, she very much wished to know how Harry was doing. When she met people from the village, it was the name she most wished to hear from their lips.

"I will not pretend that I do not know to what you are referring. Mr. Aston and I were particular friends, but it seems lately as though our friendship was not of an enduring nature." Anna kept her voice light, but it nearly broke her heart to say so.

"I believe friendship may be of a short order where one's heart is not touched, but it is not so when the heart is engaged. In that case, the attachment runs deep and is enduring."

Anna could not think of a suitable reply. She had given Harry her heart—perhaps not in the most traditional or elegant of ways—but it was something she had never done before. *He* chose not to take it. It wasn't her fault if he trusted her so little or if her heart were of so little value to him.

"We must enter quietly," Anna said. "The servants are tiptoeing. Their only thought is to see to the needs of—what I am sure is very shortly to be—the prince of the household. Nevertheless, everyone will be glad to see the one to whom Master George owes his existence. You certainly helped Emily with his arrival."

Mrs. Foucher followed her into the cool entryway. "Oh, I can take very little credit for myself. Mother did just fine, the baby was strong, and Dr. Carson was there. I am sure they would have been perfectly well off without me."

"I will let you think so if it makes you more comfortable; however you know he was small and not ready for some weeks yet. Your instinct to put him against his mother's heartbeat was the right one, and even Dr. Carson said so." Their soft footsteps sounded as Anna led the way upstairs.

Emily had finished feeding her son and now sat with a look of adoration as she studied every detail of his face. She lifted her eyes at last to her visitors and spoke in a low voice so as not to wake him. "Mrs. Foucher, how glad I am to see you. Isn't he perfect?"

"I can see from here that he is." Mrs. Foucher laughed. "I could not stay away. I had to see how your *jeune homme* is getting on."

Mrs. Foucher sat down by Emily, and Anna was drawn to the noise of a carriage riding along the gravel road. The other two women ignored the sound in favor of discussing the excellence of the infant before them, but Anna peered curiously through the window, hoping against hope that it would be Harry.

It was not Harry's carriage. But . . . Anna narrowed her eyes. Her heart started beating violently as the open carriage drew near. *It's not possible*, she thought, as she made out the features of one of the gentlemen. But she could not imagine that someone could look so similar. *If I am wrong . . .* Anna forced herself to keep calm as she turned to the ladies.

"I believe we have a visitor. I will go down and see who it is."

"You must say that I am not at home to visitors," Emily said, still absorbed in George's tiny features.

"I will tell the visitor," she murmured, "but I am not sure I will be listened to." There was a buzzing in Anna's ears, and she felt faint as she left the room and hurried down the hall. As soon as she reached the staircase, Anna ran down and opened the front door before any servant could arrive. She rushed down the steps.

"Captain Leatham!"

John Leatham, who was much thinner than she had last seen him, and quite tan, turned to her with a smile on his face that fell slightly when he saw it was only Anna.

"I know," she said. "I am not the one you expected to see. But how is this? We had given you up for lost."

Before she had finished speaking, Anna had time to observe the exhaustion in his features, and added, "But I must not press you for answers. You shall see your wife, who has been grieving most sadly and who is just upstairs. And what is more, you shall hold your son."

At that, John Leatham gave a start and placed an unsteady hand on the side of the carriage. "My son! Surely it is too soon. Is he well?"

"Master George decided to make his appearance early, but he is well," Anna said. "He is ever so well. You shall see for yourself." It was so much to take in, and Anna saw the captain was not looking stout after his ordeal.

"I must go at once." Captain Leatham bounded up the stone steps before stopping short. He turned back and said, "No. I have waited this long, and duty must come first."

Anna followed his gaze toward the second gentleman whom she had barely noticed in her excitement. The man descended from the carriage with the hint of a smile on his face and handed the reins to a waiting groom.

"*Non, allez-y,*" he told Captain Leatham. "I can wait."

With a restraint Anna could not imagine, Captain Leatham shook his head. "I will see that you are settled first, Antoine. I owe you that much, although I ask only to see my wife before taking you to the rectory."

Anna was impatient to rush inside and prevent any servant from spoiling her surprise by announcing to Emily the life-altering news, but she forgot about that when John made the introductions.

"Miss Tunstall, this is *Monsieur* Antoine Foucher."

"Antoine Foucher?" Anna opened her eyes wide. A heady sensation descended upon her as though they were on the brink of something divine—the maelstrom sweeping through their lives once again. But this time, instead of bringing grief and destruction, it tossed tragedy aside to make room for promise and hope. Mrs. Foucher's husband was *here*?

"*À votre service.*" The elegantly clad gentleman with dark curls and side whiskers stepped before her and bowed.

Oh my, oh my. I won't miss this reunion for the world. Anna knew without a looking glass that the joy that had been spreading over her face approached incredulity. It was simply too astonishing to be true. Mr. Foucher had climbed the steps to join Captain Leatham, but Anna intercepted their progress with quick steps.

"Allow me to enter the room first and make your presence known." She turned with a pleading look to her eyes. "Please. It will be a shock. Let me prepare her."

Captain Leatham gestured forward, and they climbed the stairs in haste. She heard John assuring Antoine in French that happy reunion notwithstanding, he would waste no time in taking him to the rectory. Anna raised her fingers to her lips before she opened the door.

"Emily, I regret to tell you I was not able to turn away the visitors. They were most insistent." Anna stepped just inside the doorway, and Captain Leatham walked in first.

"John!" Emily's voice was more of a whisper, a strangled cry, and Captain Leatham was across the room in two steps.

Mrs. Foucher instinctively took the baby from Emily before her hands went limp from the shock. Captain Leatham lifted Emily to her feet, wrapping his arms around her and putting his forehead to hers. Emily was crying, mouthing the words, but no sound came out. Next to Emily, tears poured down Mrs. Foucher's face as she rocked Master George in her arms. She smiled and wept and reached up to draw her sleeve across her eyes, whispering to the baby that his father had come.

Anna's gaze went back to the door. Antoine had entered and stood just inside, his gaze fixed on Mrs. Foucher, not saying a word. Her attention still on the baby, Mrs. Foucher turned away to the window to give the Leathams privacy.

I had better come to her aid as well, Anna thought, *though she does not know she needs it.*

Anna walked over and took the baby out of Mrs. Foucher's arms before she could protest. She gave Anna a look of confusion and then whirled her head in shock when Antoine took another step into the room.

"Marie-Madeleine." Antoine opened his hands, but he was frozen in place. He tried to form words, but nothing came out.

"*Mais . . . je rêve.*" The color drained from Mrs. Foucher's face, and she wavered on her feet.

Antoine was shaken out of his stupor, and he ran forward to grab his wife before she fell. "*Non, ma colombe,* you are not dreaming. *C'est moi.*" His arm around his wife's waist, Antoine kissed her soundly.

Anna had never been made privy to such an intimate scene, and their kiss stirred something in her. *I wonder if Harry had truly loved me, if he would have kissed me like that.* She turned away.

"Well, George." Anna smiled at the sleepy form and pulled him closer. "I am happy to have you in my arms. Otherwise I might begin to feel that I am quite unnecessary." Her cheeks ached from smiling, but she was blinking back tears as well. There was something so touching about couples who reunited, whose pain had ended and whose future held hope. *What it must be like to live without heartache.*

"It seems everyone has their happy ending," she whispered. *Except me.*

Anna left with the infant and went to the library, eventually wearing down the carpet as her steps went back and forth. The baby slept on. It had all worked out in the end and better than she could have imagined. How odd that the only time in her life she had ever given up hope, she was to be proven wrong. It was as if a message was being sent to her: there is still goodness to be had in the land of the living. Perhaps even for her.

A servant came to fetch Anna, saying her presence was requested in the drawing room. It was just as well. Master George had awakened and was becoming increasingly fussy. The two couples were seated when she entered, and Emily reached out her hands for her son. Anna slid the baby gently into her arms.

Mrs. Foucher broke away first, saying in her efficient way, "We must have the story. As surely as the Leathams wish to be left alone, and as surely as I wish to make up for ten years, I believe it is only fair that Miss Tunstall, too, may know how this came about."

"Let me do something so prosaic, then, as to ring for tea." Anna smiled at the Leathams on her way to ring the bell.

Emily took the opportunity to leave the room and see that George was fed. And when the tea set arrived, she handed the baby to her husband and began to prepare it. John examined his son's features with pride.

"I can bear the suspense no longer, John. Why did you not write?" Emily now looked at Antoine. "What happened, and how did you find each other?"

The two gentlemen exchanged a look, and it was Captain Leatham who spoke. "I was on my frigate headed for a rendezvous that we were supposed to have with the HMS *Liberty*. We were moving in the direction of Gibraltar when an enemy man-of-war came toward us at full speed. There were no other friendly ships about, we had no protection, and—pinned as we were to the coast—we could not outrun them. They fired upon us, destroying our masts, and I believe their intention was to take us as prisoners and seize our frigate. But in a stroke of bad luck, one of their cannons landed on our guns, causing an explosion that took out the stern and part of the hull."

Emily set the teapot down with a sharp clatter, and Captain Leatham put his arm around her and pulled her closer. "The winds and undercurrent were very strong, and we were dashed against the rocks before we could weigh anchor. The man-of-war could not draw so near to the shore and gave us up as loss. They did not send rescue ships for our sailors, and I believe it was because of the strong current. It was a difficult day and night spent, I own, with several dead and many more injured and no hope of rescue—or so it seemed."

Captain Leatham smiled at his son, adjusted him in his arms, and then looked up. "Help eventually came in the form of a privateer, who was small enough to draw near. They boarded our ship to take what they could of supplies and information, and although our frigate was badly damaged, they managed to tow what was left."

He indicated Antoine with his chin. "Antoine here, as you may have guessed, was captain of the privateer. And although he was from the enemy's side, he was just as interested in coming to our rescue as he was in getting his share of the plunder." Captain Leatham gave an ironic smile then.

Antoine raised his two hands. "It is a point of honor. We are fellow humans."

"As I was saying," Captain Leatham continued, "he pulled his sloop up next to ours and boarded our ship. What wounded he could help he did, and he brought everyone over to his ship, even if he knew they were not long for this world. It was an act of mercy not to leave those souls to die alone."

Antoine took over the story, his French accent so strong Anna had to listen carefully to understand him. "The matter of English prisoners was not an easy one to settle on my conscience. As a Frenchman, I must be loyal to France, although I was not given the letter of mark making my duty to the emperor official. And England had welcomed my beloved wife a decade earlier when I feared for her life."

He took a moment to kiss his wife soundly in a way that should offend English sensibilities. Anna felt a blush forming on her cheeks from such an open display, but she was not offended. She wished she might know what it felt like. Antoine broke away from the kiss and picked up his story as if public displays of passion were an everyday occurrence.

"In the end, the matter was settled by Jean's ability to speak French. He told me about his wife, who was expecting a baby." Antoine bowed in Emily's direction. "And I, knowing what it was to leave a wife behind and not be able to go to her, had compassion on his situation. I offered to help him and the other English sailors get back to their soil."

Captain Leatham interrupted with a laugh. "And since he had not sent an official letter requesting a bounty in exchange for his prisoners, his method of getting us home was creative."

Antoine gave the ghost of a smile, and with a look at his wife that encompassed a separation of years, said, "But we are getting ahead of ourselves. Once Jean had been open with me about his wife, I began speaking of mine, a long-lost love who I thought I would never see again.

"I reminisced about a Marie-Madeleine, who I had searched for in every corner of London—she, who was fair of skin, with the red hair not so often seen on a Frenchwoman, and crystal blue eyes of the brightest cast on earth. And when, over the course of days together, I spoke about her petite, comely stature and how she was the most beautiful woman in the world that not even the little scar on the side of her cheek could diminish . . .”

Antoine leaned over to kiss Marie-Madeleine’s scar. “Jean surprised me. He told me he knew of such a woman in the village of Avebury and that if I could help them get to English soil, he could help me get to my wife.”

“What was your creative method, Monsieur Foucher?” Anna asked, a smile lurking. It was impossible not to like him.

“Since we were given no letter of mark—and a man needs to earn a living—we carried on a bit of smuggling between Saint Malo and Dartmouth. I left my sloop in the care of my brother and rowed the English soldiers to a quiet place on the shore. Jean, here, is conscientious and immediately presented himself to the naval officers at Portsmouth, who gave him a short leave to see his wife.”

“And although I neglected to tell them that Antoine had come ashore, I do not feel bound to do so since he is not, currently, fighting for the French. He is here as a gentleman, not as a soldier,” Captain Leatham said.

“He is indeed a gentleman,” Emily said.

Antoine shook his head modestly. “A gentleman smuggler. We made a fair trade when we brought your husband home, and I do not think my brother will *râler* over the delay. He gave Mrs. Foucher a wink. “That is the story in short order. Next comes the rebuilding of ten years of absence, which will take more time.”

Captain Leatham held his baby close, and Emily rested her hand on his knee. “Thank you for saving my husband.”

Antoine bowed. “It was nothing, madame.” And he shared another look with Mrs. Foucher.

It will take years, Anna thought. *The story you can get in one day, but it will take years before John and Antoine’s absence becomes a distant memory to the wives in whose hearts they are anchored.*

Chapter Thirty

Harry's steps echoed in his nearly empty house. Mrs. Foucher had only stayed the night as she set the kitchen in order. She assured Harry that she had trained the kitchen maid, Abigail, well enough for her to take over the duties, at least until Harry found someone he thought more suitable. She was gone before Harry's mind could grasp the sudden apparition of her long-lost husband. Now, there was only the distant sounds of the maid-of-all-work and the scruff of boots outside from the stable lads who had taken over some of Tom's chores in the fields.

He had not seen Tom in nearly a week and could only conclude one thing from Tom's absence: he was guilty of *something*, even if he was not mixed up with all the doings of the highwaymen. It was the only logical thing to conclude, yet Harry had trouble doing it. There must be some other reason for Tom to stay away. His absence weighed on Harry, making the house seem even more empty.

Harry was no fool, though, and could not deceive himself. It was the loss of hope regarding Anna's suit that had deflated him most of all. Although he should be ready to strike her from his heart after what he'd seen, there were enough seeds of doubt over whether she had kissed his brother willingly, despite what Hugh said. God only knew how likely it was that his brother would lay claim to something that did not belong to him and leave the repercussions to work themselves out.

The sound of a visitor shook him out of his reverie, and he answered the door himself. The squire was on the other side of it, his horse tied to the post nearby.

"Won't you come in?" Harry asked, more from courtesy than from heart.

"I won't be keeping you, Aston. I promised George I'd take him out shooting, and I like to keep my word. I came only to tell you that the Runners have got their men."

A flash of fear came over Harry. *Tom.*

He tried to keep his voice even. "That is good news, indeed. Were they from Wiltshire as the Runners expected? From Avebury?"

The squire nodded. "They were, and they were easy to identify as the highwaymen because of the pistol they had stolen from Lord Ramsworth."

"How so when they had left it behind?" Harry asked. "What did Lord Ramsworth say? I assume the Runners questioned him."

"They tried, but Lord Ramsworth has been dead these three years in India. His successor has no interest in a run-down estate, so that was of no help. But the connection led them to focus more specifically on the inhabitants of Haggle End and those on its outskirts."

Harry again thought of Tom but was reassured by Mr. Mayne's next words.

"In the end, they had a stroke of luck. The highway patrol happened upon a robbery in the course of action, and as the patrol was greater in number, they quickly subdued the two criminals. Jerry Madling and Ambrose Bailey were the men. Locals to Haggle End, just as the Runners suspected. They said they were working alone, and Jerry had on his person other items of Ramsworth's property, connecting the two to the other robberies."

The squire reflected on that for a minute. "Not that they needed the evidence, for they caught the men in the act. But it closes the case that has been troubling us all for some time."

"My mind is relieved," Harry said. "Thank you for coming to deliver the news."

Mr. Mayne looked into the distance, his jaw set. "They'll hang, those two, for what they did, but I can't say they don't deserve it, not after killing an innocent victim besides scaring half the residents of the very county they hail from this year past."

The squire soon left, and Harry was left to think over the news. So Tom was innocent. At least he appeared to be, although he could have been a party to it all and happened to miss being caught. Harry wondered if the Runners would remain in the area in the hopes of catching him. If only Harry could question the man himself.

He retired to the stillness of his library, sitting with his gaze fixed on the garden and fields through the window. He stayed like that for some time, his mind not fixing on any definite thing. Just when he thought he should set out to occupy himself, Tom crossed the fields outside the window. He stopped to speak a few words to the stable lad, who handed the rake over to him.

Harry leapt out of his chair and strode outside, climbing the rows of vegetables where Tom had already begun to work. "You've returned."

Tom whipped off his cap, his eyes on the ground. "Ay."

"Did the Runners leave? Is that why you've come back?" When he received no answer, Harry fired off another question. "Do you know that they caught the criminals?" He searched Tom's face, looking for some clue as to the inner workings of Tom's brain. Not a very private man himself, Harry could not understand what made Tom so closed.

Tom furrowed his brows. "'Twas caught, was they?" He handled the gardening hoe nervously. "Nay, I did not know. I come even if it be a risk, seeing as how I looked guilty, though I *did* put that barker back in the Runner's room, along with my kerchief. I come because Miss Tunstall had the right o't when she said I ought not to vamp off."

The shock with which Harry greeted this announcement was great. "Miss *Tunstall*? When ever did you see her?"

"She followed my sissy, Beatrice, and I be there." Tom had lifted his gaze from the ground and gave Harry a side glance to better see how he took this news. Harry felt like the world had spun on its end.

"Beatrice is your sister? All this time you knew where she was?" Harry took the tool from Tom's hands and dropped it on the ground. "Tom, I think you'd better start from the beginning."

And Tom did just that. When he got to the part about clubbing Anna on the head by mistake, Harry winced. *How her tender head must have ached. She was lucky to have survived.* He remembered how woozy she had been, which led to memories of holding her and how soft she was as he held her to his chest.

Tom rubbed his face, leaving streaks of dirt on one cheek. "I be terrible sorry about that. But Miss Tunstall says as how she'd forgiven Beatrice for taking her gewgaws—Bea told me that; I'd vamped off by then—and said as how we shouldn't go back to our old ways. So I took it 'pon myself to come back to work."

Anna sought Tom out? She forgave Beatrice for the theft of her jewels and then urged her to stay on a righteous path? Harry's head was reeling, and his heartbeat quickened with this fresh information. Perhaps he had not fully tried to understand Anna. *Maybe there is still hope.*

"Tom, those robbers. Did you know them?"

Tom looked him fully in the face then. "Ay. I rode with them. We be friends since we was babes—Jerry, Ambrose, and me. I tried to turn 'em proper after I met you, but they wouldn't listen. We had a parting o' ways in the end."

Tom's look said so much—the sorrow of losing his friends and fear over their fate, regret that he had not been able to help them change their course.

Harry reached out and put his hand on Tom's shoulder. "You have no idea how thankful I am you're back. The rectory grounds fall into disrepair faster than one could imagine without such a diligent servant."

A smile flashed across Tom's features and was just as quickly gone. Harry left Tom to his work and entered the house thoughtfully, where he was about to return to the library. He paused in his steps. Had he not blackened Anna's name, even if only in his own mind? When would he make amends?

What was he still doing here?

"Jasper," he yelled. When the servant hurried from the back stairs into the corridor, Harry said, "I must have a shave, and I'll need a stack of neckcloths. There is no time to waste."

When Harry set out for Durstead Manor, he was freshly shaved, wearing cream pantaloons, newly polished Hessians, and the Spanish blue coat Weston had made for him. He hadn't realized until he was again properly turned out to what point he had allowed himself to be slipshod in his dress, a carelessness his father had always drilled into him was inexcusable. The duke would not have made allowances for a broken heart.

Harry found Anna seated on the bench behind the Leathams' house. She leaned back on her hands, and her eyes were trained on the meadow that rose on an incline to meet the sky in the distance. The hill was flanked on either side by a row of trees, but the stretch of lawn in the middle seemed to touch the sky so that the clouds appeared to begin at the horizon and climb upwards. It had always been a beautiful view.

She had not noticed him, and he stood for a minute, absorbing the sight of her. Perhaps he should have taken the time to prepare a speech, for as it stood, he did not know where to begin. Could he simply beg her pardon and tell her he loved her? That he had always loved her from the moment she had opened her eyes in his cart and turned them on him?

Anna did not appear to have heard the sound of his boots on the pebbles as he drew near. Or she was ignoring him. Harry was forced to announce his arrival.

"May I sit?"

By way of answer, Anna moved over on the bench and gave him a fleeting glance. She had heard him then. "By all means."

The half-hearted welcome made Harry's heart sink. He began to think he was too late until he saw her fingers tremble as she clasped them on her lap. He sat and stared ahead, searching for how to begin. The unexpected news Tom had shared of her visit to Haggle End had given him the boldness to come, but that did not mean he dared hope the battle was won. Anna Tunstall, he had come to learn, was anything but predictable.

"What a reunion you witnessed yesterday," Harry began. She gave him a brief smile before looking away again. "John's return is astonishing, and I am overjoyed for Mrs. Leatham. I find Foucher's return to be even more shocking, I must say. Given the length of time they were separated and the death of all hope, it truly *is* as though the dead has returned to life."

"It is," Anna replied with the smallest of smiles, this time of reminiscence. "And for him to return with Captain Leatham is beyond anything. How funny coincidence is at times. It almost makes one believe there is a grand design."

Harry was so relieved that Anna had unbent enough to speak he almost missed the nuance of what she said. Then it dawned on him.

"You are teasing me, Anna. You are much more devout than you let on. It just doesn't suit your notion of dignity to wear your heart on your sleeve." She did not blink at the free use Harry made of her name, which gave him the courage to surge forward.

But he still needed to tread delicately. The misunderstanding between them had been too great and, he suspected, filled with unfair recrimination on his side. "The grand design." Harry sighed, and with a quick glance at her face, said, "There is, indeed, a grand design, and sometimes it is such that allows us to have our heart's most earnest desires come true."

Anna put up her nose at his words. "Enough of such talk, else we might be accused of being pious." He hadn't missed the hint of teasing in her voice or—and this filled him with regret—the sheen of moisture that came over her eyes.

"A most deplorable trait in a parson," Harry said in an attempt to keep up the light interchange. Anna fixed her eyes ahead of her and went silent. This was not going to work, not like this.

"Would you . . . would you walk with me a bit? I find I cannot sit still right now and would very much like your company."

Anna lifted her eyes to his as he stood and held out his hand. She accepted it and allowed him to help her to rise. After a breathless moment, they began walking. Harry took her hand and placed it in his arm, and still she did not resist. Their nearness and their intimacy as they traced the garden path emboldened him.

"I have not apologized for keeping the nature of my family's position hidden from you when our sentiments for each other were becoming more clear," he began.

Her eyes were downcast, and he felt her shiver at his side. He wanted to slip his arm around her waist, but he held back. "And I have never apologized for not having asked to hear your version of the events when my brother kissed you. I am aware . . ." He took a sustaining breath as they walked. "I know the latter was particularly unfair since I—better than most—must know what a scoundrel my brother can be. I accused you unfairly, did I not, Anna? You did not desire his kiss?"

Anna tightened her grip on Harry's arm, as if unconsciously, although it came with more trembling.

"I am not innocent, Harry." The force of her words, coupled with the sound of his name on her lips, nearly felled him. Before he could react or respond, she continued. "I encouraged Lord Brookdale's advances in a spirit of retaliation, for I was not pleased with you. But I have long, *long* regretted the folly of that maneuver, for my feelings for your brother have never run deep."

She stopped short, and Harry halted their progress so he could turn to face her. "I am the one at fault, Anna, not you. Let me rectify my errors at once. Upon my oath, I will *not* keep anything from you in the future, and I will not mistrust your intentions again."

Anna shook her head and moved forward once again, her expression hidden in the rim of her bonnet. "These kinds of promises are quite difficult to keep, and oaths must not be taken. Therefore, let it be said that I will not hold it against you if a moment's doubt should assail you, or if you should wish to keep something private."

Harry's heart began hammering in his chest. Anna was speaking as though they would have a future. After weeks of forcing his desires into submission, it was now as if Harry had been riding on a narrow path for too long and suddenly came into a clearing where he could sprint. *Now* was the moment.

He took a deep breath. "Men and women are apt to keep secrets when they do not know one another well; it is only natural. But when a certain intimacy has been established, a man and his . . . a man and a woman begin to desire no secrets between them."

He shot Anna a quick glance. "*I* desire no secrets between us, and I hope for a return to the intimacy we had. In fact, if I may be so bold, I hope for a deepening of it."

Anna did not speak, but her steps had slowed. *I just need to speak the words.* Harry took her by the arm and gently turned her to face him, waiting until she raised her eyes to his.

"Anna, will you marry me?"

Anna stood completely still. "Just like that? No flowery speeches?" He watched as a gleam of mischief appeared in her eyes. She was teasing him.

She had come back to him. His Anna who teased and provoked and made his life both living misery and heaven on earth, usually depending, he realized, on the extent of his own sins. Harry shook his head, the corners of his mouth lifting with the hope that was just within reach.

"I cannot give a flowery speech for something that matters so much to me."

When she didn't answer, Harry knew that he had not said all he needed to say. He owed her an explanation. "I did not declare myself when I intended to. You were expecting it, I believe, but then my brother arrived. And when he was here, I was reminded how much you loved Society." He paused, searching her face to see what it would reveal. "My love, I held back because I was afraid that in declaring myself I would be forcing you to choose."

Anna's face revealed nothing, and Harry could only go on blindly. He took her hand in his and held it. "You always desired a life in London, did you not? Leading the ton, as you said, at the side of a man in politics—a position of which I have no doubt you would not only accomplish but excel at. My declaration, or so I thought, would force you to choose between your dream and a life with me. Love is not meant to be a selfish thing. I could not force you to remain in Avebury, where I have every intention of staying, if it is at the cost of your happiness. So I held back."

Anna was silent still, and he was glad, for he needed to get all the words out. "But then, I've grown so miserable without you. I thought . . . well, I never asked if your dreams had changed and if, perhaps, a life with me would be more to your liking than it once was."

Harry moved closer and would not let her break his gaze until he had said it all. "I never asked if accepting my declaration would make you happier than any original pursuit you had once envisioned."

"It would," Anna said quietly.

"It would," Harry repeated. His breath froze in his chest. "*It would?*"

Anna nodded, her lips curving into a smile—the first full smile he had seen since his brother appeared on his doorstep, a smile that reached her eyes. It was too much. In a rush, Harry pulled her close, touching his lips to hers in a heady experience that was soft and tender—that was, until Anna responded with an eagerness that stunned him.

The thought that it was he who had awoken such passion in Anna made Harry deepen the kiss, amazed at the sides to her that shone with brilliance—first one facet, then another. How had the gentlemen of the ton overlooked this woman? *Thank God* the gentlemen of London had overlooked this woman. Harry kissed her cheeks and her nose, then claimed her lips again, with Anna meeting his kisses just as eagerly.

Then, he thought that, perhaps, he should probably stop. Reluctantly Harry pulled away, buoyed by joy and grinning foolishly, he was sure.

"Miss Tunstall, that was a 'yes,' was it not?"

Anna put her hands on her hips. "Mr. Aston, that was a yes."

"I suppose my behavior just a moment ago was not very parson-like." Harry looked heavenward in mock contemplation but felt a twinge of uncertainty all the same.

"I should hope when we are married, Mr. Aston, that it would not always be. I should hope you are not always a rector but sometimes simply a man. That is what your congregation needs, especially when they face daily the limitations of their own humanity." Anna was smiling at him and her words were teasing, but they struck Harry as particularly true.

"Then you must remind me," he said.

Unable to resist, he kissed her again, and this time put his arms around her waist, lifting her to spin her around.

"It is a matter of pride," he said. "I want to be sure you are properly dizzy after you've received the kiss of a man who has not a great deal of experience but enough enthusiasm to make up for it."

Anna laughed. "There was no need to be spun about. I was properly dizzy."

"Then it was just to have you in my arms again." Harry held her gaze and grinned. He took a sharp breath when struck by a thought. "We should tell someone," he said and started moving.

He led her back in the direction of Durstead Manor, Anna's arm in his, pausing again, as if to turn to the rectory. "But whom? I believe the Leathams are busy, and we are without family members who would care to share the news."

"If we don't find someone who is in the least bit concerned in the matter, we may grab the next unsuspecting passerby and force them to wish us happy," Anna murmured.

Harry laughed. "I believe that will do very well."

Chapter Thirty-One

$\mathcal{A}$nna floated at Harry's side, although they did not seem to have a clear direction of where to go. Her limbs were loose, and her heart soared high above her, as Harry hesitated between going to the rectory or Durstead Manor and what, exactly, should he do next.

In the end, he walked with her back to Durstead, where they stopped. Harry stood close and held her hand in a way that felt both intimate and right when—coming from the distance—what sounded like a cavalcade made them both look up. There was enough dust coming off the road to indicate that more than one carriage was en route. Anna, by instinct, stepped away from Harry.

"Let us see who it is before we announce to the world."

"Not stop the unsuspecting stranger to wish us happy?" he teased, but Anna's distress must have shown because he quickly reassured her. "As happy as we are in the discovery of our mutual feelings, we want to tell the appropriate people before some stranger is made aware of it."

Anna nodded in relief, although this did not stop them from grinning rather foolishly at one another. Anna did not care. She was quickly learning that love broke through all carefully constructed façades.

They turned again to watch the carriages hastening toward them, and she narrowed her eyes. *Was that not . . . ?*

Anna turned to Harry in surprise. "If I am not very much mistaken, that is my brother, Stratford. Harry, what shocking thing could bring him here now? His wedding is only two weeks away and will be followed by an extended honeymoon. He cannot take time away from his estate at this juncture."

225

Both carriages rounded the final stretch and pulled to a stop in front of Harry and Anna. The footman jumped off the back of the first carriage and pulled the door open, allowing her brother to step down. Stratford bowed formally, a gesture meant to encompass both her and Harry, before turning and reaching inside the carriage so that he might help his fiancée, Eleanor Daventry, and her aunt to alight.

Despite years of training in proper decorum, Anna's mouth dropped open when not only did her twin sister, Phoebe, exit the second carriage, but also her indolent Aunt Shae. At the sight of her dear twin sister, Anna was no longer rooted to the spot but ran over to Phoebe and threw her arms around her.

"I am so terribly happy to see you," Anna said. Her voice was muffled in the embrace, and she tried to hide her tears.

"What's this?" Phoebe asked in a gentle voice of surprise. "Avebury has worked wonders on my sister. Or perhaps it is Avebury's rector." Phoebe turned mischievous eyes to Stratford, avoiding Harry's gaze all together. "I am referring to his doctrinal guidance, of course. What say you, brother?"

Stratford had been studying both Harry and Anna, unsure, perhaps, of how much he could assume and was not as easily led into flights of levity. "Anna, I believe there are introductions to be made."

She wiped her eyes before turning. "Of course, Stratford." And with the measure of self-control at her command, Anna took her place at Harry's side. "The Lord Henry Aston, second son to His Grace, the Duke of Kirby, and known to the village of Avebury simply as its rector, Mr. Aston, please allow me to present The Right Honorable, the Earl of Worthing—my brother, Stratford."

The two men assessed one another with curiosity. Both inclined their heads in a similar stately manner, and Anna wondered if this was what it was like before a cock fight. Not that she was supposed to know about such a thing. She was then struck with a thought. How had their family known she and Harry had managed to reach an understanding when they had only just discovered it for themselves?

Phoebe answered her question without Anna having to ask it. "I, for one, was not surprised to travel up the lane and find you nearly holding hands with Mr. Aston. I am only glad to know that the affair is happily resolved so that we might enjoy our stay here without needing to set out at once to repair the state of things."

"Hmph!" Anna had already grown weary of rolling out her emotions for display and was ready to resort back to more comfortable ways. "I've never needed you to do anything. I have always been able to handle my own affairs."

"We allow you to persist in this false thinking," Phoebe said with a smile. "Mr. Aston, I am Phoebe, Anna's sister. I suspect we are to be on a first-name basis?" She waited until he nodded. "Then allow me to present our soon-to-be sister-in-law, Miss Eleanor Daventry; her aunt, Mrs. Renly; and my aunt, Mrs. Phillips."

Harry bowed over Eleanor's hand. "I am delighted to make your acquaintance and happy to see that your introduction into the family is a circumstance we share." He then turned to bow over Mrs. Renly's, then Aunt Shae's hands with the grace that was inherent to him. Harry Aston would make any woman proud.

Eleanor, looking fresh despite the carriage ride, appeared radiant under Stratford's devotion, and Anna had to admit she had been wrong about how much Eleanor brought to Stratford. Only Phoebe had seen how perfectly suited they were. Like a flower to the sun, Eleanor blossomed simply by the fact that she was loved. Now Anna could see for herself how such a thing came about.

"How glad I am to hear of your engagement," Eleanor said, addressing Harry. "If I might say this, though I am not quite a member of the family, I have yet to have met a man capable of understanding the deeper current of Anna's feelings. Lucky is the gentleman who has won her."

Eleanor sent a twinkling smile Anna's way as if to say she knew how much Anna disliked public praise, but she was going to hear it whether she liked it or not.

Anna attempted to divert their attention. "I must ask, though. What brings you all here?" She hailed one of Emily's footmen, who had appeared from inside, gesturing for him to unload the luggage from both carriages. She stopped herself when she realized she no longer needed to—or should—run Emily's household for her.

"We were concerned about your happiness and decided to take it upon ourselves to ensure your well-being." Phoebe tucked her arm through Anna's. "I sent a letter to Emily proposing we visit and see for ourselves how you are doing, promising her we would not trouble her to stay here. We have taken rooms in the village. That reminds me . . ." Phoebe turned to the footman. "You may leave that trunk where it is. We shall not be staying."

Stratford had not forgotten Anna's question. "In short, we came to make sure you did not make a mull of it."

Anna turned as the front door opened and had only the time to say, "Thank you for your confidence in me, brother."

Captain Leatham and Emily came to the front door, their newborn son in Emily's arms. Phoebe hurried up the steps.

"Emily!" Although she had not been as close to Emily as Anna was, theirs was an affectionate relationship. "I had not had word that you delivered or that your husband is home. Good afternoon, Captain Leatham. We thought to come as a support to you, Emily, never dreaming that we'd find such happiness instead. We will not incommode you both, I promise. We have already engaged rooms in the village inn."

"But of course you must stay here," Emily began.

Anna turned on Stratford with a frown. "You know, with it being so close to your wedding, I do not think this visit at all wise. Had you written to advise me of it, I would surely have told you not to come."

"Perhaps it was not wise, but you are family, and families look out for one another. Not to mention the fact that . . ." He shot Harry a look. "We will need the services of a rector as ours was called away suddenly for a death in his family and had no time to find us a replacement. Mr. Aston, do you think you might?"

Harry grinned. "If you agree to my suit, I suppose we can reach an agreement for your ceremony."

"Agree to it?" Stratford exclaimed. "I thought she was past praying for." Anna leveled him a glare.

"Welcome," Captain Leatham said, lending his voice of reason to what was quickly degenerating into sibling absurdity. "Perhaps we should make our way into the house, where I'm sure we can summon up refreshments, can we not, my love? Then, although I believe we've deduced the matter, Aston can inform us of the reason for such a large reunion." He escorted his wife inside, leaving the crowd to follow.

Stratford brought in both Eleanor and Mrs. Renly, and Phoebe came behind them with Aunt Shae on her arm. Harry took Anna's hand in his and held it discreetly, his face brimming with quiet joy.

In front of them, Phoebe cared for their aunt, slowing her pace when the exertion of climbing the stairs was too much for her. She had always been the solicitous one—beautiful, if Anna did say so herself—and kind. She was so much more *good* than Anna could ever hope to be. Phoebe deserved to be happy, and Anna hoped she would soon find a love of her own, especially now that Anna knew what a wonderful thing it was.

Once inside, the drinks were brought, with Aunt Shae and Mrs. Renly served first. Emily turned sparkling eyes to the assembled crowd, her gaze lingering on Anna. "Well?"

Harry encompassed the crowd when he gave the formal speech they were all expecting. "Miss Anna Tunstall has done me the honor of agreeing to become my wife."

"*No!*" Emily stared. "In all my wildest dreams . . ."

"Emily, stop teasing." Anna could not hold back the laughter that bubbled up in her. "It was your plan from the very beginning. To think you likely orchestrated the highwaymen just to arrange our meeting in a more dramatic setting."

Both Stratford and Phoebe turned to her in alarm. "Highwaymen?"

Anna had forgotten they knew nothing about it. "I will tell you later," she promised under her breath.

Emily gave her a speaking glance. "You have not told them yet, Anna? But no. That treat was not by my design. It is only that from the moment of making Mr. Aston's acquaintance, my one thought has been to coax you to Avebury so that you might meet him, too."

Harry turned his head to Emily. "You have earned my gratitude and my debt."

The room buzzed with talk on all sides, and Anna refused the attempts from her siblings to learn more about the highwaymen. "Later," she muttered. Listening to snippets of conversation, Anna participated where she could, but her eyes were on Harry and her ears were attentive to what he was saying to Stratford.

"I would have requested an audience with you as soon as my feelings for Anna had become clear, but the matter could not wait. I'd hoped I might call upon you to discuss the particulars."

Stratford gave a smile that held more warmth than it used to, Anna thought. "I understand the feeling of not wanting to wait. And yes, we can discuss the details as soon as Leatham might spare us a room. Is your lawyer in London?"

"It is still my family's lawyer, but yes, the firm has their main offices there." Harry beamed at Stratford. "Excellent."

"Business aside, let me both welcome you"—Stratford crossed one leg over the other and shot Harry an ironic glance—"and also warn you.

Anna is not the easiest person to live with. Are you sure you have thought this through?"

Anna sent him a wry look. "I am sitting right here, Stratford. However, Harry is not deceived about my true nature, and he loves me."

Harry held her in a warm gaze. "Anna could not have said it better. I knew from the moment I met her that I would have no other."

Stratford shrugged and met his fiancée's gaze, the hint of a smile in his eyes. "Then I suppose there is nothing to be done. You must marry her."

The Leathams made it perfectly clear that under no uncertain terms would Anna's family stay anywhere but at Durstead Manor, and the guests were shown to their rooms to freshen up in short order. Emily grew urgent to feed Master George, who had become unrepentantly insistent, and Anna accompanied Harry to the door, stepping outside with him and letting him lead her down the stairs.

They had walked a few paces when Harry took her hand and intertwined his fingers with hers. The gesture alone held all the intimacy Anna could wish for—friendship and the promise of more. They walked only a few steps more before Harry stopped.

"I must go."

Anna nodded, smiling as his gold-flecked eyes scanned her face with undisguised yearning.

He leaned down and dropped a kiss on her lips. "But one day," he said, squeezing her hand and letting it go, "a day in the not-distant future, for it will be as soon as I can arrange it, you will go with me to *our* home."

She nodded a second time, her heart too full for words. Harry kissed her once more before turning to walk down the path to the rectory. Anna watched his broad shoulders as he left, the boyish curls that spilled over his coat collar, his determined steps that—*in the not-distant future, as soon as he could arrange it*—would come back to claim her. She squeezed her hands in little fists of excitement before darting up the steps.

Phoebe!

She had to find Phoebe. There was so much to tell.

About the Author

Photo by Caroline Aoustin

Jennie Goutet is an American-born Anglophile who lives with her French husband and their three children in a small town outside Paris. Her imagination resides in Regency England, where her romances *A Faithful Proposal, A Regrettable Proposal*, and *The Christmas Ruse* are set. Jennie is author of the award-winning memoir *Stars Upside Down* and the modern romances *A Sweetheart in Paris* and *A Noble Affair*. A Christian, a cook, and an inveterate klutz, Jennie writes about faith, food, and life—even the clumsy moments—on her blog, aladyinfrance.com. You can learn more about Jennie and her books on her author website, jenniegoutet.com.